Praise for th

MW00794881

"This inaugurates a trilogy that young fans of the fantastic will like for its fast-paced action."
Publishers Weekly

"Shades of Jules Verne, J. R. R. Tolkien, and a little George Lucas."
Reflections in Hindsight

"Betrayal, deception and danger are in every corner this is a series that will have you engaged and drawn in!"
5 Star Books & More Newsletter

"An exciting action-packed fantasy thriller."
Harriet Klausner (#1 Amazon Book Reviewer)

"This is a page turning thriller. . . . I am impatiently waiting for the next book in the series."
Vic's Media Room

"This book has a slight C. S. Lewis or Ted Dekker feel . . ."
The Christian Manifesto

"Combines energy, creativity, and familiar fantasy characters and tropes that will appeal to readers."
CBA Magazine

City of Gold

By Daniel Blacraby

Published in Boise, Idaho by Russell Media
Web: http://www.russell-media.com

This book may be purchased in bulk for educational, business, ministry, or promotional use.

For information please email info@russell-media.com.

ISBN (print):?
ISBN (e-book):?

Library of Congress Control Number: ?

Printed in the United States of America

Dedication
To Chevy,
King of the Mutts.
May your bark be ever fierce.

Table of Contents

Prologue   1

PART ONE: PREPARATIONS   **5**

  1. Confined   7

  2. The Pawn   13

  3. A Beautiful Voice   19

  4. A Mole   25

  5. The Point of No Return   27

  6. Fallen Sanctuary   30

  7. Murky Motives   36

  8. A Veiled Romance   40

  9. Forming The Company   42

  10. From Dust to Dust   47

  11. The Journey Begins   51

PART TWO: RESCUE   **55**

  12. Darkness Closes In   57

  13. An Ill-Fated Departure   59

  14. Discord   64

  15. A Torn Heart   69

  16. Carvings and Ink   75

  17. Redtown   79

  18. Ominous Feelings   82

  19. Clash of Steel   84

  20. Trust No One   89

  21. Starting Fires   93

  22. The Caves of Revelation   95

  23. Bones and Corpses   99

24. The Den of a Killer 102

25. The Prophecy 105

26. A Passionate Heart-to-Heart 110

27. Exchanging Destinies 114

28. The Garga 119

29. Summoning the Hound 123

30. Through the Portal 127

31. Missing Pieces 129

32. The Ageing City 134

33. Hidden Pasts 139

34. The Journey Continues 145

35. Changing the Board 151

36. Flore Gub 153

37. Gone 157

38. Unleashing the Flood 161

39. Battle of the Borderlands 164

40. Of Loyalty and Disloyalty 168

41. The-One-and-Only Igg 171

42. Across the Great Sea of Lava 175

43. A Golden View 180

44. Out of Time 184

PART THREE: A PERFECT CITY **187**

45. Changed 189

46. The King's Court 192

47. The Two are One 194

48. Stirrings 198

49. Confessions 200

50. A Perfect City 205

51. A Pull-and-Shoot Kind of Guy 210

52. Of Air Density and Fancy Clothes 214

53. The Banquet 217

54. Welcoming Party 224

55. An Under-Earth Fortune Cookie 229

56. Missing 232

57. A Deeper Training 236

58. Ulterior Motives 240

59. A Sacred Glen 243

60. The Price of a Good Story 249

61. Disagreements 253

62. Two of a Kind 258

63. History Erased 263

64. In Search of Answers 267

65. The Heart of the Orb 270

66. A Living Sacrifice 273

67. Death and Life 275

68. One Final Task 280

69. Packaged 283

70. Stranger in the Night 287

PART FOUR: ILLUSIONS AND REALITY **291**

71. Phase Three 293

72. Resistance 296

73. Illusions Dispelled 299

74. Danger 304

75. A Special Girl 306

76. The Desire to Kill 309

77. The Dream Ends 313

78. An Intimate Connection 316

79. Visions 320

80. A Tight Spot 323

81. A Fool's Plan 327

82. A Secret Language 331

83. The Fortress Falls 335

84. Waiting for the Sign 338

85. The Piercing Sting of Love 340

86. Less Than Perfect 344

87. From Under the Rug 347

88. Of Daggers and Arrows 349

89. Randilin's Dark Deeds 351

90. History Repeated 355

91. Unforeseen Events 357

92. One Simple Word   361
93. Trapped   364
94. An Icy Prison   367
95. Forged in Hatred   369
96. Duel of the Book Keepers   372
97. A Strange World   376
98. Safe   378
99. Unmasked   381

GLOSSARY   383

ACKNOWLEDGMENTS   388

ABOUT THE AUTHOR   389

Prologue

They were coming. He felt it in the marrow of his bones as clearly as the breath hastening over his lips. Fleeing was pointless. He would be caught; he had foreseen it. But he was prepared for this day.

The pattering of footsteps echoed through the tunnel. Time was short. He glided across the room to where a lone table rested against the damp rock wall. He smiled; he had constructed the table with his own hands—many years ago. He ran his fingers across, caressing the brittle surface as its legs wobbled beneath. *We've grown old together, haven't we?*

The approaching footfall grew louder. With a deep sigh, the elderly man grasped the object resting on the table. He gazed at it longingly, as though looking into the eyes of a loved-one for the last time. He had no doubt that it would, indeed, be the last time.

Cradling the object against his chest, he lowered himself into a wooden chair. His eyes focused toward the room's lone entrance where flickering light, growing brighter and brighter, bounced off the walls. His solitude had been compromised. He allowed his weary eyelids to droop over his pupils; he could do nothing but wait.

The faint sound of the intruder's steady breath prickled the hair on his arms. The trespasser, concealed only by the pirouetting shadows, now stood motionless in the entrance. The elderly man felt a small grin hijack his aged face; his visitor's eyes sweltered with flame. *The recklessness of youth.*

"Are you here to kill me?" he asked calmly.

The man nodded. "I am," he uttered without hesitation.

The old man motioned to the object in his lap. "The conviction of your mouth has yet to take hold of your muscles, boy. Why delay what is so certainly to be? I am ready to accept my destiny. Are you?"

The figure in the shadows shifted. "Do not mistake my lack of action for hesitation or mercy, for I am friend to neither. As a gentleman of honor, I owe any man I execute, and there have been many, the satisfaction of knowing why. Is this knowledge not desired?"

The old man chuckled. "What good is knowledge to a corpse? I know what drives you; you seek the truth, and find it you may. But spare me one more question, boy."

"Proceed."

The old man bent forward, pointing a bony finger toward the stranger. "If the truth you obtain turns out to be not what you were searching for—what next? There is no rewriting the truth. Are you prepared to accept what you find?" He reclined into the chair. The man in the entrance shuffled once again.

"Unfortunately, my crusade for truth no longer concerns you. The more appropriate question seems to be whether the truth *you* have found is one worth dying for?"

A shimmer of light glimmered off the metallic pistol as it emerged from the shadows.

A shiver trickled down the old man's spine. He gazed at the object in his lap once more. Raising his eyes to the intruder he spread his arms like the wings of an eagle. "There is a time for summer and a time for winter. Life is but a vapor in the wind. Live well, boy. Live well."

The deafening crack of gunfire was echoed by a thump as the old man's lifeless body crumpled to the floor. A trail of blood stained his wrinkled forehead.

The assassin emerged into the light and stood over the body. Two more shots rang out in the small room. He lowered his smoking pistol. *Senile old man.* Bending down, he retrieved the object that had fallen from his victim's lap. He stroked his hand across it; he had waited a long time for this moment.

Reaching into his pocket he pulled out a smooth silver disk. With a soft pop the object split in half, revealing five dime-sized notches. The fingers of his right hand slid perfectly into the holes. There was a low drone as he brought the metallic device to his ear. The moisture in his mouth evaporated and his heart jumped as the tone ceased.

"Report," came an icy voice.

The assassin inhaled slowly. "The deed has been accomplished."

The sound of puffing smoke crackled against the device before a response came. "And, The Thirteenth?" the speaker questioned, equally void of emotion.

"Eliminated. That which was his is now ours."

"Did he beg for mercy?" questioned the cold voice.

"Yes, master. Like a whimpering pup," replied the assassin. The lie produced the desired effect. The killer could feel pitiless pleasure oozing like tar through the apparatus.

There was a silence before the master spoke again. "Well done, Dunstan. Your service and obedience to CROSS will not be forgotten. The day of justice is within our grasp. The bloodshed between Atlantis and El Dorado is only the beginning. The truth at last will be unleashed upon the land. You have done well. Don't lose my trust." Static once again sounded in his ear.

Dunstan returned his gadget to his pocket. With a final glance at the face of the corpse lying on the floor, he turned and disappeared. Silence once again engulfed the small room, leaving only the bitter stench of blood to testify to the violent event. Dunstan knew the balance of power had shifted and the order of the cosmos had been violently hurled into limbo. And, yet, the world remained blissfully oblivious.

Dunstan chuckled. *Oh, but they will know soon enough. The Day of Reckoning is coming.*

PART ONE
PREPARATIONS

1
Confined

The phantom dashed down the abandoned alleyway, blanketed under the shroud of midnight. He cast a quick glance over his shoulder to confirm he was not being followed. Reaching the end of the lane, he threw his back against the stone wall and peered out at the comatose courtyard. It was eerily tranquil—and that worried him. He carefully scanned his surroundings for any sign of life. He halted—his suspicions affirmed.

Two sentries paced militantly across the lofty wall overlooking his position. Both were garbed in full battle armor and broad swords dangled by their sides. He crouched down low against the wall; he would have to be cautious.

With trance-like silence, he scampered from the alley before taking refuge behind the base of a fountain that dotted the middle of the courtyard like a bulls-eye. He held his breath.

The sound of the guards' casual conversation floated down to him, assuring him that he had remained undetected. With another deep breath, he scurried out of the courtyard. Passing under a large arched gateway, he ducked down low in the shadows cast by the wall. He could now see his destination before him; his mission was almost complete. *Just a little farther.*

Suddenly his ears spiked—somebody was approaching. Quickly inching farther into the haven of the shadows, he locked every muscle. Seconds later he was looking at the hefty silhouette of a man, the outline of a double-edged axe resting against his shoulder. Another man appeared beside the first, both inspecting their surroundings.

"I'm telling you…all the captain told me was that it was urgent. Think it's an attack?" asked the first in a gravelly voice.

"Anything is possible these days. Perhaps it's a spy or an assassin. Let's have a look around. Stay alert," suggested the second. The larger guard grunted in affirmation and they set off, turning out of sight from the concealed figure.

The phantom readied himself. If he timed it correctly, he could make it with one final dash.

He could feel the cool damp air rushing through his hair as he bolted into the clearing, moving closer and closer to his target. Out of his peripheral vision he observed the shapes of the two guards, both walking the opposite direction. He had made it…*UMPH!*

A sting against his chest sent him tumbling to the ground. Two firm hands ripped through the dark and clutched onto his collar. Before he could reorient himself he was jostled up. His back stung as it was slammed against a solid stone wall.

"I'm disappointed," spoke the captor slowly. "I thought we had a deal. You gave me your word." The grip on the detainee's collar loosened as the man released a weighty sigh. "But it seems that you, Cody Clemenson, are going to require a *much* closer watch."

Cody rubbed his throbbing chest where the man's arm had struck. "Was the tackle *really* necessary, Dace? How did you know what I was doing tonight?" asked Cody irritably.

The handsome captain gave a roguish smirk. "Because fate seldom befriends the untrustworthy, my young, scheming friend. As it happens, the Queen has summoned another red-eye war council tomorrow; I was tasked with informing you but found your room abandoned. As this is now your *fourth* attempt to flee Atlantis, it didn't take much to hunt you down. Now, let us go before anyone else witnesses their savior Book Keeper fleeing the city."

"How much longer do we play this game, Dace? You gave me *your word*, remember? The night of the ambush, the night...they took her," Cody replied, his voice distant. "You promised me we wouldn't abandon her to the enemy. It's been almost *two weeks* since Jade was stolen from me. Two weeks! How do I know she's safe? How can you, in honest conscience, expect me to attend a relentless parade of pretentious councils when it's *my* fault she's gone!?" yelled Cody, his rage awakening from its shallow repose.

Dace gave Cody's shoulder a sturdy squeeze. "You *know* my word is good. We *will* rescue Jade...but not tonight. Passion does not negate wisdom. One more council. Besides, you can't abandon me. Without you, I'm deserted to withstand the dreadful ramblings of the politicians alone!

Come on champ, I sent my superior to jail, wrongly I might add, for *your* sake. Stay another night for mine."

After a moment of silence, Cody sighed. "One more night."

The two turned and began wandering back to the palace. "Oh, and Dace," added Cody, "there's probably no need for the Queen to hear of my...sleepwalking tonight."

"Aye?" Dace responded with a hint of amusement. "Perhaps we can arrange a bargain," he said with a wink.

They came to a halt before an iron gate separating the Outer-City and Mid-City districts. Two large turrets spiking up like spears flanked the entrance. Cody could faintly perceive the glimmer of arrowheads emerging from the narrow slit-like windows.

Blockading the entrance were the two bulky figures that Cody had earlier evaded. They gave a slight bow. "Captain Dace, Book Keeper." Dace returned the gesture. "Wolfrick, Sheets." As the guards stepped aside to allow passage, Dace frowned. "Your lax attitude is unacceptable, soldiers. *No one* enters without the proper password. Including me."

"But Dace...it's *you*! We've served under you for hundreds of years."

Dace's hand silenced him. "Times have changed. We are at war. The Golden King is as cunning as he is malicious. He has already infiltrated our city with mocking ease. Comfort and trust are no longer luxuries we can indulge. Now, carry on."

The guards crisscrossed their weapons, although their faces exposed clear discomfort. "Password," they demanded half-heartedly. Dace replied without hesitation. As the final word slid from his tongue there was a loud popping sound, and the gate began to lift.

They proceeded through the Mid-City, which was unnervingly silent; the residents all inside their homes having long-since closed their scattered factories. Since the onset of war, citizens rarely ventured out into the night.

At the Inner-City gate Dace relayed a new password, representing higher clearance. General Levenworth devised the system following the ambush. Passwords were changed every five hours. Those with clearance were delivered the new password thirty minutes beforehand. No exceptions. The Queen herself would be denied without the proper passphrase.

Dace stopped at the foot of the royal palace. "I trust you can make it to your chambers without detour?" It was an order, not a question. Taking leave of Dace, Cody scurried up the stairs toward the large, double palace doors.

He abruptly slowed to a stop. Something grabbed his attention. Even before his eyes located the movement he knew what it was. The alluring smell floating on the stale air was unmistakable. Cody found her concealed in the shadows. Her flowing blonde hair hung gently over her shoulder and the fairness of her skin appeared to glow in the dark night. Her red lips were pressed firmly together and her ocean blue eyes held steady.

"Tiana!" Cody exclaimed in surprise. "What are you doing here at this time of night?"

The girl tilted her head, her thick hair falling loosely over her eyes like a fresh sheet of snow. She silently examined Cody. "I was watching your escape. Even from my dwelling on top of the Sanctuary, I could tell it was you. Your movements are predictable; they give you away," she answered emotionlessly. Cody felt the brisk drumming of his heart through his throbbing temples.

"Ti, we really need to talk. I don't understand what went wrong between us. We need to..." Cody didn't get the opportunity to finish his plea; without a sound, Tiana disappeared, leaving him, once again, alone.

2

The Dawn

Mornings are the foulest abomination, thought Cody as sharp light beams poured through his window and burrowed through his eyelids. He pulled his shaggy, brown hair over his eyes. It was not so much the *morning* which was so detestable—it was the *living* which followed. He massaged his temples; it had not always been this way. Just one short month ago everything in his ordinary life was meandering along as usual.

Like every other morning, his hand instinctively slipped beneath his pillow, brushing against the cold sleekness of worn leather. A shrilling jolt of static energy scaled his finger and raced down his spine. Pushing aside the pillow, Cody gazed at the ancient Book—the scarlet 'A' radiating like smouldering coals: *The Code.*

The Book had obliterated everything *normal* in his life. It had given him unimaginable power...but at a great cost. Cody exhaled a pained breath. If not for the Book his dearest friend in the world would still be with him. She had been stolen from him—and it was entirely *his* fault.

I miss you, Jade.

He snatched a smooth, ruby-coated object from the nightstand—Wesley's mysterious pocket watch. The clock's golden hand remained firmly pointed at 3 o'clock. Cody wondered whether Jade had arrived in El Dorado yet. What he tried *not* to imagine was what dark, unknown fate awaited her when she did.

A burst of knocking on the door startled him. "Come in," he called out. The door creaked open and a plump, pear-shaped head oozed through the narrow crack. "M-m-master Clemenson? Oh, there you are!" the man muttered, as though somehow surprised to find Cody in his own room. "Th-th-the Queen reminds you that your presence is required at the war council in precisely thirty-two minutes."

"Thanks, Poe. I was just heading there now."

Poe gave a quick, clumsy bow. He opened his mouth to speak but, seemingly losing his train of thought, turned and waddled out of sight. Cody kicked off his blanket. Normally he'd seize another thirty-one minutes of sleep, but lately slumber had become scarce and contaminated with nightmares—every night the same one.

Cody was still rubbing his baggy eyes as Queen Cia commenced the assembly. As always, she looked radiant, transmitting intoxicating grace with every motion. Her twin brother, Prince Kantan, was perched beside her like a vulture patiently waiting for something to die. To the Queen's other side was a conspicuously vacant chair: that of the traitorous murderer, Prince Foz.

Filling out the table was the grizzly General Gongore Levenworth; Captain Dace; the panther-faced Sli Silkian, head of the Atlantis Rule Enforcement Association or AREA as it's called by Underlings; and lastly, Private Tat Shunbickle, the borderlands' scout who had provided first intelligence on El Dorado's swelling war camps.

"These are dire days," began Cia solemnly, "the faith of our people is in an epidemically fragile state. So again, I must advise that the information revealed in this council not be shared. Our citizens must continue to assume that there is hope, even if that hope is bleak. General Levenworth..."

The stone-faced General stood. "Word has come from Flore Gub through the tunnel-phone network: Captain Eagleton's forces arrived just in time to repel the initial assault on the borderlands...*however,* rumor spreads that a new legion of enemy soldiers has emerged on the battlefield. Warriors referred to in hushed whispers as *The Rephaim:* hollow wraiths impervious to fear and pain; men who are not men at all—but unholy demons. Where they trek, the ground ripples with the blood of our men."

Cody saw Tat's face drain of color. It had been he who had first seen the warriors up close. Levenworth continued, "I fear El Dorado is using these assaults merely to gauge a lesser foe's strength. The Golden King now knows the extent of our weakened state. His strike will be swift and furious. As such, I will not risk wasting our soldiers in unnecessary open conflict or in an indefensible outpost such as Lilley. I have ordered all fighting men to fall back to the fortress of Flore Gub immediately...."

"And what of Lilley?!" Tat cried. "It's just a peaceful outpost. You remove the troops and you assure its doom!" The suddenly animated Tat Shunbickle thrust a finger at the General. "You heartless fiend, it will be a bloody massacre!" his voice cracked and his eyes moistened. "My wife…"

General Levenworth stood silently against the outcry like a rocky shore withstanding the violent crash of the ocean's waves. Rage drained into fatigue and Tat collapsed back into his chair. When Levenworth spoke again his voice was calm and steady.

"The fate of Lilley is a tragedy without equal since Sir Randilin's *dark deeds* in the First Great War. Captain Talgu evacuated as many people as possible but, regrettably, many still remained when the dark shroud of El Dorado fell over it. I'm sorry, Private. Unfortunately, the price of victory is often the willingness to sacrifice some for the greater good…."

"Repeat that tonight while you rest in your luxurious palace chambers," spat Tat venomously.

At this Kantan broke his silence, "Enough, Private! Step out of line *one* more time and you'll earn a date with the gallows. The decision is made. Lilley is now lost behind enemy lines and thus out of our control. We will not let Lilley's sacrifice be in vain. As much as it pains my soul, our greatest hope now rests in our Book Keeper." His beady eyes fixated on Cody. "Regardless of how utterly incompetent he may be," he added spitefully.

"Indeed, brother. Cody is the key," declared Cia. "He alone is the symbol that unites Atlantis against El Dorado."

Sli Silkian cleared his throat, producing a high-pitched wheeze. "Symbol or not, Kantan is correct. Valuable as he may be, Cody remains an amateur Creator at best. Potential alone does not win victories. He doesn't stand a chance against the immense power of the Golden King. Let him return to the Brotherhood of Light and complete his training under High Priest Lamgorious Stalkton..."

"There is no time!" Kantan interjected. "Every moment we delay means more soldiers slaughtered on the borderlands. Flore Gub is strong but not impenetrable. It *will* fall, and when it does, the wrath of El Dorado will pour into our land like a plague. Cody's connection to *The Code* is all that can tilt the ever-slimming odds in our favor. Peace is a time of knowledge—war is a time for action. Cody should be..."

"*STOP!*" The room faded into silence. All eyes turned to Cody, who was now standing, the veins in his neck bulging as they pumped blood to his reddened face. " Everybody just *stop*! You talk about me like I'm invisible. It's been thirteen days since El Dorado's ambush. Two weeks of *councils*. Two weeks of *bickering*. Two weeks of arguing over how to best deploy me like a game piece. *Enough*! Every second we delay, Jade is dragged closer to El Dorado. I want to help, I really do; but I'm not abandoning Jade to that fate. I'm going after her, with or without this committee's approval." Cody slammed *The Code* onto the table. "And don't even *think* about trying to stop me."

For a moment the unexpected tirade lingered in the air. The unusually tender voice of Cia was the first to venture into the silence. "We have not forgotten Jade. I swear upon this royal crown that we will do everything in our power to rescue her. But you *must* understand, you are very special. You have been given a marvelous gift—but it is always the greatest men who pay the highest price in troubled times."

"I never asked for this," Cody said bitterly, still standing defiantly.

"But you received it, nonetheless. The moment you placed your hand on that Book, your life became destined for a higher purpose. The only question is—how will you respond? The fate of our world hangs on how you, and you alone, answer that question."

3

A Beautiful Voice

Sharp pain jolted through Cody's forearm as his fist slammed against the wall. *Ouch!* He had stormed out of the council, paying no heed when Dace called after him. He was in no mood to talk—with anyone. *Why can't anyone understand?* Suddenly Jade's image filled his mind as clear as if she were there in the flesh.

Cody forced open his eyes; the vision brought unbearable pain—and guilt.

Somebody shouted his name from across the hall. Cody sprinted down the corridor and rounded the corner. He needed privacy. He didn't care that he was being childish. He skidded to a halt. Several voices sounded from around the bend; Cody recognized one as the grating voice of the irritating, nosey editor of the *Under-Earth Rumblings*: Fincher Tople. From the other direction, the shadow of the original pursuer approached.

Cody glanced around desperately. There was only a lone, windowless door staking claim to the lengthy hallway. He jerked the doorknob—it was locked.

Both the shadow and the voices continued their steady collision course toward him. Cody dropped to his knees. *"Sellunga."* A gooey, silver substance bubbled out of the keyhole. Cody cupped his hand, allowing the molten material to spill out onto his palm. He scrunched his eyebrows together. As he did, the silver matter thickened like dripping water into an icicle. *"Gai di gasme."* He grinned—being the Book Keeper definitely had its perks. He twisted the newly formed key and hustled through the door, latching the lock behind him. He was safe. And alone.

The room overloaded his senses. Like a long forsaken attic, it was a congested stockpile of trinkets and neglected objects. Dust blanketed the room like morning snow after a wild blizzard. The ceiling curved in a majestic arc and was adorned with a collage of detailed artwork that time had faded beyond recognition.

Cody strolled deeper into the chamber, examining the vast assortment of treasures. He paused before an elegant royal coat on a hanger. The purple tone gave the robe a kingly appearance. Cody pulled it over his shoulders. He couldn't help but walk with an exaggerated strut—he needed to find a mirror.

"All, hail, Lord Cody Clemenson! Noble Book Keeper and powerful creator! All foes quake before him!" he exclaimed in a booming voice.

"Hail!" said a gentle voice in response. The unexpected sound sent Cody leaping into the air. Blushing beet red, he yanked off the coat. He lost his balance and stumbled into the coat hanger behind him, sending it clattering to the floor.

Standing before him, wearing her gentle smile, was Princess Eva.

"Eva! I didn't see you...you scared me! What are you doing here?" Cody asked exasperated while using his foot to nonchalantly flick the purple robe out of sight.

"The same reason as you—to hide away," Eva replied softly. "I come here often."

"How do you know I'm hiding? I didn't...never mind. What *is* this place anyways?" Cody questioned as his breath settled back into its regular rhythm.

Eva was an enigma. He had only shared an extended conversation with the modest Princess one other time— the night she had appeared unannounced at his chamber to warn him that her siblings were dangerous. The counsel she had offered had been wise. Cody felt surprisingly comfortable in her presence and the tension in his muscles ebbed away.

"What it once was is no longer," Eva replied as she motioned to a stone structure in the room's center. The rustic construction, surrounded by a mosaic platform, resembled the periscope of a submarine, with the shaft opening at face level—one of Atlantis' famed tunnel-phones.

"In ancient days this was the royal communication chamber. But this channel has long since been decommissioned. Now it's no more than a storage closet for things that belong nowhere else...like us," she finished with a tender smile.

Cody stroked his fingers along the polished surface of the appliance. "Where did the channel lead?"

Eva hesitated before answering. "It's the prototype; the first ever constructed. It leads, or rather, it *led*, directly…" she paused again as Cody leaned forward in anticipation, "to the throne room of El Dorado."

Cody stumbled back a step, rubbing his dazed eyes. His surprise morphed into anger. "You mean…we have direct communication with El Dorado…and nobody informed me?! Don't you understand what this means?" Cody didn't wait for a reply; his face was already at the chute. "Whoever hears this, I demand to speak to your prisoner, Jade. Let me hear her voice! Answer me…ANSWER ME!" Cody bellowed.

Silence.

Eva placed her hand upon Cody's clamped fist. "I was trying to tell you; this channel hasn't been used in a thousand years. It's either caved in naturally or El Dorado filled it in centuries ago. I'm sorry." Cody suddenly felt embarrassed by his impulsive theatrics.

"Don't be ashamed. Jade would have done the same for you," Eva comforted, as though reading his thoughts.

Jade would be stronger. She's always been stronger, Cody thought bitterly. He scanned the room, anxious to change the subject. "What's this for?" he asked, grabbing the first object within his reach.

Eva smiled, offering no resistance to the shift. "One of my favorites; another of Lamgorious Stalkton's long-forgotten experiments. It's called *The Speaking Sands.*"

Cody examined two pewter bowls and a small, transparent vial containing white sand. Eva chuckled. "I'll show you." She set the dishes on the floor. Removing the vial's lid, she poured sand into each basin and began tracing her finger through the sand in one of them.

"I still don't und…" Cody reeled in his tongue and rubbed his eyes to assure they hadn't been deceived. Within the second bowl lines were carving through the sand on their own accord. Eva stood and joined Cody in looking at the two dishes that now perfectly mirrored each other in displaying a jagged mountain range sketch.

"*Hello?*"

Cody glanced to Eva in surprise. "Excuse me?" The Princess stared back blankly. "I didn't say anything."

"You must have; I heard a…"

"*Hello?*"

This time Eva's eyebrows elevated as well. The voice was being projected from the tunnel-phone.

"I thought you said…" Cody began but Eva cut him off. "It's not *supposed* to work."

Cody stepped to the chute and cleared his throat.

"It is I, Cody Clemenson, Book Keeper and protector of Atlantis. I demand to speak to Jade." He grimaced, having sounded painfully more timid than intended.

A rumbling echo sounded in the distance. Then a puff of dust blasted from the shaft like a deep cough, as though foretelling the coming reply. "This is certainly an…*unexpected* surprise. What an honor to meet the Book Keeper at last." A chill ran down Cody's spine. The voice was beautiful. It had the purity of a child and the melodic chime of a songbird. Cody felt drawn to the voice like the seducing call of a siren.

"Where's Jade? Who are you?" Cody probed, fighting to break the spellbinding trance. Neither Cody nor Eva released a single breath as they awaited the reply. The distant rumbling came bouncing down the tunnel. Cody clenched his sticky fists. "One who has eagerly awaited meeting you," replied the angelic voice. "It is I—the Golden King."

4

A Mole

The man's eyes fell to the gleam of the smooth dagger. The cloaked figure reclined in the chair across from him and continued to pet the circular blade as though it were a lazy house cat. He gave no heed to his counterpart's discomfort.

"Is that really necessary? I won't conduct business with a weapon pointed in my face, Mr...." the agitated man questioned. His words dangled in the air like a fishing lure.

"Agent Two. That is my name," the other responded flatly as he continued to stroke his blade.

"Well...*Agent Two*, perhaps your master is accustomed to lording his power over the meek; but I trust he is prudent enough not to underestimate me. If I deem our arrangement has lost its luster, then I *will* walk, regardless of who or what your master presumes to be."

The figure in the chair raised his head for the first time. "Indeed," he replied, offering no further response. The indifference in the bladed man's voice infuriated his listener, although he concealed his rage behind an equally stoic expression. He took a seat across from the agent.

"Our bargain stands? I have your master's word that it shall be as promised?"

The hooded one nodded. When it became apparent that no further words would follow, the man leaned forward toward the agent and spoke in a whisper though they were alone in the dim room. "Levenworth has conceded Lilley. Our forces blockade themselves within the fortress at Flore Gub. As for the Book Keeper, he remains set on El Dorado to rescue his lady friend. His creation powers remain relatively unspectacular. Queen Cia remains in control; however, her grasp is weak and opposition from her twin brother awaits but a push. As they are equal heirs to the vacant throne, uprising is inevitable."

Agent Two raised his blade to inspect the polished surface. As he did, light beams reflected off its surface. Extending his finger, he pressed it lightly against the dagger's edge. Instantly a bead of blood bubbled out and rolled down the weapon.

"CROSS appreciates your cooperation. You say nothing that has not already been seen by our Master's omnipotent web—but your loyalty has been noted, as has your willingness to sell out your own people. Be assured, when the time comes, you shall be rewarded handsomely: The Forbidden High Language words will be yours. As for the royal family, it is being...*handled. Agent One* is seeing to it personally." The hooded agent raised his gaze from his blade. "Above all else, keep your eyes on the boy. He is the key to everything."

5

The Point of No Return

Fear gripped Cody like a merciless leech, sucking every ounce of courage. The haunting words hung suspended in the musky air—the words of the Golden King. Cody's tongue sagged under the weight of the sticky saliva foaming in his mouth.

"What have you done with Jade?" he murmured.

After a moment, the tunnel-phone rumbled to life. "Ah, yes. Jade...such a pretty girl. A shame I must torture her—keeps shrieking your name, day and night."

"You're lying!" Cody yelled without conviction. The image of Jade confined to a cramped, desolate prison cell filled him with wild rage.

"Am I?" the Golden King replied steadily, his voice trailing off. Cody tried to swallow, but could not.

"Cody?" came a weak voice. "Cody? Is that...really you?" Cody's eyes welled. "Yes, Jade! It's me! It's me! Tell me you're okay!"

"Cody?" replied Jade faintly. "Cody, please help me. *Please...*" her voice drifted away.

"That was…touching," returned the calm voice of the Golden King.

"What have you done to her? If you touch *one hair* on her head I swear I'll…" Cody stopped, his mind swirling too fast to pull his words together.

"If you want that question answered—you will have to come see for yourself. I eagerly anticipate the opportunity to welcome you to my throne room. In fact, you have *one week* to do so. If you are not standing in my court by dusk on the seventh day—your Jade will suffer a most agonizing death. You *will* come to El Dorado." Cody clenched his hands into tight fists. He knew, as the King did, that it was true. There would be no more delays, no more excuses— Cody was going to El Dorado.

"You did *what*?!" Cia cried. Her perpetually calm face contorted into a fusion of anger and fear. "You *spoke* with the Golden King!?"

Cody stood defiantly before the Queen's throne.

The shadow that drifted over him was accompanied by a familiar, exotic scent. "Indeed. Your actions were ludicrously foolish," Prince Kantan uttered, circling into view. "You've done nothing but affirm his wishful suspicions. What was once his elated hope is now his assurance; he now knows without a doubt the extent of your affection for Jade; that you would do anything, or *go* anywhere, to rescue her."

After the Golden King's ultimatum, Cody had shouted into the tunnel-phone several more times to no avail. The

Golden King did not respond, not that Cody expected he would; the terms had already been set—the next time they spoke would be face to face. It was a challenge Cody was ready to oblige.

"He's right. I won't stay here and let Jade die. Seven days—the clock is already ticking. You may be Queen of Atlantis, but I'm not your subject. I'm a Surface-Dweller—not an underling. There's *nothing* you can do to stop me."

Cia's heavy glare remained solid; her pencil thin lips pressed firmly together and her jaw clamped. All the while, Prince Kantan remained motionless, eyeing Cody with raw contempt.

The Queen stood. She took a purposeful stride toward Cody. "My subjects trust me both for their safety and for the protection of our glorious city. Sending you to the Golden King as our only feeble hope for victory accomplishes neither."

Cody readied his rehearsed protest, but Cia continued. "*However...*" her eyes shifted boldly to her brother before returning to Cody, "I suspect this mission *will* take place—commissioned or not. Therefore, I relent. But you will not be going alone."

6
Fallen Sanctuary

𝒜tlantis. Cody felt like a child after the Christmas fervor subsides and the excess of new toys no longer captivates. Weaving down the dusty alleyways of the Inner-City, he sensed a thousand scrutinizing glares directed toward him. The looks teemed with disappointment, despair, and blame. His inability to prevent the fatal ambush and preserve their fallen King's honor had not gone unnoticed.

A droning gong propelled sound waves across the city. Like an obedient pet, Cody knelt and began chanting the Hymn of the Orb: "Hail the Orb of holy light, humbled we by its eternal might, hail the Orb, let it shine forever bright..."

As he mechanically uttered the refrain for the seventh time he looked around. Most people were kneeling as expected, although many mouths were unmoving. Several other citizens hadn't even slowed their pace and ignored the gong's call entirely. One woman passed with exaggerated strides and a brazen face. As Cody uttered the closing *amen*, two bodies pushed past. The scarlet sashes around the men's torsos left no doubt to their identity—Enforcers: grunt men of the AREA.

In an instant they were on the insubordinate lady, tackling her to the ground. When the dirt settled, the woman's head hung feebly on her shoulders and her hands were bound. As the Enforcers dragged her away her swollen eyes met Cody's. Without strength to speak, she mouthed, "Is *this* worth fighting for?"

Cody broke the stare, resuming his path, anxious to leave the troubling scene—Atlantis was crumbling into chaos.

An immense, oval-shaped structure towered before him. The Sanctuary of the Orb—the source of unending power; a power that two legendary cities would spill a sea of blood to claim as their own. The image of the bruised lady skulked into his mind. He wondered just how far the two cities would go to achieve their prize.

Cody's knees buckled as he stumbled off the flimsy lift onto the balcony. A knot wrenched his stomach; it was his first return to the Monastery since the Hunter had pitilessly preyed upon the monks. The repulsive stench of dried blood caused Cody to gag. Only the derisory, timid scent of mint vainly sought to mask death's awful stain.

The instant Cody entered he knew something was wrong. The room was eerily silent. The ten balconies corkscrewing up the expansive chamber toward the domed ceiling were empty. *Where are the remaining monks?*

A coughing sound made Cody jump and fling his hands into a defensive position. "Chill out, you coward," Xerx snarled, retreating a step. Cody maintained his fighting stance.

Whether by jealousy or simple unpleasantness, Xerx had been a regal pain. But their shared near-death experience at the jaws of the Hunter stirred unfamiliar emotions in Cody. He scrunched his face; was he actually feeling a sense of loyalty or even *friendship* toward him? The jarring collision of the young monk's shoulder reoriented Cody's thoughts. "What? The colossal weight of your inflated ego makes you flat-footed? Master Stalkton is expecting you; don't keep him waiting...as always." Xerx spat on Cody's feet as he passed. Cody shrugged. *It's comforting that some things never change.*

As he stepped into the pitch-dark spherical chamber a vile stench assaulted him. Cody covered his nose. The odor wasn't blood; it was something worse—*much* worse.

"Hello?" questioned a creaky voice. "Is that you, Tiana? I've been waiting all day for that hot dirt smoothie...."

"Um, no, Master Stalkton. It's me—Cody," he responded uneasily. The mention of Tiana caused his heart to skip. The two had rarely spoken since the ambush; and even then, it had been stiffly formal. *What was Tiana doing inside the Monastery?*

"Cody, you say?" the wheezy voice replied suspiciously. "Hmmm...never heard of her."

"Excuse me? I'm the Book Keeper and your *apprentice*! And I'm not a *she*!"

There was an agonizingly long pause. "Well, *Cody*, who-is-not-a-she...did *you* bring me my hot dirt smoothie?"

Cody grabbed his forehead. *"Illumchanta"* Bright light ascended to the ceiling like a midnight star. "Master, I've come to...oh, my gosh!"

The light exposed the High Priest for the first time. Three flakey black scabs stretched diagonally from his left ear to the bottom of his gawky chin. The wounds stood out like neon signs against the backdrop of the albino's pastel skin. His regular skeletal figure was even further emaciated, the flesh hanging from his frail bones like wet tissue paper. Looking to the cushion where the elder master sat, Cody yelped in surprise—Stalkton had no legs.

Only two, smooth, rounded stubs remained where his arthritic kneecaps used to be. The Master chuckled. "Wasn't anything they could do, not without the expertise of that Prince...oh, what's his name...the plump one...." The priest retreated into his mind, preparing to conduct a laborious investigation for the elusive name. Cody cleared his throat, thankfully causing the priest to forget his quest.

"Legs are overrated!" Stalkton declared. "Legs can never take one everywhere that a mind can, but one's imagination can effortlessly transport you anywhere your legs could, and beyond...besides, pretty maidens love a man with battle scars! Although it *has* made it rather problematic to wash myself...." The mystery of the room's vile smell was, unfortunately, a mystery no longer.

"Master, I'm afraid I can't continue my training. I am going to El Dorado." Cody braced himself for rebuttal, but Stalkon simply nodded pleasantly.

"Oh, how splendid. Be sure to pack several pairs of underpants. I never seem to remember; gets *so* breezy, especially when I customarily forget to pack pants as well and..."

"Master, did you hear me? I'm going to *El Dorado*, to rescue Jade from the Golden King."

At the mention of the Golden King, the revelation finally registered. "If you face the King...he will kill you." The absolute certainty of the statement was unsettling. "You've only just begun your training. The Book is all that separates you from being an average, or even below average student. Indeed, it's actually rather embarrassing to call you my pupil...perhaps in public you could only refer to me in code...."

"*Thanks*, Master, but I have no choice. Jade needs me. If I can just hold the King off long enough..." Stalkton began to chuckle.

"What's so funny?" Cody demanded, offended by the outburst.

"You!" Stalkton laughed, aiming his boney index finger at Cody. "You *still* don't understand. For a millennium the Golden King has obsessed over the Orb. It's his addiction. He has exceeded all boundaries of possibility. He has no code, no ethics, no morality—only unquenchable desire. Even I, in all my shameless brilliance, would be nothing but an inconvenience to him. He cannot be beaten."

Cody felt sweat rise through his pores. "If he's invincible, why doesn't he just march to Atlantis himself?" asked Cody.

"Simple. Despite unequaled power, he remains bound by the Covenant of the Books. King Ishmael was a gentle man—but not a guileless man. Whatever power he wielded in forming the Covenant remains elusive to his brother." Stalkton's voice died to a murmur. "Although I fear for not much longer. The Golden King has sought to produce *The-Creation-Which-Should-Be-One's-Own*. When he succeeds, the Covenant will fall and he will let loose his full, unrelenting power on Under-Earth."

"*The-Creation-Which-Should-Be-One's-Own*?" Cody probed with a raised eyebrow.

Stalkton shook his head. "I would not tell you more if threatened with certain death. I refuse to speak plainly of it even to myself. It's the first step on the road to destruction. It would be nothing but a temptation; a burden I won't willingly bestow upon you. We will never speak of it again."

Cody nodded in reluctant agreement, although the temptation already had seized his curiosity. He committed to discover more, one way or another. "Master, I must begin my preparation. I just wanted to visit you before I left." Cody turned to leave but stopped, again noticing the silence. "Master...where are the other priests?"

Stalkton sighed. "You already know the answer to your question...they are dead. You and Xerx are all that remain of the Brotherhood, our last hope...a reality so dismally depressing it makes me tingle...oh...or perhaps that's because I just urinated my pants."

7

Murky Motives

The ground beneath his feet swayed. As the balcony shrunk smaller and smaller, Cody's stomach tightened and his limbs became jittery. He wasn't sure whether it was due to his life-long phobia of heights—or because of what awaited him at the top.

The platform jerked to a stop, sending Cody tumbling against the rails. He stepped off onto the Sanctuary's domed roof. Peering across the smooth, metallic surface, he saw her.

Tiana rested on her nest-like bed. Her back was turned and her thick blonde hair, which was accented by a scarlet rose tucked behind her ear, was draped over her left shoulder. She wore a white nightgown that flowed out around her like a marvelous snowflake. Cody had never seen her so peaceful.

She held up a smooth stone tablet that she was painting. The art depicted a large, blooming, silver flower. Each of the four petals formed the shape of a heart.

Cody couldn't bear to disturb her privacy. He inched back toward the elevator. But the moment his foot pressed against the frail wooden planks, a brash creak exploded.

Tiana's head perked up like a deer at the sound of danger. A hint of surprise instantly gave way to anger. Hastily pushing her artwork out of sight, she flung aside the drapes hanging over her outdoor chamber. Cody's mouth went dry. It was the first time he had seen her without her heavy makeup or wild clothing; she looked more radiant than ever.

Tiana pulled a robe over her shoulders to cover her nightgown. "I told you not to come," she issued with chilling steadiness.

"I just need to know what went wrong," Cody said. "Ever since the courtyard you've been avoiding me. I don't understand." He paused, unsure whether to commit to his thought. "And, I miss you," he added tentatively. The minute the words left his mouth he wanted to reel them back. They sounded ridiculous when spoken out loud. Whatever emotions Tiana had about the comment made no impact on her blank expression.

"I avoid you because it's how things must be. We have nothing more to talk about. Go away." Without waiting for a response, she spun back toward her tent.

Cody grabbed her shoulder. "Please," he pleaded. Tiana remained still for several seconds. Then, without a word, she shrugged him off and continued walking.

"Is it because I discovered your talent as a Creator? Or skill with a sword?" Cody pleaded, without realizing he was following after her. "If you think I'm angry because you didn't tell me, I'm not. If you ever want to talk about your past I'm here..."

Cody's words finally struck a nerve. Tiana whirled around and shoved him backwards. "You honestly think I'm avoiding you because I think you're *upset* with me? Why should I care? You stay the blazes out of my past, hear me? I don't want to talk to you about anything. *Any*thing. Now leave me alone before I *force* you to leave." The boiling anger in her eyes validated the threat.

As Cody returned to the elevator he glanced over his shoulder. "You know, Ti...I really care about you. I'm leaving Atlantis; I wanted you to know that." He waited for a response that never came.

The stench of sweaty body odor made Cody retch. The potent aroma gripped his skin. He grinned; he never thought he would be so grateful to smell such an awful stink.

"*Illumchanta.*" Light filled the room.

Cody's eyes followed his nose toward the frumpy little man who wore an ugly smirk on his leathery face. "About bloody time," the man barked in a scratchy voice.

"I hate to admit it—but I actually think I've *missed* you, Randilin. No one else decimates my self-esteem with such precision."

The dwarf's plump, chapped lips changed into a smile as he soaked in what he evidently took to be the highest of compliments. "It ain't ruddy hard when ya' provide such excellent source material. So, what news from the land of freedom and cozy beds?" Following the ambush, all access to Randilin's cell had been restricted. Prince Kantan personally enforced the decree, claiming Randilin's checkered past made it unwise to allow visitors during wartime. Thankfully, Cody's creation ability made it remarkably easy to bribe the prison guards.

Cody recapped all that had transpired since the raid. He briefly shared of Tiana's sudden attitude shift, but Randilin shrugged. "Can't blame her. My stubby left, big toe has more charm with the ladies than you."

Ignoring the slight, Cody explained El Dorado's capture of Lilley and the retreat to Flore Gub. Finally, he stated his decision to rescue Jade and the Queen's surprisingly easy accommodation.

Randilin's head tilted like a curious mutt. "Odd," he muttered, half to himself, "it's not consistent with her character. She holds the ruddy *glory of Atlantis* in higher regard than her own privileged life. For her to just send the city's only hope on a suicide mission and risk surrendering *The Code* to the Golden King...it doesn't feel right."

"Maybe she has faith in my ability..." Cody began but stopped, realizing the absurdity of that claim.

Randilin shook his head. "*You* don't even have faith in your ability. Nor ruddy well should you. *Hmm*. It doesn't make any sense, unless..."

Cody pressed his head between the prison bars. "Unless what, Randilin?"

"Unless...she's not actually sending you to rescue Jade. The Queen's dogmatic, but she's no simpleton. If she's sending you on this reckless quest, then she must have her reasons for doing so. And the longer I think about it, the more I conclude that none of those reasons have your best interest in mind."

8

A Veiled Romance

Cia peered out her window. Atlantis rested in its nightly hibernation, with only the flickering of torchlight to illuminate the thatched rooftops. The lighting glimmered off her ice blue gown. The Queen left the window and retreated into her chambers where a table was positioned and polished silverware precisely placed. A vase of brilliantly colored blooms served as an elegant centerpiece. The wait was excruciating. *Why does he always make me wait?*

She slowed her breathing, allowing her thoughts to drift elsewhere. *Would my father have made the same decision?* Only time would tell; she had no other choice but to wait patiently. *All I ever do is wait*, she thought, glancing again to the door. On cue, the doorknob twisted and her heart jumped—*he's here.*

She smoothed her dress against her slender body, double-checking one more time that the table was properly arranged. The visitor's familiar scent infiltrated the room.

Cia turned to face the man. "I've been anticipating your arrival," she greeted softly.

"As have I," the man replied. "Your presence is always a prize worth waiting for." He removed his hat and gave a slight bow. "As always, you look lovely." Cia's face flushed; she fought to block the sensation.

"And, as always, you are the perfect gentleman. Please, come in."

Complying with the invitation, the man entered. Reaching the Queen, he placed his hands gently on her curved hips. Leaning forward, he pressed a soft kiss against her forehead. "I look forward to our dinner together, my beautiful Queen."

Cia could no longer control the blush that overtook her powdered cheeks. She gazed into the man's eyes.

"As do I, my noble Dunstan."

9

Forming The Company

Sixteen eyes peered impatiently as Cody emerged into the immense room. He scurried across the Great Hall toward the assembly, the rows of majestic pillars flanking his path like a forest of redwoods.

Queen Cia perched on the simple wooden throne, her powdered face taut with a frown. Joining her were Kantan, Levenworth, Dace, Tat, and Sli Silkian, who looked slimy and smug as ever. Cody's eyes bulged; rounding out the group were the last two people he expected to see—Lamgorious Stalkton, who sat merrily in a wooden wheelbarrow swinging his stubbed legs like a child on a swing set and Xerx, who held the wheelbarrow with a spiteful glare as though daring Cody to make jest of the situation.

"Let us begin," Cia said calmly as Cody arrived. The beautiful Queen stood. "This quest balances on the furthermost edge of lunacy, with a myriad of dangers and opportunities to fail. Do you maintain your unwavering decision to proceed?"

Cody nodded without hesitation. "I do."

Cia stroked her thin bottom lip. "Very well." She motioned to Levenworth. The husky General plopped a tattered scroll onto a circular table, allowing it to unroll and dangle over the edges.

"A map of Under-Earth." Levenworth dropped his heavy index finger onto a red star marking Atlantis. "In better days, the logical route would be to go south and follow the river to Azelc's Parish, the Ruins of Sal-Gazta, and then Flore Gub." He traced the path as he spoke. "However, time is short and necessity demands a more direct route." His finger returned to the Atlantis emblem. "A straight course to Redtown, circling the northern perimeter of the Fiery Plains to Du-Morgar, Flore Gub and through the Labyrinth Mountains to El Dorado. The journey will be perilous, but it's the fate we've been given."

Cia touched Cody's chin and tilted his face toward her own. "I will not risk the Champion of Atlantis undergoing this journey alone."

"I pledge my sword to the Book Keeper!" proclaimed Dace, kneeling and presenting his sword in outstretched hands. "For three generations this blade has protected Atlantis and has never been bested in combat. I will protect the Book Keeper to my death."

Cody felt an immense sense of relief; the unfolding scene was like a fragile dream that he had dared not voice for fear it might be snatched away.

"Elegantly spoken, Captain," Levenworth replied. "But your collateral trail of judgment lapses is undeniable. You are young and rash. A mission like this is no place for noble ideals; it is one for wise action."

"As it happens," said Kantan, speaking for the first time and silencing the room, "unreliable or not, Captain Dace is the greatest swordsman in Under-Earth. His skill equals that of ten seasoned soldiers." Kantan nodded to Dace. "I will hold you to your oath. From this moment forth, you are the Book Keeper's blood protector."

"So be it," Levenworth uttered, clearly displeased but lacking any notion of a grudge. "Select the five most capable, trustworthy soldiers in your legion to accompany you."

Queen Cia circled around Cody, tracing her index finger across his back. "The Company is now seven strong. However, the wastelands of Under-Earth are expansive. You lack a guide."

Tat Shunbickle cleared his throat. "I've completed fourteen successful covert missions in all four corners of Under-Earth and have spent two seasons studying under the legendary map-maker, Zilar Dask. I can escort The Company as far as Flore Gub. From there I will then report back to Captain Talgu—and my family...." A violent inferno smoldered in his eyes. Despite his disciplined demeanor, it was clear to everyone that an emotional dam was ready to burst.

Cia peered at him like a maddeningly indecipherable painting before finally relenting. "Offer accepted—The Company is eight."

The excruciating noise of off-pitched humming sliced through the swelling tension in the room. All eyes turned to Stalkton, who was looking absently to the ceiling while swaying back and forth. Sensing the stares, the pale priest smiled. "Does anyone else *love* that song!? Such a heart-wrenching waltz of romance and tragedy! The three-legged horse truly loved that blind spider. True passion, heartbreakingly, never to be realized."

"Touching," uttered Kantan in disgust. The priest took a deep breath, preparing to dive into the second verse but, to the relief of all, Cia spoke first.

"High Priest, what wisdom do you impart to these questers?" Stalkton glanced around the room for a moment before his face lit up. "Golly, is it somebody's birthday! How splendid! I do hope there's cake." With a flushed face, Xerx leaned forward and whispered into the priest's ear. Stalkton's face drooped; now reminded of the actual occasion for the gathering. Gone was any jubilant hope of cake. He sighed. "The Book Keeper's ability remains *agonizingly* amateur. If we are to cling to our cloud of hope, he must continue his training. If not here, then on the journey."

"Wise Master!" Cia cried. "You are in no condition to accompany Cody..."

Stalkton chuckled. "How ridiculous! I haven't quested in ages! Not since the time I awoke in an uncharted cave, naked, holding a cooking spoon, and with the distinct smell of animal dung on my fingers...." The crowd waited impatiently as the rest of the nauseating story played in his head. "No, no, no. I'm not leaving my Monastery." The crowd exhaled a collective sigh of relief. "I will remain here and send Xerx in my place."

"What!" yelled Cody and Xerx in unison.

"With the Brotherhood purged, Xerx is the most versed in the High Language. The final stage in his training can

45

only be achieved through the teaching of others." Cody's eyes locked with Xerx's, who shared his dread.

"The Company is nine."

A low cough rattled as Silkian slithered before the Queen. "Ten...I will be sending my own pupil, Llyi Chazic as AREA representative." Silkian spoke with firm authority; and although Cia and Kantan's faces exposed clear opposition, neither voiced a challenge.

"Ten it shall be," Cia concluded.

Cody dropped his eyes to the floor. "I request that Randilin accompany me as well. He has been..." His voice trailed off, realizing his breath was being wasted.

Kantan sneered. "Request denied. The last time Randilin journeyed to El Dorado, it was as a heartless traitor; to sell out his people and rip away what was most precious to them. He will stay in his cell and rot." Cody saw the Prince's jaw clamp tight.

Cia stepped forward to douse the escalating flames. "Agreed; it is too risky. This war will prosper or crumble on the outcome of this quest. We can trust no one else. You shall depart tonight under veil of nightfall. Upon the ten men of this Company does hope rest."

"*Eleven!*" shouted Tiana from across the Great Hall. Before anyone from the surprised audience could respond, she vanished.

10

From Dust to Dust

I t was unbearable. Like the leisurely change of the seasons, the evening slogged along too slowly. Cody picked at his long-since pillaged fingernails and gazed out his bedroom window, impatient for the vibrant daylight to disappear. A thin, stone tablet on the nightstand caught his attention. Brushing aside the ruby pocket watch, he retrieved the object. His eyes ran over the smooth calligraphy:

THE POWER OF FULL DIVINITY,
RESTS ENCODED WITHIN EARTHLY TRINITY.
WHERE SACRIFICE OF THE PURE ANGEL WHO FELL,
IS THE WAY TO RETRIEVE THE PEARL WITHIN THE SHELL.
WITH HUMBLE HEART AND GOLDEN KEY,
THE UNIVERSE'S MOST POWERFUL FORCE IS REVEALED TO THEE.

He had long since abandoned pursuit of the tablet's prize; in part due to his mistrust of its giver, Dunstan, but also because of his dismal lack of talent with riddles. He exchanged the slab for the worn leather Book, allowing the energy to swim through his veins and revive his fatigue.

Confirming that his door was locked, Cody pressed his palm against the Book's cover.

"Dastanda."

Thousands of dust granules began sweeping across the floor from all corners of the room like an army of tiny insects ambushing an unsuspecting picnic. Colliding in the room's center, the dust stacked like bricks, climbing higher and higher toward the roof. Then the room was still.

Standing before him, like a phantom, was Jade. The dust incarnation took a stride toward him, grime sprinkling down with its every movement. The apparition of Jade pointed her finger and narrowed her eyes. Cody began to tremble. Her finger pivoted until it was fixated on the Book. No words were needed; Cody understood perfectly. "I'm sorry. I should've chosen you," he whispered.

"How long are you going to blame yourself for a decision you can't undo?" asked a stranger's voice from the corner of the room.

"Gai di gasme!" The silhouette of Jade crashed to the floor. Standing in the frame of the window were two men garmented in black robes, both of which were embroidered with a crest and a solitary word: CROSS.

Dangling from the speaker's hips were two polished, circular blades. The second man towered above the first, standing at least seven feet tall. A bushy beard billowed from the shadows of the hood and two elongated, pure silver pistols were tucked into his belt.

"You!" spat Cody in an accusatory tone, "where's Dunstan?"

"Your importance in the unfolding events is significant, but you are far from our only concern. As it happens, Dunstan is...otherwise occupied." The speaker rested against the windowsill; however, the silent giant remained unmoved, his thick fingers resting uncomfortably close to his large pistols. Cody could feel the man's intense stare digging a grave into his forehead.

"Dunstan sends his regards—and a message."

Cody sat up attentively. "Go on...."

The man motioned toward the stone tablet on Cody's nightstand. "He says that your appointed journey will lead to your desired location, but away from your destiny. The answer to questions not yet asked waits at *the place where it was discovered*. Find the northern caves where The Thirteenth dwells; there you will receive understanding."

Cody ran his fingers through his shaggy hair. "What on earth does Dunstan expect me to do with all that mumbo-jumbo? What's in the caves? What's The Thirteenth? And why should I trust you? I don't even know your name."

At this the shorter man chuckled. "What is a name? A name represents individuality—a vice I've long since forsaken for the greater cause. I am Agent Two, no less and no more. My associate," he motioned to the seven-foot behemoth, "is Agent Four. That will be sufficient." He turned to face the window. "The time has come." With that, everything went black and the Orb's light extinguished behind the metallic eye of the Sanctuary.

"Illumchanta!" A bright light filled the room, but the two hooded men had vanished. How they had managed to disappear was of no concern to Cody; he had more pressing

matters on his mind. He scooped up the Book, the ruby pocket watch, and the stone tablet and stuffed them into his backpack. Without looking back, he vanished out his door. Darkfall had come at last—the wait was over, but there was one essential thing left to do.

11

The Journey Begins

Hushed, reverberating whispers exposed the only trace of life as two figures hastened down the darkened alley. A creaking noise brought a sharp *"shhh"* upon the guilty culprit. Exiting the alley, the first figure pushed aside a rock, revealing a narrow corridor. Without a sound, the two figures ducked inside.

Scurrying toward the end of the tunnel they were greeted by the vast horizon. Red soiled dunes stretched across the immense landscape and faded into the distance. Lingering on the threshold view were the titanic pillars of the Labyrinth Mountains: the gateway to El Dorado.

"Cody, you're late. We have no time to spare. Hurry!" Dace hissed toward the men in the tunnel. A congress of people waited, tucked against the city's forty-foot wall; The Company was ready for departure.

Dace looked fierce in full battle armor; a bright Orb crested on the breast of his rock-mail chestplate. His helmet narrowed to an arrow point between his eyes, and a feather draped from the top like a horse's tail.

Five equally adorned warriors flanked Dace. Cody recognized them as Wolfrick, Sheets, Lacen, Kingsty, and Tryin. Their horse-hybrid creatures flared their black noses, clawing at the dirt with their front hooves, anxious for the journey.

Unlike the others, Tat wore only a loose-fitting blue tunic and a tattered brown hat. A polished bow draped over his shoulder and a quiver of arrows rested on his back.

The next man was unfamiliar, although the scarlet sash wrapped across his chest confirmed him to be Chazic—Silkian's representative for the AREA. The Enforcer had a hardened square face, with only the vanguard of morning stubble detracting from his otherwise methodically-groomed appearance. Two C-shaped, hooked scimitars hung from his saddle. Across from the Enforcer was Xerx, exhibiting his usual melancholy demeanor.

At the end was Tiana who stood beside her snow-white stallion. A white headband managed her flowing, lush hair. A leathery-brown corset outlined her narrow figure and the small, elegantly decorated hilt of a knife was visible from the scabbard on her hip.

The three royal siblings, Levenworth and Silkian approached the group. Kantan's face registered confusion at the sight of the man standing tentatively behind Cody. "My servant, Poe Dapperhio, has been an invaluable service to me. I have requested he accompany me to help bear the burden."

General Levenworth huffed. "The Under-Earth wasteland is no place for a bumbling servant. I forbid it." To validate the accusation further, the stumpy servant collided against a horse, blinded by the tower of baggage tottering in front of him. His oversized robe was two sizes too large, making a humorous mockery of his attempted stealth.

Cody stepped toward the massive tactician, his forehead failing to reach the General's chin. "Poe's under oath to me. That places him under my authority—not yours. He is coming." Cody surprised himself with the courage in his voice.

Levenworth shrugged indifferently. "So be it. The time you spend burying him will doom *your* girlfriend. Just don't allow him to speak or show his face; maybe an amateur scout will mistake him as a warrior."

Dace reared his horse. "With all due respect, we have but seven days to save Jade's life. We must depart before the light exposes our mission."

Levenworth whistled. As he did, a majestic black and white horse cantered into the circle. Without slowing, the horse rolled to the ground, scooped Cody onto his back, and shot back to his feet. Cody grasped the horse's thick neck to keep from sliding off.

A tug on Cody's pants brought his attention to Eva's guiltless eyes. He immediately felt her soothing aura. She handed him a dish-sized pewter bowl and a small vial of sand.

"The Speaking Sands?"

Eva nodded. "I'm here for you." She gave no other explanation.

Tat's voice sounded over the gathering, "It's two-days' ride to Redtown. Time is our deadliest foe. We journey steady from darkfall to darkfall. Ride!" Rearing his horse,

Tat slammed his heels and burst away at a gallop. Dust clouded the air as the others set off after him. Cody looked at the majestic city of Atlantis, the Sanctuary towering over the walls. Without a second glance back, his horse rose to its hind legs and bellowed an echoing neigh. The thunderous drumming of hooves sent Cody's world blurring. He clutched the horse's neck and settled into a smooth rhythm.

Somewhere, sitting alone in a dark cell, was Jade and she was counting on him. The clock was now spinning at rapid pace: in seven days she would either be rescued...or dead.

PART TWO
RESCUE

12

Darkness Closes In

Thump...Thump...Thump.

The earth rumbled with each *boom*. The sky dimmed and all visible color drained away like wet paint dripping to the edge of a canvas. Under the gloomy canopy, frantic footsteps and alarmed voices stained the air with the smear of fear.

Hustling from the barracks, Nocsic emerged into a fortress consumed by chaos. Soldiers rushed madly in all directions, many still in the process of dressing. The elevated shouts of commanding officers were suffocated by the mass commotion.

Thump...Thump...Thump.

The ground continued to quiver, sending Nocsic stumbling into a passing soldier. "Private Nocsic, what's happening?" Regaining his balance, Nocsic pushed the soldier aside without responding; there was no time for unnecessary discussion. Weaving through the mob, he scaled a flight of stairs to the top of the wall.

Thump…Thump…Thump.

"Captain Talgu, Sir. My orders?" He called to a tall, gray-haired man who was standing with one leg perched upon a crenellation, gazing onto the horizon like the skipper of a ship. His casual face resisted any trace of apprehension.

"It has begun." At his words, the sky completed its solemn retreat. Nocsic joined the Captain's side, staring silently into the dark. His cheek tingled as a soft flake fluttered against it…then another. Soon the two men were surrounded by a blizzard of white bits. Nocsic rubbed the substance off his nose and pressed it against his tongue. "Ash."

Talgu nodded. "Lilley has fallen."

"Any survivors?" Nocsic asked without conviction.

"The Golden King is merciless, as is his High General—*The Impaler*. If the General leads the offensive…I dare not ponder the unholy fate of the Lillians. The unstoppable flood of El Dorado now crashes toward Flore Gub…." Talgu's voice faded into introspection.

Thump…Thump…Thump.

Nocsic took a deep breath. "Is there any hope…Father?"

Talgu placed his hand upon the younger soldier's broad shoulder. "Son, we have long since forfeited our hope. I swear a blood oath upon my father's blade that Flore Gub will not fall while I have the power to defend it. We are but a leaf in a hurricane. The Golden King's sight is set, and our time is up. They are coming."

Thump…Thump…Thump.

13

An Ill-Fated Departure

Something was wrong. Cody felt it immediately. The ominous sense of peril was tangible. He glanced over his shoulder at the blurry silhouette of Atlantis fading into the distance. Only the small, floating orb of created energy that hovered over his head offered any light to his night-darkened path.

The monotonous drumming of hooves against the rough terrain spoiled the otherwise nocturnal vacuum. Cody squinted through the haze. Tat rode directly in front, his head pivoting on a swivel. *He feels it, too.*

Cody's skin grew cold. A light gust of wind rolled over the upright hair on his arms. *What was that?* Cody could feel his breath hammering against his chest. *Something's not right; there's no wind in Under-Earth.*

He felt another quick chill against his cheeks. Then he sensed it; an unexplainable, yet undeniable feeling—*I'm being watched.*

He began to tremble. Noticing movement above, Cody peered toward the cave's ceiling. A colossal shape hovered over him like an enormous bat and two scorching scarlet eyes punctured the darkness and were glaring directly at him.

"The Hunter!"

A piercing shriek ripped through the sky. Cody grasped the reins just in time to keep from tumbling off as his horse bolted forward, casting dirt into a thick cloud.

Another shrilling screech resounded from the Hunter as it circled above; its immense wings propelled it across the cave's celling. Blinded by the haze, Cody lost his bearings on the winged demon. His heart beat in sync with the horse's powerful strides. *Where is it!?*

Whoosh! An agonizing scream rang from somewhere in the dust. The cry was followed by a wet, crunching noise—then silence.

Cody dug his heels in. *Faster! Faster!* He didn't know which direction he was heading; he was completely caged in the nightmare. "Tiana!" he screamed into the blur, but it was the voice of Dace that responded, "The light! Cody, kill the light!"

It took several seconds before the order registered—the glowing sphere over his head was like a beacon pointing the Hunter directly toward him. *"Gai di gasme!"* he yelled. The orb exploded like a firecracker and vanished, leaving him engulfed in the blackout.

Whoosh! The yell of a second victim echoed—then silence. The Hunter was picking them off like a bird of prey snaring helpless mice.

"Split up! Lead the demon away from the Book Keeper!" Dace ordered. Cody felt a tingle wafting against his neck. Cranking his head, he saw the Beast burst through the smoke, its iron, blood-stained jaws gaping.

"*Ahh!*" Cody nearly was jerked out of the saddle as his horse thrust itself abruptly to the left. The Hunter's powerful wing whizzed over Cody's head. Cody's stomach lurched as his horse hurled through the air and resumed its mad dash down the ridge of the steep dune.

Two shapes appeared at Cody's sides, falling into steady stride: the broad-shouldered Chazic galloped to the right wielding his mighty scimitars. Looking left, Cody exhaled a sigh of relief—Tiana's fair skin seemed to glow in the night. Her blonde hair had broken free from the headband and was now streaming in a wild train behind her.

CRASH! The sound echoed like dynamite. The Hunter had landed and was now racing on all fours down the dune after them—and quickly gaining. Reddened saliva gushed from its open mouth as it howled in hungry ecstasy.

Cody slammed his heels repeatedly, but the Hunter was too fast. The creature's long talons ripped into the ground as it careened down the hill. Its voracious panting grew louder as it lowered its shoulders. Cody winced. With another wild shriek, the Hunter pounced.

In a blur, Chazic propelled himself off his horse and rammed into Cody, sending them both soaring through the air. They crashed to the ground and skidded to a rough stop.

Cody grabbed his chest, fighting to regain his wind. A staggering Chazic was already on his feet; a bloody gash pumping from his side. The Hunter rolled to its feet; its blood-red eyes burning with rage. It surveyed its challenger; then, without hesitation—it sprang. Chazic dodged left and swung his blades in a powerful arc—but the Beast was faster. Its gargantuan wing bashed the Enforcer against the dirt. Launching onto the fallen attacker, the Beast sunk in its claws. Retracting its talons, it hurled Chazic out of the way, a smear of blood tracing his path. The Hunter returned its lustful gaze to Cody.

"Dastanda!" The earth shook as enormous soil pillars burst up, imprisoning the Beast. Tiana emerged into the clearing wielding her jeweled dagger in one hand, and the other palm open to the Beast. Her pale skin glistened with sweat. *"Gai di gasme,"* she finally uttered. She knelt beside Cody. "We have to run!" The Hunter immediately burst through the earthly prison.

Tiana jumped between the creature and Cody. With one swift thrust of its wings, the Beast propelled forward. Tiana sidestepped the first attack. A splatter of black blood squirted onto her face as her knife sliced the predator's wing.

The Beast howled in rage. Its hind leg smashed against her, knocking her over. Tiana's forehead struck against the solid ground and her body instantly went limp, blood pooling around her head.

Cody shuffled backwards as the Hunter approached. He could no longer think. He knew he should resist and fight, but he had become incapable of unscrambling his thoughts. The Hunter's gore-soaked talons stretched out toward him. He felt the prick of the claw slowly puncturing his skin—then nothing.

The Beast released a fierce wail. Its giant wings spread out and with one powerful flap it soared away into the night.

Cody clutched his throbbing forehead. *Tiana!* He pulled himself weakly to where she lay unmoving. A stream of blood trickled down the side of her head, staining her beautiful golden hair. He scooped her into his arms. "Help! Somebody, please help!" Cody looked up. Standing across the clearing was a stranger.

He had long, stringy gray hair that merged with a thick beard to form a matted mane. His garments were tattered and grimy, and his face was filthy. The man's wide, dilated eyes gazed unblinkingly at him. Cody realized the man had no eyelids at all.

"Cody! Cody!" Cody spun to the top of the dune where Dace was racing toward him. Turning back to the clearing, Cody saw that the stranger had vanished.

Everything went black.

14
Discord

S ir, we can't linger—it could return any moment."

Cody pushed himself up and winced as a stinging sensation raced through his shoulder. As he did, the hushed voices around him ceased. Dace and Tat turned in unison toward him. "The Book Keeper wakes. *Now,* we *must* move on," Tat urged.

Dace examined Cody curiously. "It appears that the miraculous has befriended you. You're lucky to be alive."

Memories of the nightmare crowded Cody's mind. "Ti! She's hurt! And..."

Tiana stepped into view. The gash on her temple had vanished although dried blood stained her fair hair. Her expression was one of relief—but not for her own life. She clearly was as relieved to see him alive as he was to see her.

"Fortunately for both of you, Chazic is trained in the art of healing," Dace noted. The Enforcer stood silently beside the Captain, his torn cloak damp with blood. "Although the sacred Book worked its own wonders on you."

Cody squinted and rubbed his eyes, fighting to make sense of what had occurred. "In the haze, I heard screams."

Dace's eyes hardened. "Lacen and Kingsty."

"A sacrifice in vain if we don't move quickly," pleaded Tat.

Dace agreed. "Mount up!"

The remaining Company members scurried to prepare their horses. Poe pushed himself in front of Cody with a clumsy bow. Attempting to ready Cody's saddle, the servant fumbled with the straps causing it to slip off the other side.

Tat scoffed. "*Mistaken as a warrior,* indeed. Two seasoned soldiers fall yet the bumbling slave remains."

Poe puffed his chest but Cody's hand on his shoulder quieted him. "It's not worth it, Poe." The servant gazed silently downward as the scout trotted away.

Cody noticed that Dace was standing several feet behind. "We *both* know that it was more than dumb luck that has you alive. The Hunter doesn't abandon helpless prey. It must have had a reason. Cody, did you see anything? Anything...*unusual*?" The haunting image of the eyelidless man replayed in Cody's mind. *Had he been real?*

Cody shook his head slowly. "No...nothing at all." He lied, unsure why he felt the need for secrecy. His head was still spinning. *What could scare off a monster that, by its very nature, was fear itself?* He wasn't sure he wanted to discover the answer to that question.

Six Days Remaining...

The sky exploded, flinging streaming light shards across its vast canvas. Like an invited guest arriving early to a banquet, the sudden transformation from night to day startled the ten riders as they galloped across the rocky wasteland.

Cody peered over his shoulder; the immense stronghold of Atlantis was now a pebble on the crest of the skyline. They had put ample distance between themselves and the city before daybreak...although at a steep cost: the lives of two honorable men.

Like hail shelling against a tin roof, the drumming of the horses' hooves filled the air. A cramp clenched the left side of Cody's butt. He shifted his weight with a groan but the ache soon migrated to the right side. After what seemed like several eternities, Cody was relieved when Dace raised his fist and reeled his reins. They had arrived at a water station.

With a sigh of relief, Cody flopped off his horse onto the cold ground. The others dismounted with exponentially more grace, and scanned the surroundings. No one needed to acknowledge the watchful action; they all shared the same fear—the Hunter. It was still out there somewhere. Its savage hunger would only be contained for so long. It would find them. For all they knew, it was stalking them at that moment.

"Stretch your legs and water the horses. We depart in ten minutes," Dace barked as he dunked his face into the refreshing water of the well.

The imposing figure of Chazic gave a fluid bow. "Captain, let us offer up the Hymn of the Orb in thanksgiving...." His steady voice was deep and richly toned.

Cody instinctively bent to his knee, but Tat tugged him back up. "*Thanksgiving*? For the slaughter of two good men? We don't have time for your nonsense if we're going to make it halfway to Redtown by darkfall. Let's go." He turned his back, muttering, "Hail to a powerless orb..."

In a soundless instant one of Chazic's scimitars was leveled against Tat's neck.

"*Whoa!* Everybody relax!" Dace commanded, jumping forward. "Chazic, lower your weapon...that's an order. We can ill-afford disunity. Our enemies are numerous enough as is...we will chant the Hymn."

After a few tense seconds Chazic lowered the blade. He pressed his face an inch from Tat's. "Your eyes are a glassy lake..." The Enforcer turned to leave but Tat grasped his shoulder and swung him around. "You have something to say? Then speak!"

Chazic's eyes narrowed. "You care nothing for our mission, Jade, or this war. You blaspheme the Orb in a personal crusade to rescue your wife...."

In a blink an arrow was fitted into Tat's bow. Wolfrick dove forward and tackled him as the arrow discharged, ripping a chunk of flesh from Chazic's cheek. Voices raised as the others rushed to break up the commotion.

Cody leapt back to avoid the conflict. In the periphery he caught sight of Tiana alone by the water well. She made no motion to acknowledge his presence as he approached.

She stroked her fingers though the downy mane of her white stallion and wet its brow with the cool water.

In that moment, an idea consumed Cody's mind—a *horrible* idea. The instant it materialized Cody knew he should reject it. But before reason could deter his rashness he took a deep breath. Turning, he placed his hands on Tiana's cheeks and planted a wet kiss.

15

A Torn Heart

Tiana made no effort to pull away. Time slowed to a stagnant halt. When Cody finally broke the embrace his breath was ragged and his forehead burned. He braced himself for the inevitable explosion of rage—but it never came. Instead, Tiana's face was tender for the first time in weeks. Drying her lips with her sleeve, she grinned. "You should probably water your horse."

As she turned to leave, Cody touched her shoulder gently. "That...felt really good," he blurted. *What are you doing!? Pull yourself together!* "I'm sorry, that sounded stupid. I mean...thank you...for earlier. I wish... " he stuttered. Tiana placed a finger on his lips. "Tonight." Without another word she leapt onto her horse and trotted away.

Cody was hypnotized as he watched her leave. His stare was broken as Poe led his horse by the reins. With the servant's help, Cody mounted.

His face was beaming. *Wasn't such a bad idea after all!* The kiss *had* felt really good. He searched for Tiana again, but instead looked straight into the burning eyes of Xerx. The young monk's usual spiteful expression was replaced by a glare of pure hatred.

"You can teach *yourself* the High Language, you filthy pig." Xerx reared his horse, but only moved several feet before turning back around. "Two men have *died*—for *you*! The men in this Company risk their lives on this suicide mission—for *you*! How do you respond? By frolicking around like a love-sick child." Xerx was quaking. "You make me sick." He spat a mouthful of saliva and departed.

They rode hard, occasionally pausing at water stations but never lingering long. Each time, at Chazic's request, everyone would recite the Orb's Hymn; everyone except Tat who used those moments to disappear on unexplained scouting duties.

Throughout the day, Cody's attempted eye contact with Tiana was unsuccessful. The same could not be said for Xerx, whose continual glare burned a hole into his back.

Dace decided it was too risky to ride through the night again, as the necessary light to guide their path would too easily expose their position to the Hunter. So when the daylight finally vanished Cody released a sigh of relief.

The tents were quickly erected. Tat was assigned first-shift watch duty. The rest of The Company retired to their dwellings. Cody felt savage butterflies raging in his stomach recalling Tiana's earlier promise—*Tonight*. He stared unblinkingly at the entrance of his tent—and waited.

But Xerx's outburst continued to resonate. Why *had* he kissed Tiana? It was as though he temporarily had lost control of his body. Was it because their first kiss, the night of his first Atlantis *sunset*, had been the greatest moment of his life?

He heard the deep rumbling of Wolfrick's snoring from the adjacent tent. *Why isn't she coming? Did she lie to me?* Cody sighed in disappointment and rolled over. *I should have known. Maybe Xerx was right.*

A cool chill washed over him, tickling the hair on his arms. He sat up. "*Illumchanta.*" The faint light filled the tent, steaming around Tiana like an eclipse. She looked angelic. "I thought you weren't..."

"*Shhhh...*" Tiana cooed, crawling toward him. "We have more important things to...*think about.*" Without warning she pressed her lips against his. She inched closer, backing him against the edge of the tent.

Breaking the kiss, Tiana smiled. "Did that one feel... *really good*?" she purred.

Cody's heart beat in a wild frenzy. "Ti...I thought we were going to *talk* about..." His words were muffled by another passionate assault. Cody felt the warmth of Tiana's body next to his.

"Stop!" Cody shouted, shoving her away. "What are you doing?!"

Tiana's face hardened. "What's *wrong* with you?! I thought this is what you wanted."

Cody bundled his blanket around himself as a barrier. "I wanted to *talk*. This isn't talking. It's *wrong*..."

Tiana pursed her ruby lips and ran her fingers through her thick hair. "Are you telling me...you didn't *like* that?" She crawled toward him again, but Cody forced her back with his legs.

"*Stop*! Yes, it felt *amazing*. I think you're absolutely beautiful. When we kiss I can't even think straight..." Cody stammered, speaking faster than his ability to pronounce the words, "but that's not the point. Obviously, I care about you; but I want to go back to how it was before the ambush; before everything became so complicated. What you're doing tonight isn't right."

"What *I'm* doing isn't right?" Tiana spat. "Don't you dare blame *me*. It wasn't *me* who started smooching *you* at the water well!" Her cheeks were scarlet. "Why can't you understand? Things *can't* go back. Never..."

Cody found himself smiling. "If you really believe that then why are you here?"

Tiana turned and left without answering.

"Go to bed," Tat issued flatly. Cody froze his silent approach toward Tat who was keeping watch outside the tents. When it was clear Cody wasn't leaving, Tat finally shrugged. "Oh, *very well*. Have a seat if you must." Cody found a rock beside Tat and joined him in staring into the darkness. For the next several minutes neither spoke. The silence was soothing.

"Is it true?" Cody asked quietly. "What Chazic said today; about your real mission to find your wife?"

A small smirk came across Tat's face. "I suppose it is." He pulled an arrow from his quiver and began twirling it through his fingers. "You of all people should understand—when that piercing sting of love exposes everything else as dull and colorless...."

"What was she like? I mean…"

Tat laughed. "What *is* she like?" he corrected. "She's the most beautiful woman alive, Upper-Earth or Under-Earth alike. Her eyes are glittering gems and her laughter could light the darkness to Atlantis and back…my precious Rali. I don't deserve her. I never have," he chuckled. "When I asked her to marry me, I felt so unworthy. I saved my earning for *three* years to buy her a bracelet with a heart-shaped pendant. To the Inner-City folk it would be a cheap trinket, but for me it represented everything I had to offer."

"Did she like it?" Cody asked.

Tat shook his head. "She couldn't stand the thing! Oh, she never *said* it, but I could tell by the look in her eyes. She wasn't one for expensive clothing or excess. But she's worn it every day since then, even to sleep. To her it represents something more priceless than anything money could buy—true love." His voice trailed off, but his face continued to glow.

Cody shifted uncomfortably, keeping his eyes downcast. "How did you…*know*?" He felt his face flush and was thankful for the shadows.

Tat grinned. "How did I know I loved her?" Tat began drawing a heart in the sand with the arrowhead. "I knew it the day I realized I couldn't live without her; that life apart from her *wasn't* living…."

"Oh." Cody responded for lack of anything better.

Tat began to chuckle. "Kid, I earn my living by reading the signs and connecting the pieces. You're conflicted. You care about Jade like no one else. She understands you in

73

ways that no one else ever has. But whenever Tiana looks at you or touches you, you get this feeling…"

Even the night couldn't hide Cody's scarlet face. "How did you…" he stumbled, but Tat laughed. "You wear your affections like a banner flown high." Tat snapped the arrowhead from the shaft and tossed it to Cody. "We don't know each other well, and it's certainly not my place to decide for you. But there will come a time when *you* will need to decide between the wild lightning storm you desire and the steady mountain you need. The question is, when that time comes, which one will you choose?"

16

Carvings and Ink

Sand trickled through his fingers into the dish. Cody shook the bowl gently, spreading the sand evenly. *The Speaking Sands.* His thoughts were racing too fast for sleep. He needed comforting, and Eva had the special knack of doing just that.

This is so strange, he thought, staring at the dish. He began tracing—**First day. The Hunter. Two Dead. I Am Safe.** He leaned back. *Now what?* Suddenly the sand began shaking, washing out the words like an Etch-a-Sketch. He watched in amazement as letters were drawn into the sand by an invisible hand. **Hail!**

Cody blushed, recalling their embarrassing encounter in the storage room. The sand in the bowl shuffled as Eva drew the words: Was worried. Who was lost? Cody quickly recapped the journey's first day. In turn, Eva updated the affairs of Atlantis. With Cody now out of the picture, Kantan had made a heavy push for the crown and the people of Atlantis were divided.

Thinking for a moment, Cody began writing earnestly: **Do you know anything about the creation-which-should-be-one's-own?** He had spent much of the day's travel pondering Stalkton's cryptic revelation.

Never heard of it. Cody sighed. *It was worth a shot.* A yawn forced his jaw open. **Goodnight** he wrote, then headed to bed.

The moment his head touched his pillow he was blinded by the sting of light—it was morning. He groaned.

Five Days Remaining...

"No-no-no! *Feel* the rhythm," Dace lectured as Cody bounced like a rag-doll in his saddle. "*You* control the motion; don't just go limp...well, at least you're not the *most* miserable rider..." Dace winked at Poe who was clinging to the side of his reins for dear life, flopping repeatedly against the horse's ribs.

Several hours later Cody actually was starting to find good rhythm; or at least rhythm that wouldn't leave his butt black and blue. Despite his outward jesting, Cody knew Dace was deeply disturbed by the previous day's events. Lacen and Kingsty had been handpicked for the operation. Their swift death was a sobering reminder of their mission's unfavorable odds.

"Seems like just yesterday I was a' riding alongside ya' in a convoy just like this. Only back then you were a dangerous fugitive." Cody turned to acknowledge the husky guard Wolfrick as he came alongside.

"A lot has changed since then," Cody responded gloomily. Wolfrick cackled, "Aye, suppose so...although I'm still a lousy drunkard and Sheets still smells worse than dried horse dung. Ain't that right, Sheets?"

The red-haired Sheets appeared on Cody's other side. "We're nothing if not commendably consistent!" he responded proudly. Wolfrick gurgled as he took a long sip from his flask. Cody didn't ask what was inside; it was safe to assume it wasn't water.

"Dace is taking the deaths really hard," Cody observed, more as a statement than a question.

Wolfrick lobbed the flask over Cody's head to Sheets. "That he is, indeed. Good men, both of them. When you live as a soldier death always finds you in the same way. We've seen many comrades fall, but ol' Dace has never grown numb to it. It's what separates men like him from men like Levenworth."

"Aye, two more ticks for the sword handle," seconded Sheets.

"Two more ticks?" Cody asked.

"Every warrior slain under his command gets his initials carved into the hilt of Dace's sword. He remembers every one by name."

"Symbolic in a way; every enemy life he takes avenges one of his fallen soldiers," finished Wolfrick.

Cody gazed at Dace who rode alone at the front of the convoy. He felt honored to have the Captain leading the mission.

Cody wiped his glistening forehead. The temperature increased with each step The Company took. He felt like they were plunging deeper and deeper into a blazing furnace.

Chazic had removed his shirt, fully revealing his impressive physique. Sweat shined off his back, highlighting each muscle and revealing an expansive tattoo. The faded ink depicted three equal rectangles, positioned together to form an upside-down arrow. The arrow was surrounded by a runic sun.

Sensing Cody's stare, Chazic flung his shirt over his shoulders, concealing the image.

"What's it mean?" Cody asked. When Chazic didn't respond Cody probed further. "It looks significant…."

"It only has as much significance as it is given," Chazic responded in his rich voice.

"When did you get it?" Cody persisted.

The Enforcer turned to face him. "I don't know."

"How can you *not know*? It probably hurt like crazy!"

Chazic shrugged. "I was dedicated to the AREA as an infant. Silkian says it was already present then. That's sufficient for me."

"You sure don't talk much," Cody observed.

"I speak when something is worth saying," A sudden snicker drew their attention. Tat had reared to face them. "He prefers speaking with magical orbs."

Chazic grinned. "If you talked to the holy Orb half as much as you shot your mouth, you might almost be a pious man."

"Children, stop your bickering," interrupted Dace. "We've arrived at Redtown."

17

Redtown

The Fiery Plains. A hazy cloud of scorching heat hovered overhead and served as a warning to all unfortunate trespassers to stay away. The barren grounds stretched as far as the eye could see. Resting on the edge of wasteland was a small cluster of buildings.

Who would ever live in such a miserable place? Coming to a stop in the town square, Cody received his answer—*absolutely nobody*. The doors and windows of the rundown buildings were bolted up; and by the look of it, they had been that way for a long time.

"War doesn't just stain human life," Tat explained. "An epic battle during the Great War scorched the land with fire and blood. This crumbled parish was once teeming with vibrant life."

Dace's long hair clung to his neck like a wet mop and his face was inflamed. "But now, no one passes through Redtown, which is to our advantage. Night soon will be upon us. Find shelter from the heat. We depart at first light." The Company dispatched, fervent to escape the unbearable temperature.

Cody found the building farthest from the square. He was eager for a little privacy; not to mention ample distance from Wolfrick's resounding snoring. The two-story building had once dually functioned as a store below and a living quarter on top.

Finding the bedroom, Cody flopped onto the tattered bed. As always, he removed the Book from his backpack and slid it under his shirt for safekeeping. The flowing energy felt refreshing after the day's ride.

"*Byrae*," he whispered. A cool draft came streaming through the window. The breeze was frigid as it rolled over his sweaty skin. He gazed out the window. *Jade, where are you?* He had only been gone two days, but already the journey felt an eternity. *I miss you....*

Cody's eyes shot open and he sat up. His heart was racing and he was drenched in sweat. It was dark outside but he was fully alert. He turned to the doorway. Standing in its frame was a man; two lid-less eyes peering directly at him. "*Ahhhh!*"

"Cody, it's okay!" Cody's eyes opened. He was lying down again, although still soaked in sweat. Tiana stared down in concern. "It was just a nightmare." Cody sat back up and glanced to the empty doorway.

"There was a man...in the doorway." Cody tried pointing but Tiana pushed his arm down and pulled him toward her. "It was just a nightmare."

"It felt so...*real*. What are you doing here anyways?"

Tiana stood from the bed. "I was sleeping downstairs when I heard screaming. I thought I was alone in this house so I came to investigate...." Cody grinned; he was seasoned in the art of excuses. As a master, he saw right through Tiana's amateur lie.

"Why would you sleep downstairs if...*He's back*!" Cody pointed to the door. Tiana seized her dagger. A large silhouette filled the open door.

"Show yourself!" Tiana demanded. The figure stepped forward—followed by another man, and then another. Dozens of men poured into the room; each one with skin armored with gold platelets.

Tiana swung her knife up just in time to block a savage blow.

"We're under attack!"

18

Ominous Feelings

Atlantis had already drifted into its nocturnal slumber; the creaking of ancient buildings rattling like deep, rhythmic snoring. Eva gazed down on them from her chamber window. Like the city, the citizens had succumbed to the need for rest, every worry and care set aside to be picked up and worn the following morning. For the time being, however, pleasant dreams blinded them to despairing realities. For Eva, it usually was her favorite time of day—but not tonight.

She paced back to *The Speaking Sands*. As it had been all night, the sand was tranquil and undisturbed. The silence affirmed what she already knew to be true—something had gone wrong. She could tell; she could always tell. It was her curse.

Prince Kantan stroked his chin as he gazed absently toward the flames dancing in the fireplace. The quiet night was soothing. He reached into his desk and unlocked the bottom drawer, retrieving the only object inside: a framed picture, with the simple caption—*Kantan and Arianna.*

The woman's playful smile caused his stone face to soften. He brought the picture to his lips and kissed her forehead gently.

"Brother…." The startling voice caused him to jolt. He flung the picture back into the cabinet and slammed the drawer.

"Sister, you are not to enter unannounced!" His face was flushed, but he felt his anger slowly ebbing out. "What is it, Eva?"

"Something's wrong with the quest."

Kantan's eyebrows pulled toward his nose. "One of your feelings?"

Eva nodded.

Kantan stood. "Then we must consult our sister."

Suddenly a large shadow engulfed Eva. General Levenworth appeared from behind, blocking the entire door frame. "I apologize for the untimely intrusion—but there's been an incident."

Kantan exchanged glances with Eva. "With the mission?" Levenworth's face was hard as rock. "No, sir, with the prison…Randilin has escaped."

19

Clash of Steel

Sparks erupted with the sound of clashing steel. Tiana's dagger danced in smooth arcs through the air. The three bodies littering the floor were instantly replaced as warriors continued funneling into the room. Despite Tiana's furious defense, they were being backed against the wall inch by inch.

Cody watched helplessly. "Help! Help!" he screamed out the window. Tiana winced as blood smeared down her cheek from a newly-carved gash. The golden golems engulfed them in a semi-circle.

Cody's stomach began to tingle. He clutched his chest and felt the outline of the Book still tucked under his shirt. The sensation raced toward his head. Closing his eyes, he took a deep breath and relaxed his jaw. Like a distant spectator he heard himself whisper, *"Duomi."*

Then the entire room exploded.

Dace was instantly alert. The ground still trembled from the roaring boom. He tightened the grip on his sword.

Without a sound, he crept to the front door. The smell of smoke polluted the air—across the clearing a building was engulfed in flames.

His trained ear instantly recognized the low whistling noise ringing out beside him. Without hesitation he flung his body backwards—half a second before an arrow lodged into the wooded archway an inch from his face. Emerging through the shadows a legion of golden warriors swarmed into the town square.

Dace allowed the tension to drain from his body and willed his muscles to relax. Pressing the cold hilt of his sword against his forehead, he mouthed a soundless oath. He could now smell the charging assailants. With a deep breath, he flung himself at the front line of attackers.

Cody shoved off the rubble that imprisoned his lower body. A gaping hole in the ceiling exposed the bedroom above. They had fallen through into the bottom storefront that now was aflame. The scorched bodies of the soldiers had been blasted around the room. *I definitely need to remember that word!*

"Hurry!" He was yanked to his feet by his collar. Tiana's face was smeared black with ash and her blonde hair powdered gray with grime. "We need to get out of here before..." A loud cracking noise sounded from above as the ceiling sagged. *"Run!"*

Cody bolted after Tiana across the room. He felt the intense heat of the fire as he dodged a collapsing piece of flaming debris. Then came another loud crack from above. "*Jump!*" Cody hurled himself toward the door. "*Umph!*" Falling debris slammed against him mid-jump, pinning him to the ground.

Dashing back through the flames, Tiana grasped Cody's hand and pulled with all her strength. She dragged Cody through the fiery door as the roof came crashing down.

As Tiana heaved Cody to his feet, he saw that the entire courtyard had been consumed by furious combat and already several slain soldiers lay crumpled on the ground.

Tat perched on a rooftop picking off warriors with his bow; each arrow perfectly penetrating between the embedded golden platelets. Below, Wolfrick, Sheets, and Tryin formed a shield around the building.

Approaching footsteps stole Cody's attention. Three golden golems charged toward them. Tiana flipped her dagger into the air and caught it by the blade. With a fluid motion she sent the blade whirling across the clearing. *Thud*. The knife plunged up to the hilt into the lead soldier's neck, killing him instantly.

The two remaining warriors continued the charge, but their path was unexpectedly blocked by the hulking mass of Chazic. Before the surprised golems could react, Chazic's giant scimitars ended their lives. The Enforcer positioned himself in front of Cody, daring more challengers to attack.

Dace was seasoned enough in battle not to be blinded by success. He recalled General Levenworth's favorite proverb: *"It's not the hundred conquered foes that determine your fate; it's the remaining one who plunges his dagger into your back as you admire your victories."* They had fought valiantly; but the waves of enemies were relentless. *There are too many of them.* Tat's quiver would eventually run dry and even Chazic's brawny arms would tire. *We need to flee.*

"Dace! Behind you! A Dark-Wielder!" Xerx dashed toward him pointing urgently. Dace pivoted and braced himself. Approaching slowly was a bald being whose entire body shone as though made of diamonds. It wore a dark purple robe that trailed behind it as a cape. Its expressionless face tilted. As it did, Dace's legs stumbled and he plunged waist-deep into sinking sand. He fought to climb out, but every move pulled him deeper into the earth. Dace stretched his neck to keep his face above ground.

The Dark-Wielder opened its mouth and boiling lava poured out like a waterfall, streaming toward Dace.

"Colania!" Xerx shouted. The flowing lava began to slow, hardening into an icicle in front of Dace's face. *"Gadour! Gadour! Gadour! Byrae!"* Three fist-sized stones appeared, circling above Xerx's head in a whirlwind. He flung his arms and the stones launched like bullets toward the diamond foe.

The first rock chipped off a large shard from its shoulder. Before the other two stones could strike, the Wielder's eyes focused and the rocks imploded into dust. The Wielder sliced its arm through the air. Xerx gagged as he felt something hairy forming on his tongue. Soon a thick fungus filled his mouth, obstructing his breath. Xerx collapsed, his head burning for air as the mold climbed into his nose and out his nostrils.

The Wielder stood over Dace. A thick cleaver grew into the man's hand. Dace winced as the blade came swinging down.

Thump! A body collided with the Wielder, sending both toppling to the ground. Poe rolled to his feet swinging a sledgehammer. The adversary was equally as quick, jumping up and launching a lightning-fast strike toward the stubby servant. To Dace's surprise, Poe ducked, allowing the blade to swing over his head. Pirouetting in a full circle, Poe threw his full momentum into a weighty swing of his hammer. The diamond foe's head shattered into a thousand glittering shards.

Poe stumbled back. As he did so, his hood fell from his head. Dace gasped. "What in the name of...*Randilin*?!"

Randilin's dry lips formed an ugly smile. "A thank you wouldn't ruddy hurt...."

20

Crust No One

O pen the door," Kantan commanded. He shoved past the two flustered guards and through the thick, stone entranceway of the prison. "Light." One of the guards handed him a lit torch. The Prince marched to the jail's lone cell, his furious eyes burning brighter than his torch.

"P-p-p-prince K-K-Kantan?" stuttered a meek voice from within the cell. "Th-th-thank heavens! Are you here to let me out?"

Without responding, Kantan turned and exited the prison.

"What shall be done?" questioned Levenworth.

Kantan fought to slow his breathing and quench his billowing rage. "Find Randilin. Bring him here *alive*. I want the satisfaction of killing him myself."

Four Days Remaining...

"You had better have a good explanation, boy!" Dace scolded. Cody looked sheepishly to Randilin who sat wearing an unnaturally large, amused grin.

The Company had managed to fight its way to the stable and charge through the enemy mob out of Redtown. Although bloodstained and heavily wounded, none had been lost in the ambush. Their miraculous survival did little to quell Dace's anger.

Cody shrugged. "I trust him. When Cia prevented him coming, I guess I just took matters into my own hands the night we departed." Dace strode to where Randilin, whose hands were bound by thick rope, was sitting.

"The Queen forbade it because he's a criminal. His *dark deeds* are not called so without reason. It's too dangerous for him to return to El Dorado. Not after last time."

Randilin huffed. "Dace, I know you. You're too ruddy noble to abandon me here, and I'll be hornswoggled if you weren't smart enough to realize you can't afford even a single man to escort me back to Atlantis. Sorry, lad, but I'm afraid you're bloody stuck with me."

Dace thought a moment before nodding. "Flore Gub. You will accompany us, under close surveillance, to Flore Gub. From there you will be turned over to Captain Eagleton and escorted back to your cell."

Randilin shrugged indifferently. "Anything beats playing a blasted servant."

Chazic stood, having finished healing Tryin's wounds. "Randilin's fate is not our chief concern," he announced. "We're lucky to be alive."

Dace nodded, pacing back and forth. "We've been betrayed. That's the only explanation. That was no small force. They knew our route and were ready. Somebody's leaked our plans."

"Randilin!" Xerx accused.

The dwarf huffed with disgust. "You better watch your filthy mouth, you lousy..."

"Enough! Randilin is the obvious choice," Dace cut in, "but he was in his cell during the council. An ambush of this scale demands time and planning. I fear Atlantis has been infiltrated by a mole."

Tat came galloping into their midst. "We must make haste. The enemy closes in from beyond the next dune. Two more Dark-Wielders are with them."

"If our plans have indeed been compromised then we must take an alternative route," Dace concluded.

Before he could stop himself, Cody spouted, "We should head north to the caves." Dace and Tat became serious. "How do you know of the Caves of Revelation?"

Cody took a step back. "I...uh...probably just...well..." he stammered.

He was shoved aside by Randilin. "The boy's suggestion is folly! I wouldn't step within a thirty-mile radius of that accursed place!"

"Unfortunately, for you," Dace responded, "a prisoner has no voice in the matter. Tat?"

The scout adjusted his pointed hat. "The route to the Caves will bring us perilously close to the Garga Territory."

"Garga?" Cody interrupted.

"Pagans," Dace offered as explanation. "Defectors of Atlantis many, many years ago. They are no friends to any who worship the Orb. They are strictly territorial, but they will attack if they feel threatened. And, they are ruthless demons in combat."

"In other words, their cult is not a beehive we can afford to disturb," Randilin groused. "We should take another bloody route."

Dace glanced to Tat. The guide nodded. "A man can only cross one bridge at a time. Our more pressing concern is the platoon of golems and Wielders behind us. Our small band would have the decided advantage of speed through the cavernous terrain."

Dace agreed. "Mount up. We head north to the caves."

Randilin's beady eyes narrowed. "So be it."

21

Starting Fires

L et me out!" the female's voice was coarse and her words muffled by a coughing fury. Her knuckles were white as she yanked on the solid steel bars of her encasement. "How long are you going to keep me here?!" Her pleas received no reply. She slumped back in exhaustion.

Across the room a tall man reclined in a padded chair filing his nails. He held out his manicured hand to inspect his work, completely unaffected by the prisoner's desperate shouting.

The woman took a deep breath as she prepared for another tirade. Her plans were foiled when three hooded figures silently appeared. Their sudden presence had no effect on the lounging man.

The tallest of the three was hidden except for his exposed, thistly beard. The body shape of his associate established her as an exceedingly thin female with red hair flowing from her hood to her chest.

The third figure stepped forward. "Lord Dunstan," he began, addressing the man. "The boy's path is set. He will reach the caverns by nightfall."

Dunstan smiled. "Glorious news, Agent Two. The master will be most pleased."

The red-haired woman shook her scoped rifle toward the tiny jail across the room. "How long are we going to keep the hostage?" she questioned in an edgy voice.

Dunstan chuckled. "Patience, Agent Six. There will be plenty of time for killing later. As for now, our prisoner is leverage. Until the moment that our contact requests this package to be delivered, our prisoner will remain as décor. A shame really, as I think I'm starting to like her."

The cage rattled violently as the detainee heaved on the bars. "You devils!" she shouted. "You and your *almighty* master think you're so clever. You have no idea what you're dealing with. Consider yourselves warned. You're playing with fire!"

Dunstan grinned. "Actually, my dear lady, we're not playing with fire...we're starting one."

22

The Caves of Revelation

_____

They appeared on the horizon like ghosts; invisible one instant—towering over the landscape the next. The mountains cut through the air violently like edges of a broken mirror.

"This place gives me the creeps," Cody whispered to himself. Despite the convoy's persistence, the rocky fortress remained tauntingly distant.

After several more long hours, the group finally slowed to a halt at the base of the imposing rocks. Like a honeycomb, a matrix of caves dotted the mountain side; each one fading into oblivion and venturing to a thousand unknown ends. The air was filled with the sudden chorus of neighing as, in unison, the horses yanked at their reins, fighting to flee.

"Our speed has bought us valuable time. Catch what rest you can; we cannot linger," Dace ordered. His command was greeted with hearty acceptance; no one minded a shortened rest if it meant escaping the menacing shadow of the caverns.

"We shouldn't have come here, mark my ruddy words well!" muttered Randilin as he stomped away from the camp and settled a hundred yards away. Dace signaled to Tryin who quickly followed after the disgruntled dwarf.

Dace beckoned Wolfrick and Sheets. "Watch the east for any Garga activity. They move like silent demons so stay alert. No dozing...and no ale, Wolfrick." The bulky guard groaned as they set off in obedience.

As the others set to the task of pitching their tents, Cody tugged on Tat's sleeve. "Tat, you've traveled more than anyone. Why are they called the Caves of Revelation?"

The guide paused, and turned to face him. "Aye, and as all experienced travelers know best, some places are best left avoided." He motioned toward the caverns. "All roads may not lead to the same place, but you take any one of those ill-omened passages and find the same end: death. I shudder at the number of souls forever trapped within these endless channels."

"Then why would anyone enter?"

Tat smiled mischievously. "*Legend.* According to ancient Under-Earth lore, it was in *these* very caves that the original tablets containing the High Language were found by Ishmael and his traitorous brother. *The Caves of Revelation,* the place..."

"where it was discovered," finished Cody, his voice trailing off. He mentally recalled the words of the CROSS Agent: "*The answer to questions waits at the place where it was discovered. Find the caves where The Thirteenth dwells, there you will receive understanding....*"

Cody traced through the sand in the bowl. **Hail! Ambushed. Redtown. Safe.** He began to write their current location but paused. Dace seemed convinced that the Redtown ambush was the result of a mole within the inner-circle of Atlantis. *Eva? Surely not!* The young Princess had a gentle simplicity to her that made it impossible to imagine any underlying malice. *I also thought Prince Foz was a peaceful gardener.* Cody's finger remained frozen. He *had* communicated with Eva the night before the ambush.

Detour, he finally wrote, deciding it a good compromise. Shaking the bowl, he waited. Eva's response came quickly: **Hail! Worried. Randilin escaped.** He watched as a smiling face formed into the sand, suggesting that she was under no delusion as to the escapee's current whereabouts. Cody grinned. *Not so simple after all.*

After several more minutes, Cody finally poured the sand back into the vial. As he pulled his bedding over him a shadow darted past the wall of his tent. Cody froze and held his breath; there was no sound other than his racing heart. The shadow briefly flashed along the other side before disappearing. *Something is out there.*

He pressed his face to the tent's wall and peered through the blur, but there was no sign of movement. Turning, he yelped before he could stop himself. The shadow was now directly in front of the tent's entrance.

Sweat slid down his forehead. *What do I do!* The shape remained deathly still and silent. Cody inched forward as gently as he could manage. The sillhouette on the other side remained motionless.

Cody halted an inch from the door flap. There was chilling silence. Whatever was on the other side was not breathing. Cody rubbed his clammy hands and grabbed the flaps. Taking a deep breath, he threw them open.

Two glassy, lidless eyes peered back at him.

23

Bones and Corpses

Agonizing screams filled the air. She strained her eyes, but all she could see was the rocky ceiling hanging over her. She heard a familiar voice but couldn't locate the face. A silver flower with heart-shaped petals dangled above her, blocking her sight.

With a shake, she felt herself floating through the air. Hurried, frightened voices called out all around her. Shadows raced across the walls and people were shouting. Unsure why but convinced it was the right thing to do, she, too, cried out.

She was being carried quickly but couldn't see the face of who was lifting her. She could feel the rapid breathing as her head rose and fell against the carrier's chest. Then, from behind, came a piercing cry.

Tiana jolted up. Her heart raced and her thick hair was sticky against her neck. *A dream.* It was the same dream that had consumed her for the last few weeks. Every night she had awakened at the same point, the terror of the final scream haunting her.

She stepped out of her tent, stretched her arms and allowed her heart to slow. At moments like this, she longed for the solitude of her rooftop hideout. Now fully awake, she surveyed the cavernous mass—and paused.

Two people were scurrying up the side of the mountain.

Cody's eyes stayed fixed on the stranger ahead of him who was darting up the mountain with impossible ease. The ground behind Cody's foot suddenly broke, sending a mass of rocks avalanching down the slope. He lunged forward, grasping the next niche with his fingers. He didn't dare slow down for fear of losing sight of the stranger.

Heaving himself onto the ledge, Cody found himself at the mouth of a giant cave. He searched both directions but the man was nowhere in sight. He looked down the slope, scanning the horizon. In the distance, a spattering of lights confirmed his fears. *The enemy.* They had been pursued since Redtown, and by the look of it, their trackers had not slowed during the night. *They will overtake us in a few hours.*

Cody turned back toward the ominous cave. *The stranger must have brought me here for a reason. I have to know.* "Illumchanta," Cody whispered; a beam of light shot forth from his index finger like a torch.

He cautiously journeyed into the tunnel. Despite his light, the darkness of the cave was overwhelming, each step carrying him farther into a blind abyss.

He froze after a brittle crunching noise sounded under his foot. He took another nervous step. *Crunch.* He halted and illuminated the ground. "Ah!" he yelped. He had stepped on a human skull.

"*Illumchanta!*" Light burst throughout the cave. The wind in Cody's lungs was sucked out.

The room was filled with hundreds of human skeletons.

24

The Den of a Killer

Hollow sockets and fleshless faces shared their silent agony. Cody was petrified under the accusing glare of the deceased. Tiny insects scurried over the bones, weaving in and out of the crevices. The carcasses were in many sizes; both adult and children. Cody felt sick.

Rusted spear blades and fragmented arrow shafts were lodged between the exposed ribs of many. Fear seized Cody as realization hit—*These people didn't just die; they were murdered.*

He paced backward; he needed to leave—and fast. Taking another step he collided against something solid. Two stout arms wrapped around him, muffling his shout, and dragging him to the ground.

Eva was fully alert the moment she woke. She winced as a sharp sting pinched in her chest. *Oh, please, not again.* Her back arched as her body convulsed in pain. She was helpless, paralyzed by the violent jolts pulsing through her. Then, as unexpectedly as it had begun, the throbbing ceased.

Trembling and weak, she managed to open the window and inhale the outdoor air. The seizure had been worse than usual. *The Book Keeper is in danger.* Suddenly her legs gave out and she collapsed to the floor, unable to move. She gazed up through the window. *Cody, wherever you are, may the power of the Orb watch over you.*

Cody skidded across the ground, briefly freeing himself from his captor. His hand fell into a pile of bones. Steadying himself with his arms, his reach found a detached *humerus*. Grasping it, Cody twirled and batted his attacker square in the jaw, sending the man reeling to the wall. Cody wound up for another swing. "Who are you!? What do you want from me? Why did you lead me here?!"

"You ask a lot of bloody questions," replied a scratchy voice.

Cody paused. "Randilin?"

The ugly dwarf stepped into the light and swatted the bone from Cody's hand. "You bet your zit-infested, over-sized nose it is. If you ever hit me like that again I'll use your own scrawny bones to make dust outta ya."

"Wait just a second...*you* attacked *me!* I thought you were...someone else. What are you even doing in this horrible place? You shouldn't be here."

"Neither should you," said a third voice. Cody and Randilin turned to the cave's mouth where Dace, Tiana, Xerx, and Chazic had appeared. "I know not what made either of you come here, but now you must leave—that's an order."

Cody scampered to join the group, more than eager to comply and leave the haunting den. As he did, a shining piece of metal caught his eye. He knelt and retrieved it, shoving it quickly into his pocket.

Tiana examined two skeletons lying side-by-side. She released a soft gasp and backed away. "These bodies...they all seem to be female. What happened here? What could commit such evil?"

Cody grabbed her hand. "We should leave."

As he turned to go he realized Randilin hadn't budged.

Dace's fingers wrapped around his sword's hilt. "I gave you an order."

Randilin's eyes glazed over as though in a trance. He motioned indifferently to the skeletons littering the room. "I can't leave...I...*owe it* to them to stay," his voice dissipated into a distant mumble as though he were speaking to an invisible audience.

Cody shivered. "Randilin...what are you saying? Why do you owe them?"

The dwarf's face went stone cold. "Because I'm the man who killed them."

25

The Prophecy

The flickering mass of torchlight marched steadily toward the mountains; the golden warriors were on the move. Cody glanced at Randilin who walked alone, his eyes as lifeless as the cave's decomposed skeletons. Cody knew the dwarf's past was blemished; but a mass murderer? Another question floated repeatedly in Cody's mind: *Why?*

"The enemy will be upon us in thirty minutes. We must move quickly," ordered Dace. "Chazic, retrieve Tryin from his watch. The rest of you, follow me to camp and…"

"Wait!" Cody cried, halting at the mouth of another tunnel.

"We can't afford to linger," urged Dace, but Cody brushed him off. "Look at these markings!" Faint engravings marked both sides of a narrow entrance. Even from close range, the identical inscriptions were nearly invisible. Each one displayed three equal rectangles positioned as an upside down arrow, surrounded by a runic sun.

"The same as Chazic's tattoo!" Cody observed.

The Enforcer's eyebrows raised, but he merely shrugged. "Curious indeed; but my past is less valuable than the success of our mission. Dace is correct, we must be swift."

Cody slapped his forehead in disbelief. "How can you say that?! It can't be coincidental. Chazic's tattoo; the CROSS agent's message; the eyelid-less stranger. I think I was *meant* to discover this!"

"What are you talking about? CROSS agent? Stranger?" questioned Dace sternly. It was too late. Cody had already disappeared into the cave, swallowed by its tenebrous shroud.

The room was wallpapered by row-on-row of rustic shelves; each one exhibiting a corpus of stone tablets. The only other adornments in the small hovel were a brittle table and a broken wooden chair. And, acting as the room's centerpiece—a dead body.

The elderly man's skin was ghostly and a trail of dried blood streaked across his forehead. Yet, somehow he appeared peaceful.

"His body hasn't begun decomposition," observed a voice from behind. Dace knelt by the man. "He died no more than four days ago. A metal pellet was projected into his..."

"A bullet. Upper-Earth weaponry," Randilin declared, joining them in the chamber. Dace frowned. "Impossible. El Dorado has no such weapons."

Randilin ignored him. His face had gone completely blank. "Impossible indeed..." his voice trailed off. *"The Thirteenth*? It *can't* be." All eyes narrowed on Randilin.

Cody motioned to the body, "You *know* this man?"

"Maybe he killed *him,* too," Xerx coughed, but Randilin wasn't listening. The dwarf knelt and pulled the dead man into his arms. *"The Thirteenth,"* he mumbled to himself.

"Guys, come look at this," called Tiana. She swiped her finger across the surface of the table, cutting through the thick layer of dust. "There was something here." She pointed at a box-shaped outline in the dust.

"Perhaps it's what the killer was after?" Cody suggested. "What about these stone tablets?" He grabbed two from the nearest shelf. Although similar, both were seemingly written in different, unknown dialects. Cody's head tilted—there was something familiar about the engravings.

He sighed and tossed the tablets aside. Chazic's hand launched out and caught the tablets before they dropped. "The Prophecy." At his unexpected words, everyone became silent.

"You can read them?" Cody asked, voicing his surprise. "What language is it?"

Chazic's eyes glazed over. "It is every language—the long forgotten and the not yet developed. One tablet for every language, every language for one prophecy—*The* Prophecy."

"How do you..." Cody stammered, but the Enforcer stopped him. "I don't know why I said that. It's as though I'm reciting a script I've never read. Just like I know the inscription without reading it:

THE POWER OF FULL DIVINITY,

RESTS ENCODED WITHIN EARTHLY TRINITY.

WHERE SACRIFICE OF THE PURE ANGEL WHO FELL,

IS THE WAY TO RETRIEVE THE PEARL WITHIN THE SHELL.

WITH HUMBLE HEART AND GOLDEN KEY,

THE UNIVERSE'S MOST POWERFUL FORCE IS REVEALED TO THEE.

Cody mouthed the final words as Chazic concluded. He felt the weight of Dunstan's tablet in his backpack. "I'm getting a little freaked out...what does it mean?"

Chazic looked around the room confused, as though waking from hypnosis.

"I don't know...only that it is so."

Dace lowered his gaze to the floor. "Perhaps it's time someone revealed his secrets." Randilin was still holding the man, muttering quietly.

Suddenly the blare of a horn sounded in the air. Dace instinctively fingered his sword. "Tat's horn! We must go!"

This time nobody resisted. Drawing their weapons, they dashed out of the cave.

Golden warriors were streaming over the dune and draining down toward The Company. In the camp's center, Tat had readied his bow and Wolfrick and Sheets stood back-to-back bracing for impact.

"Quick! Down the mountain! Retreat!" Dace shouted, billowing down the slope before skidding to a rapid stop. A mob of soldiers blocked the route down. "Break through the lines!"

Cody's ears buzzed with a high-pitched whistling noise. He glanced up just in time to see the swarm of arrows rain-ing down on him. His joints locked up. He squeezed his eyes and flinched.

"Get outta the way, you idiot!" Before Cody could brace himself, Xerx's shoulder rammed against his ribs. Cody's neck whiplashed as his back slammed onto the rocky surface and skidded across the ground. He felt Xerx's firm grasp as they spiraled out of control toward the ledge.

Cody clawed at the ground as his momentum hurled him forward toward the steep cliff. Cody could see the base of the mountain miles below them. He grasped Xerx in a bear hug and screamed.

Then, with a final thump, they went flying over the edge of the mountain.

26

A Passionate Heart-to-Heart

Cody felt as though he'd been bulldozed by a fully-loaded dogsled; every square inch of his body hollered out in pain. He rapid-blinked several times to wipe away his dizziness. A smoking trail of dust traced his path down the steep mountain slope.

A low groan sounded beside him. Xerx pushed himself into a sitting position, his light hair powdered gray. Cody narrowed his eyes. "You just shoved me off a mountain!" He grimaced again as the sharp pain throbbed.

Xerx struggled dizzily to his feet. "*What I did* was save your life."

Cody chewed on his bottom lip, barely managing to force out, "Thanks."

Xerx shrugged indifferently. "Don't bother. You deserved every one of those arrows...I just didn't want any harm to come to the Book."

Cody's face flushed. "Oh, so *you're* the Keeper of the Book now? Last I checked it was *my* responsibility—not yours."

Xerx clenched his hands into tight fists. "Last *I* checked you were doing a royally-awful job of it. It wasn't *me* who allowed El Dorado to defile our beloved King's funeral and force honest men to sacrifice their lives just to fuel a selfish rescue mission. It wasn't *me* who allowed Master Stalkton to be disfigured or be led along like a naïve fool by Prince Foz. Was that everything? I apologize, it's getting hard to keep track…."

"And you would have done better?" sneered Cody, now standing face-to-face with Xerx. "After a hundred years of training, Master Stalkton tossed you aside like yesterday's trash. It took me *one* day to surpass your pitiful lifetime of work. You're nothing but an unwanted nuisance."

Xerx staggered back a step; the redness of his eyes shimmering. "You would know all about painlessly discarding outdated things wouldn't you...the way you dashed after the Book and left Jade standing alone. Right when she needed you most."

Cody felt his stomach churn. "If you say one more word about Jade so help me…."

Xerx smirked victoriously. "Makes one wonder if you ever cared about her at all…."

"*Fraymour!*" A blazing comet erupted from Cody's hands. "*Sellunga!*" Instantly a metal shield materialized in Xerx's hands just in time to repel the flare. The fire streamed around the shield causing the metal to glow red.

"Ahh! *Byrae!*" Xerx yelled, dropping the smoldering shield. A gust of wind billowed around the bend, catching the flame and hurling it back. Cody dove sideways as the inferno scorched the earth where he had been standing. *"Dastanda!"* A dust devil spiraled around Cody, bits of sand stinging his eyes.

Cody buried his face in his arm. *"Duomi!"* With a blinding explosion the ground detonated, propelling them both to the ground. *"Vapiroi!"* Cody was suddenly engulfed in dense smoke. He coughed as he inhaled black fog into his lungs. Squinting his burning eyes, he pivoted just in time to see a fist flying at his face. *Smack!*

The bitter taste of blood soaked Cody's tongue as he somersaulted out of control. Xerx leaped through the smoke swinging his fists down like a hammer. Cody tucked his knees into his chest. *"Umph!"* Xerx wheezed.

Their hands grasped each other's necks as they began rolling down the rest of the mountain. With a thud they hit the bottom and were flung onto their backs. Both were breathing heavily, too exhausted to continue. An uncomfortable silence ensued as they slowly stood and dusted themselves off. Finally Xerx grinned sheepishly. "I've wanted to do that for some time." Cody released a light chuckle. "Me, too!"

"We've been wasting valuable time. We must return to the group, come on." They scurried around the mountain's base until Xerx's arm shot out and stopped Cody. "There's a man up ahead leaning against that tree."

Several paces from their location a soldier with waist-length hair stood spying the other direction. Cody breathed a sigh of relief. "It's Tryin! He was on watch duty." Cody ran toward him. "We're in danger! The others are under attack!" Cody grabbed the soldier's shoulder. The moment he touched him, Tryin collapsed lifelessly to the ground—four arrow shafts lodged in his chest.

"Ah!" Cody screamed, jumping back. Xerx knelt beside the fallen warrior. "Look at the primitive design," he observed pointing to the shafts. Rather than wood, the shafts were made of solid stone. "These arrows were not shot from an El Doridian bow."

Cody felt panic stirring. "Then, who killed him?"

Xerx began backing away. "I think we need to get out of here...*fast.*"

A bellowing war cry erupted around them. Before Cody could react he felt tight pressure against his right temple and blacked out.

27

Exchanging Destinies

———

He couldn't move. His entire body was paralyzed. The slithering sensation of fear gripped him. Cody's eyes darted back and forth but his head was frozen still. Straight ahead, all he could see was an altar-structure covered with fist-sized stones. *Where am I? Why can't I move?*

"Xerx...you here, too?" In reply came a gruff cough. "Yeah, yeah, I'm here." Cody tried craning his neck toward the voice but was unable.

"I can't move."

"Neither can I," Xerx muttered. "I think they have us bound to poles. Won't be difficult to free ourselves with the High Language. Maybe if we..." Suddenly Cody's heart jumped. He was consumed by the feeling of nakedness, as though his soul had been ripped away.

"The Book! I can't feel the Book's energy!" Cody didn't need to see Xerx to sense that the fear had now infected him as well.

"If we burst out with the High Language, whoever stole the Book could flee with it. If they attempt to read from it they could call the Hunter. We can't afford the risk. All we can do is wait for them to return and hope they bring the Book."

Cody felt a stream of sweat rolling over his upper lip and onto his tongue. Unable to brush it away, he pursed his lips, trying to redirect its path. It seemed like they had waited hours but still there was no sign of their captor. Neither of them had restarted the conversation, but eventually the wearisome silence grew too much for Cody to handle.

"Why do you hate me?" Cody asked, immediately surprised by his own question. It was genuine curiosity, no trace of bitterness. After several moments without a reply, Cody resigned himself to the silence.

"I've never hated you."

The sudden response startled Cody. "You've hated me from the moment I arrived in Atlantis."

"That's not true," countered Xerx, but Cody pressed further. "Since *day one* in the Monastery you've had it in for me. You were against me before you even *knew* me...*why*?"

To Cody's surprise, Xerx's response was soft. "Have you ever watched somebody else live the life you were meant to live? Succeeding where you always failed? Watching all of it and being utterly helpless to change it?"

The question caught Cody off guard. Images of his childhood invaded his mind: of his neighbors playing catch with their father; of being shoved to the cafeteria floor and hearing his lunch distributed among the jocks.

"Yes, I have," he responded, "but I never meant to steal your life."

"But you *did*!" Xerx cried. "The moment your fingers pressed against that scarlet *A* my destiny became yours."

"I didn't mean to interfere with your training," Cody began, but Xerx laughed. "My training? I wasn't just training...I was being *groomed*. From the day I was born." Xerx took a deep breath. "I am the lone remaining heir in the Wesleyan line; the last seed in the Book Keeper lineage. I remember the night he told me that he and his wife were fleeing to Upper-Earth. I begged to go, but he refused. He told me there would come a day when I would be needed to protect the Book."

"I didn't know Wesley was married," Cody admitted softly.

"Sadria. A beautiful lady; headstrong and wise. Wesley urged her to remain in Atlantis but she would hear none of it. So, while the Book kept Wesley from aging; Sadria's proximity only slowed the inevitable. Can you imagine the agony of watching your true love slowly die, knowing that you were destined to everlasting life without her? It was the ultimate sacrifice for the Book's safety."

Cody recalled Wesley's tired, almost *relieved*, eyes before his death and his haunting words: *"Boy, I'm sorry it had to be you. Destiny is a sly devil, my lad."* Cody felt a tear welling in his eye. "I'm sorry...I didn't realize."

"Wesley's death was devastating, but I was prepared to take the torch, to offer my own life as a sacrifice. That is, until you pranced into the Sanctuary. An outsider; an oblivious Surface-Dweller sharing none of Wesley's burden. It was all a game to you. Each day as Under-Earth's newest celebrity you became smugger. Then, just when

I thought you'd pillaged every bit of my wasted life, you stole the one I love."

"What are you talking about?" Cody cut in, "Jade's just a friend and…"

"Not her, you idiot—Ti."

Cody's face grew cold. "Tiana? I had no idea…wait… you call her *Ti*, too?"

Xerx laughed joylessly. "You seem surprised? I still remember the way she looked at me her first morning in the Brotherhood."

"Wait…Tiana was trained by Stalkton in the Monastery?" Cody's mind was in overload trying to fit together all the pieces.

"She was special. What took most trainees years, she mastered in days. We had an instant connection. It's hard to explain, but whenever we were together she made me feel a way…I've never felt before."

"What happened?"

"I proposed."

"You did what?!" Cody exclaimed in shock. "What did she say?"

"Nothing. She stared at me for a moment, and then she just turned around and left. The next morning came and she didn't show up for training. She never came back. It was like our relationship never existed." Xerx stopped, suddenly realizing he had said more than intended. "Not that I expect you of all people to understand."

Cody's heart rate was increasing. *Oh, I do, better than you know.*

"I think Wesley was right about you."

Xerx coughed as he retracted the words already exiting his mouth. "Excuse me? Right about what?"

Cody continued assertively, "There *will* come a time when it's up to you to protect the Book—and I think that time is *now*. I'm sorry for the hurt I've caused you. I was blinded by my new power and everyone else paid the price for it. But through my many mistakes I've realized that I *can't* do this on my own. As badly as I want to be the *mighty hero of Atlantis*, I can't...not without help...." Cody hesitated. "Xerx, I need you. You are a more gifted creator than I will ever be, even *with* the Book. I'm asking you, despite the grief I've caused, to help me. Maybe this was your destiny all along."

Before Xerx could respond the air sounded with the beating of drums. Cody tensed up. A procession of men came charging just into Cody's line of sight. Their skin appeared to be painted entirely gray and red with designs spiraling around their limbs like an untrimmed vine.

One of the strange men thrust his face in front of Cody. In the place of teeth, sharpened stones had been fastened and rock shards jutted from his nostrils and eyebrows. Cody swallowed the lump in his throat—the *Garga*.

The barbarian released a blood-curdling, guttural cry that was echoed by the others. He grabbed Cody by the cheeks.

"Let the sacrifice begin."

28
The Garga

Cody winced as the eccentric warrior smeared dirt across his face. "What do you want with us?" The man paid no heed as he continued chanting and spreading the mud over all exposed skin. *All it would take is one simple word*, Cody thought, readying to strike.

"The Book..." Xerx whispered, sharing his thoughts, "wait for the *opportune moment*...." Cody grimaced as the mud sunk into his bare cuts from the mountain tumble. The tribesman raised his hand, wielding a coarse, pointed stone. With a shout he slashed the crude dagger toward Cody. *"Ahh!"*

Cody threw his hands above his head; the severed rope bindings dangled loosely from his wrists. Several more slices and he was finally free from bondage. Cody quickly scanned the surroundings. Xerx was correct; he had been bound to a stone column by his head, arms, chest, and legs.

There were ten barbarians in total; several stood just outside of vision, their spears aimed at Xerx. *Good thing we didn't try to break out!* Cody conducted a quick inventory but the Book was nowhere to be seen.

A sharp spear point pricked his back, guiding him to the stone-covered altar. The savage with rocks jutting from his nose, evidently the chief, waited with his hands outstretched and eyes gazing to the cave's ceiling. Reaching him, the chief's strong hands forced Cody to his knees.

The chief ceased chanting and peered down at Cody. When he spoke his voice was like a boxed tornado. "Lowly infidel, will you repent of your unholy blasphemy?"

Cody tried standing but firm hands pressed him down. "Who are you? What do you want from us? You're making a big mistake!" The chief flung his head back and released a piercing shriek, once again echoed by the others.

"The Great Garganton wills as He wills. We are the *Garga*, meek worshipers of His grandeur!"

As the leader spoke, Cody's eyes continued to hunt for the Book. "The Great Garganton? Never heard of him. Let me speak with him." Cody uttered, trying to buy time.

The crazed chief slapped him across his cheek. "Blasphemy! How dare you defile the Great One's name with such arrogant sacrilege! It's only by the Great One's mercy you have even been allowed to live!" As the wild man shouted, he motioned upward. Cody saw only the faint roof of the gem-dotted cave and the immense, dangling stalactites.

"The...cave?" Cody inquired.

The response drew another solid slap. "Continue with caution...your clear ignorance is all that prevents the Great One's wrath. The pagan Orb-worshipers have already brainwashed you. Your inclusive cult claims glory for itself, *blind* to the Great One's generosity. The gift to dwell within his very mouth."

Cody involuntarily laughed as things finally made sense. "You think *this*…" he motioned all around, "is the inside of some enormous stone-god's mouth?" His laughter increased as he pointed to the stalactites. "Those *teeth* are just a common rock formation in *every* cave; which is exactly where we are, a *cave*. How could you believe such *nonsense*?"

He braced for another wallop, but the chief merely grinned. "I pity your proud ignorance. How could you mock our god which is visible, while believing in a power which is not? A mystic orb and an enchanted leather book…."

Cody perked up. "What have you done with the Book!? Return it or I'll be forced to…*umph!*" Cody choked as a smooth, egg-shaped stone was shoved into his mouth. The rock-nosed chief knelt, grasping one of the hefty stones from the altar.

"Be forced to what? Spout your profane magic? We are well aware of your heathen powers, which is why you and your friend will no longer be permitted to speak." At his words, three more savages circled the altar and grabbed stones. "I truly pity you …unfortunately, your irreverence is not mine to judge…or to pardon." In unison the four Garga lifted the boulders in front of their faces. "Great Garganton, ever generous, ever strong. Your mercy great, your judgment sound…"

Cody thrashed against the grip of his capturers but they were too strong. He strained to harness the Orb's power,

but the stone in his mouth restricted his tongue from forming any words.

"We present our thanksgiving, oh Great One, with the
sacrifice of this infidel. May his flowing blood be soothing
in your mouth." The four men pushed the boulders above
their heads. "Amen."

Cody winced.

BANG!

29

Summoning the Ņound

The blood-smeared boulder crashed to the ground. The sound was echoed as the lifeless body of a Garga collapsed—a red mark dotting the center of his forehead.

A humming noise buzzed in Cody's ear. *Thud. Thud.* Cody opened his eyes as two Garga staggered with surprised faces. Embedded into each of their chests was a crescent blade. The zealots crumbled to the earth, their elevated boulders smashing down on them. Gunfire crackled as two more stunned Garga buckled over.

Free from restraint, Cody pulled the stone from his mouth and turned toward Xerx, still bound and flanked by two Garga. *"Dastanda!"* At his command, the zealots' eyes bulged. Dropping their spears, they grasped their necks. Then both fell to the ground, a mound of sand draining out their mouths.

Cody pulled the stone from Xerx's mouth and severed the bindings. "What's going on!? Where's the attack coming from?" There were two more jarring blasts followed by two loud thumps.

"Cease!" The only remaining Garga, the rock-nosed chief, stood upon the altar with the Book open in his arms. "May the Great Garganton's wrath fall upon you all!"

Cody held up his hands. "Put the Book down...it's over."

The Garga laughed. "Only over for you." The chief's eyes fell toward the Book. Cody's heart skipped as realization finally struck.

Oh, no! "Stop him! He's going to read from the Book!" The Garga began to mutter. There was a pop of gunfire; the chief's head whiplashed as he tumbled off the altar, dead. Cody ran toward the body. *We were too late.*

He snatched the fallen Book. "We have to get out of here, *now!*"

Xerx continued to process the rapid turn of events. "We're okay...nothing happened when he read the words."

Cody scanned the sky. "I'm not worried about when he read them...I'm worried about what comes *afterwards*. The last time someone other than the true Book Keeper read those pages it was me—and things didn't turn out so well."

A familiar British voice carried across the clearing. "A shame that necessity repeatedly cuts our meetings short, as I always find our conversations so delightful." Dunstan appeared, striding toward them; smoke still rising from his revolver. Behind him stood the Man with Circular Blades, the towering bearded man from the bedroom encounter, and a cloaked woman with bright, red hair.

Cody shoved his hand in Dunstan's face. "*Now* you show up!? Why are you following me?"

124

Dunstan's face drooped. "Now, now my boy! Your haughty tone chills my heart." He bared his crooked teeth. "Especially considering I just saved you from certain death!" He holstered his pistol. "After all this time, do you *still* not trust me as a friend?"

Xerx stepped forward. "Cody, who are these men with their Surface-Dweller weapons?"

Dunstan raised his eyebrow in amusement. "Ah-ha, you have Wesley's defined chin, my lad."

Cody brushed Xerx off, flustered. "They are CROSS. They...well...it's complicated." He redirected his attention to Dunstan. "We don't have time for games. You told me to find the Caves. You said I'd receive understanding; but all I have are more questions. What does The Prophecy mean? Who was the murdered man in the cave? What does the upside down arrow mean? What..."

"Good golly!"cackled Dunstan. "You and your bound-less curiosity. Unfortunately, it's not my place to give you life's answers—only to point you in the right direction."

Just then the ground shook. Xerx grabbed Cody for bal-ance. "What was that?"

Dunstan's cheery face became deathly serious. "*It's here.* You must go swiftly. Head east. Two of your companions are there on horseback. You must not linger," he paused, "the answers you seek reside in Randilin. Only he can pro-vide the knowledge you pursue...now *go!*"

Cody grasped Xerx's collar and sprinted across the clearing. Xerx panted. "I don't understand, what is hap-pening?"

Cody felt a chilling sensation stirring in him. The feeling was horrifyingly familiar. Floating across the glade came a soft, purr-like growl.

"We've summoned the hound."

30

Through the Portal

"D o you hear that?" Tiana whispered, stroking her white stallion's mane to keep him quiet. Tat pressed his ear against the earth.

"Footsteps—and approaching *fast*."

Tiana drew her jeweled dagger. "More golden golems? Perhaps they mean to encircle us," she suggested.

Tat promptly remounted his horse. "Possible, but unlikely. Sounds like just two or three persons on foot, and something else—something…*big*."

Suddenly Cody and Xerx came billowing around the bend; their arms swinging like crazed pendulums and their faces beet red.

Tiana's eyes widened in surprise; leaping to her horse, she kicked her heels and darted to meet them. "Cody! What's going…" she halted mid-sentence. The mammoth frame of the purple-caped Beast skidded around the corner in pursuit.

Tiana lowered herself, hugging tight against her horse's neck and slammed her heels again, galloping straight toward the three rushing figures. Reaching out her arm, she grasped Cody's collar and heaved him onto the back of her saddle. Without slowing, she turned and bolted in the opposite direction.

Cody wrapped his arms around Tiana's waist. "The Hunter is too fast! A horse can't outrun it, not with two riders!" he hollered.

Tiana pointed to the horizon to where a glowing dome-like essence rested in the distance. "If we can make it there we will be safe." Cody bit his lip as the Hunter drew closer. *That's a BIG if.*

The dome continued to grow as they drew nearer, but for every yard they gained, the Hunter gained two. It didn't take a genius to do the math. "We're not going to make it!"

"Cody, you need to make a worm hole," Xerx shouted from the back of Tat's horse. "The High Language word is *Spakious.*" The Hunter howled behind them, its hunger propelling it faster the closer it came.

"I don't know how! You do it. You're more talented!"

"I *can't*! It will kill me! *Only* the Book Keeper can do it," Xerx yelled, his voice raspy. "It's just like the water well that brought you here. Draw on the Book's power, visualize the portal's entrance *and* exit, and then shout the word with all you've got!"

Cody strained his eyes at the bubble-like structure ahead. He took a deep breath. *You can do this…you can do this…*

He heard the powerful swoosh of the Hunter's wings. "For heaven's sake Cody—*NOW!*"

"SPAKIOUS!"

31
Missing Pieces

Three Days Remaining...

The sight was utterly repulsive. Cody gasped and stared in horror. Randilin's lips curved into an ugly smile. "Rise and shine—ya' bloody sluggard."

Cody perched onto his elbows and rubbed his eyes. He was lying upon a nest-like bed in an otherwise empty room. He felt odd; as though something unusual were flowing through his bloodstream. "What happened? Where am I?" Slowly, visions of their flight came drifting back. "The Hunter! We escaped?"

The dwarf huffed. *"Did you escape*? Do I look like a revolting, savage monster to you?!" Randilin's grin stretched toward his oversized ears. "Don't answer that."

Cody rubbed his forehead. "Then where are we? What happened to you guys at the Caves?"

"As to our location, I'm afraid you are once again a slimy tadpole within my fishbowl. As for the Caves..." Randilin quickly recapped The Company's battle at the Caves, how Chazic had finally broken through the enemy lines enabling everyone to escape on horseback, and how they led the enemy on a diverted chase to buy time for Tat and Tiana to locate Cody and Xerx. "We arrived here shortly after you," he finished.

Cody noticed something odd about Randilin's demeanor. In place of his grumpy, reclusive temperament, he was strangely talkative; stumbling clumsily over his rapidly spewed words. Whenever Cody attempted to interject, he would quickly dive into another elongated monologue.

When Randilin finally paused to inhale, Cody seized the opportunity. "We still haven't had a chance to talk about earlier...about the Caves and...the bodies."

The cheerfulness drained from the dwarf like rain off a sharp rooftop. His shoulders sagged and the life in his eyes vanished. "Don't think me a bad man," he whispered; wincing, as though each word twisted a dagger deeper into his heart. "I was blind and selfish. Judge me if you want, but one day, boy, when you've truly tasted love, you will understand. I'm not a bad man...."

The dwarf's body shook and the wrinkles on his forehead tightened as though he would explode at any second.

Cody couldn't bear the dwarf's pain any longer. "What about that old man in the cave with the Prophecy?" he asked, shifting the subject. "You kept muttering something about *The Thirteenth*. What's *The Thirteenth*?"

Randilin sighed and his pupils rolled back into his head, his eyes going white. "Not a *what*—a *who*. An extremely *important* who at that: Boc'ro the Wise. The elder of our tribe...."

"The tribe of Atlantis?" Cody probed, but Randilin shook his head impatiently. "No-no-no, don't be so foolish—*Before* Atlantis."

"I don't understand," Cody admitted.

Randilin snorted. "Of course you don't. Ya' ain't the fastest ship in the fleet, are you? I speak of the mighty Alac-icacs." Cody stared blankly back, causing Randilin to shake his head once again. "Well, listen closely. I'll only explain this once."

"The Alac-icacs were the most powerful tribe, ruling over all the people of the sand. Chief Uscana the Merciless was bloody ruthless in his conquest. Blinded by his desire for land, he recklessly led his tribe into the Uncharted Deserts in pursuit of a new foe. The inhabitants withdrew deeper and deeper into the desert.

"Ignoring all wise counsel, Uscana marched onward, taking the bait until the tribe was lost in the abyss of sand and depleted of all provisions. One-by-one he watched his tribe fall dead to ambush and the violent elements until the once-powerful tribe was all but shattered. When Uscana contracted fatal blood poisoning from a spear wound, he summoned his two sons and pleaded that they not make the same foolish mistakes. With his dying breath he blessed his elder son—Ishmael.

"That very night, an unmapped star appeared in the night sky. The new Chief led the ravaged tribe over the vast wasteland toward the star; seventy-seven long days of death and sickness. When at last they arrived they found nothing but an endless sea of sand and a wild, brewing storm."

Cody moved forward on his bed to interject. "And, when the storm subsided they found the well!"

"Shush, boy! Are you the ruddy storyteller or am I?"

Cody bit his lip and Randilin continued, "The mysterious well brought the few survivors to Under-Earth. The illustrious Founders: High Chief Ishmael, son of Uscana; Ishmael's younger brother, whose name is not spoken; Wesley the Faithful; Levenworth, warrior of many victories; Tamarah the Prophetess, of the line of Boc'ro; Naadirah the Beautiful; Sadria the Plain; Shaheena, sister of Tamarah; Kael the Invincible; Evona the Heartless; The Undecided One; and of course—Randilin the Young; at least that's what they called me back then, when I was but a child and dashingly handsome."

Cody couldn't picture Randilin as young *or* handsome, but didn't interrupt. "*The Twelve*. That's what legend calls us. A catchy title...unfortunately, it's nothing but a bloody lie."

"You mean...there was another?" Cody asked.

"Aye...one more. *The Thirteenth*, as it were: Boc'ro the Wise—High Priest and counselor of the Alac-icacs. Although I reckon only the seven remaining of *The Twelve* vaguely remember that name."

"Why? If he was so important then why was he kept a secret?"

Randilin pointed a stubby finger at him. "*Because* he was so important. Until yesterday I thought him long dead. Disappeared the very night Ishmael and his brother deciphered the High Language. They must have had a good reason for keeping him hidden, although blast it all if I know what it was. Son, I'm afraid there is much more going on than we realize."

"Cody!" Dace emerged into the room. "You space-traveling lunatic," he chuckled. "There's something I want to show you."

Cody exchanged glances with Randilin before nodding. "What is it?"

Dace grinned. "Something you haven't seen in long time."

Cody followed Dace out of the tiny hut. A mass city of thatched houses blanketed the rolling hills. The entire city was veiled by a glimmering force field. The dome tainted everything blueish, as though seen through a colored lens.

Dace pulled his sword and clanged it against a hanging gong in the courtyard. Cody grasped his ears. "What was that for?!"

Then, like a raging river bursting through the dam, people began streaming out of the huts. Hundreds of people rushing and forming a mass cluster around them. Cody stared at them in shock. There was something very peculiar about them—they were short, even by Under-Earth standards. Like little men. Then it hit Cody. Dace had been correct; it *was* something he hadn't seen in a long time. The people weren't just little men or women—they were children.

32

The Ageing City

The children's faces beamed as they gazed at Cody, wonder sparkling in their eyes. The entire courtyard teemed with young people from toddlers to teenagers.

"I haven't seen children since I came to Under-Earth," Cody muttered in bewilderment. Dace grinned. "That's because you've never been to *The Ageing City.*"

Dace stepped up on a ledge. "Younglings, I present to you...the Book Keeper!" The children burst into crazed applause and began cheering. A shiver shot down Cody's back. He found himself waving to them and giving a few slight bows. His actions drew increasingly feverous cheers. *Time for a little show.*

He twirled his hands in the air. "How about some fireworks?!" he called out. The children shouted wildly. Dace grabbed Cody's shoulder. "Perhaps now isn't the best time...."

Cody pushed him off. *"Duomi! Illumchanta! Fraymour!"* He readied himself for the explosion of magnificent color, for continued cheers, but nothing happened. Nothing at all.

Cheers morphed into laughter. Even Dace joined in, slapping Cody on the back. "Nice one, hero. *Very* impressive...."

As a droning horn rang, the children hustled away in all directions, leaving Cody once again alone with Dace. "Why didn't it work? That was humiliating!"

Dace shrugged. "*I* for one was *thoroughly* entertained," he chuckled, "but before you make a complete joke of yourself, I should probably inform you that your power won't work here." He pointed to the blue haze arched over the city. "Within this bubble the Orb has no effect."

"*That's* why I feel so unusual. I can't feel the Book's energy flowing through me anymore! I feel..."

"Mortal?" Dace finished for him. "Indeed, you are standing within the only location in all of Under-Earth where you can age. An Under-Earth infant is just as immortal as an Under-Earth adult, but we wouldn't last long as a race of babies now would we? That's why all babies born in Atlantis are sent here to mature into adulthood."

Cody tried to wrap his mind around Dace's words. "I *knew* it was odd that I didn't see a single child in Atlantis. But who looks after these kids? It must be severe punishment to sacrifice immortality and become a constant babysitter!"

Dace shook his head. "Quite the contrary actually. Serving a term in this city is the highest honor and reward." Dace paused, noticing the look of utter confusion on Cody's face. "We always desire what we don't have. A mortal lacks eternal youth; but the Orb has allowed us underlings to remain unchanging forever. Therefore our greatest yearning is not for youth, but for age. It is a sign of wisdom and accomplishment. Men such as Wesley and Levenworth wear their great achievement in every deep wrinkle."

"Then why do you still look so youthful?" Cody blurted before he could stop himself. His face turned red as he realized what he had said. Dace laughed. "Because it would be the greatest tragedy to all the women in Under-Earth to deprive them of my roguish good looks," he said with a wink.

"Where did the blue bubble come from?" Cody asked, but Dace shook his head. "I wish I knew. For all we know it *always* existed. Personally, I like to think that nature itself was providing us with the necessities for life."

Cody suddenly had the sensation of eyes on him. He spotted Tiana standing across the courtyard. Dace glanced between the two. "We abandoned all our gear at the caves when we fled. I've sent Tat and Chazic back to salvage what they can. I thought they could use some *bonding* time. Regardless, we can't depart until the morning so you might as well have a look around." With a slap on Cody's back, he departed.

Cody jogged to Tiana's position. "Thanks for rescuing me," he said as he reached her.

"Same to you. Book or no Book—that was a stylish getaway," Tiana replied.

Cody stood straighter. "This is some place isn't it?" he commented nonchalantly, poorly masking his glowing pride from Tiana's compliment.

Tiana shrugged. "It loses its luster fast. I abandoned this place the first chance I could." Cody waited for her to elaborate. Instead, without notice, she turned and began strolling through the village. Cody scampered after her, matching her stride.

As they walked children would pause to stare at them like animals in a zoo. There was something very *earthy* about the city. Without the power of the Orb, the thatched buildings and dusty roads gave Cody the sensation of stepping back in time.

He looked down a lengthy road that led outside the blue shield to a large cluster of thatched buildings. "Why aren't those buildings inside the dome?" he asked.

Tiana kept her eyes straight ahead but answered, "The sleeping quarters. Consider it population control. When you live forever there's less need to grow up quickly. The children are only permitted to be within the ageing dome during their lessons. Otherwise they would grow too quickly for Atlantis to accommodate them."

Cody noticed that her tone was bitter. She shook her head in disgust. "It is obviously more convenient to keep your children in far off banishment." she added. The intensity in her eyes provided clear warning that the conversation was over.

They came to a stop in the center of the city. Whereas the rest of the buildings were thatched together, the structure in the middle was constructed entirely of stone. In fact, the building looked as though it had been carved in a single, massive boulder.

"*The Hall of Names,*" Tiana offered as explanation. "A record of every person ever born in Atlantis' realm."

"*Every* person?" Cody asked, eyeing the structure with heightened curiosity. "What sort of records are kept?"

Tiana's face was stern. "It's no more than a jewelry box of unwanted memories; records of a past I'd rather not remember. Come, let's go. There's nothing more to see here." She turned and departed the opposite way. Cody took one last glance at the building. A dozen names popped into his mind.

One name in particular.

33

Ḫidden Pasts

Cody peered out his door to the blackened courtyard. The coast was clear. Elevating to the balls of his feet, he scampered into the clearing and between the huts that flanked both sides.

He looked beyond the blue taint of the dome to the sleeping quarters. There were no lights. *Good, they're all sleeping.* Confirming the coast was clear, he dashed down the alley toward the center of the city.

Reaching the end, he halted. *The Hall of Names.* He pushed himself from the wall, sprinted to the door and disappeared inside.

The interior consisted of a single, rounded room. The outside had been deceiving, masking the room's vast size; the domed room was like a gigantic dancehall. Lining the walls were shelves reaching all the way to the ceiling. Filling the shelves were thousands of bins full of various trinkets. Each bin was labeled with a name.

Cody paced around the room examining the alphabetical names of children past and present. He stopped at one bin labeled **Fincher Tople**. *If only I had more time.*

At last his eyes found what he was searching for: **Tiana Hubrisa.** The bin was on one of the upper shelves. Cody glanced around for a ladder but there was none in sight. He pulled up his sleeves and began climbing up the shelf.

Reaching the top he drew the bin down and eagerly dumped the contents on the floor. Compared to many of the other boxes, her tub was noticeably sparse. He picked up a rock with two smeared eyes and a smiling mouth painted on it. The unsophisticated toy made him smile. He couldn't imagine Tiana ever being so young or innocent. The idea of Tiana as a child was somehow strange, as though she had arrived into the world as the same troubled, young woman he now knew.

He picked up some loose pieces of paper. They were labeled as yearly grading reports. He chuckled as he began to read them:

"Tiana is an exceedingly gifted child. However, she struggles from a very short attention span and low motivation."

"Tiana's tendency to beat up the boys remains an issue...."

Cody's glee vanished as he continued.

"Another year has passed without a single visitor. Tiana is remarkably strong willed, but her eyes don't lie."

"Her nightmares persist. She has taken to sleeping isolated from the other girls. She seems embarrassed. Still won't talk to anyone about her nightmares but the girls complain that she screams in the night."

"Tiana is always alone."

Cody dropped the paper. He didn't want to read anymore. He picked up a small nameplate carved into the stone. It seemed to be a form of birth certificate:

NAME: TIANA HUBRISA

PARENTS: UNKNOWN

GOD-PARENT: SALLY PEATWEE.

Sally? Cody hadn't seen the spunky diner owner since she had returned above ground prior to Randilin's attempted hanging. *She's Tiana's guardian? Why?* Cody racked his brain, but couldn't think of any possible connection between the two. *I'll ask Randilin.*

He heard noise from outside the hut. He held his breath until the silence had returned. *I should get out of here.* He turned to leave but paused as another bin caught his eye: **Arianna Levenworth**.

He glanced to the door and then back to the bin. His curiosity was too great. Turning back, he pulled the bin from the shelf.

NAME: ARIANNA LEVENWORTH

PARENTS: GONGORE AND TAMARAH LEVENWORTH

He examined a portrait of her. *Wait...I've seen her before.* Flipping through his memories he finally found it, *she's the woman holding hands with Kantan in the picture kept in the Prince's chamber.* Like then, Arianna was radiant despite not being overly beautiful. There was something else familiar; around her neck hung a beautiful silver necklace with a flower emblem. Each of the petals formed the shape of a heart.

Cody reached into his pocket and pulled out the metal object he had retrieved from the floor of the Caves—it was an identical silver flower necklace, although rust and grime had stolen its luster. *She was in the caves?* Cody's face hardened as he realized what that meant: *Randilin murdered her? It can't be…*

"Where did you get that necklace!?"

The voice startled Cody and caused his heart to skip. Tiana stood in the entrance to the hut.

"Ti! What are you doing here?!" Cody felt ashamed.

"I asked you a question…where did you get that necklace?" her voice was cold and stern.

"I—uh—it—caves—um…I'd forgotten about it," Cody stammered. Tiana rushed at him, backed him against the shelf, and snatched the necklace from his hands. She swiftly shoved it into her gown. Her eyes found the scattered bin on the floor with her name on it. All color left her eyes. "What have you done?"

Cody dropped to the ground and began frantically replacing the items. "I'm so sorry, I couldn't help myself. I just wanted to…"

Before he could finish Tiana's hands yanked him to his feet. "I told you to stay out of my past," she said, her voice quivering. The rage in her tone terrified Cody. With a violent shove Tiana sent Cody crashing against the shelves, causing an avalanche of bins to tumble down.

"You think you have the right to just barge into anyone's business?"

Cody found himself tumbling across the room, his face skidding on the floor.

His cheek burned as he pulled himself to his feet. "Ti, I'm so sorry." His skin went cold as he saw the gleam of a dagger across the room. He fell to the ground as the blade soared through the air and pounded into the wall just above his head. "Ti, please!" Cody raised his hands and braced himself for an attack, but instead he heard something unexpected—the sound of crying.

Tiana stood motionlessly, leaning against the wall for support, her eyes red. She pointed at him. "Look what you've done!" she wailed. She looked as never before—meek and helpless.

"Ti, what's going on? Why have you been avoiding me?" Cody probed gently.

A single tear rolled down her cheek. "Because I *care*! I actually care, and I'm not supposed to."

"What do you mean?"

"You were just a silly game; a way to pass the time; a way to make Jade jealous, to make her as miserable as I was. I showed you romantic sunsets while inside I was laughing as you bumbled about like a lovesick fool. It was perfect—until *it* happened. It wasn't supposed to, but it did. When I held you in the courtyard, after the ambush, and I kissed your cheek—it happened."

"*What* happened?"

"I realized it was no longer just a game. I realized...I *cared* about you."

Cody felt the air in his lung exhale. "Then...why... what?...If you did, then...why did you avoid me?" he managed.

Tiana released a single sarcastic laugh. "Because that's what I do—I run. You think I'm this perfect girl, but you don't know me at all! I'm not perfect. I'm a lying, scheming, selfish witch. The only person I look out for is *me*."

Cody couldn't help but smile. "If that were true then you wouldn't be here, risking your life for me…."

Tiana shook her finger at him, but was momentarily speechless. "My parents didn't want me. *Abandoned* me. Never even met them. I've *always* been on my own. *Always*. If they represent what love is, then I want nothing to do with it. *Ever*. What good is joy if it only intensifies the inevitable pain? Anytime I show such childish weakness and begin to develop that wretched feeling, I flee."

"Is that what happened with you and Xerx? Is that why you abandoned him and left the Monastery?"

Tiana smirked. "Xerx is a fool. We had a perfect thing going. I finally had a friend who could keep up with me. And then, with one foolish question, he ruined everything. That's why I don't understand…"

"Don't understand what?"

"Why you would risk your own life on this rash mission to rescue Jade, a girl who will only break your heart. Give me *one* reason how that makes *any* logical sense?"

Cody gazed at Tiana, her beautiful blonde hair sticking out like a haystack and her eyes full of so much hurt and pain. The answer to the question came to Cody unexpectedly, but was as familiar as if he had always known it. "It's not logical—but it makes perfect sense," he muttered. His face was glowing, vanquishing every shadow in the room, "Because I love her."

34

The Journey Continues

What did I just say?! Cody gazed at the roof of his hut. He felt lightheaded as though sleeping on the moon. *Am I crazy?!* His revelation had disarmed Tiana. She had stumbled out into the night speechless and dazed. Cody was no less stunned by his own revelation. *I love Jade?* The words had exited his mouth by their own accord, as though his heart had grown impatient with his bullhead-edness. His thoughts raced back to the last time he had seen her, standing in the battlefield. *What had she said?* Her last words were unheard, lost in the clamor of battle.

He rolled over in his bed as his eyes drooped. He smiled to himself; for the first time he felt confident filling in her missing word: *Love.* His breathing was deep as his body drifted to sleep. For the first time in weeks, he wasn't visited by nightmares.

Two Days Remaining...

The horses were loaded and ready. Cody rubbed his horse's muzzle, happy to see him again. The prickle of a thousand eyes struck him from behind as the mob of children crowded around the convoy.

Dace mounted his horse and headed toward the group. "Our detour through the caves has left us no room for further delay. If we don't reach El Dorado in two days' time then this mission will have been in vain. With luck we can reach the Borderlands before nightfall."

Tat pulled alongside Dace. His face was stern. "We ride hard—without stopping," his eyes pinned to Chazic as he paused briefly for emphasis. "We know not the location of the golden golems or whether the Garga has abandoned its territory in pursuit. Above all, we do not know where the Hunter rests. We ride our horses into the grave if we must!"

Cody's horse reared onto its powerful hind legs and bellowed. With a graceful leap he bolted forward, leading the charge from the courtyard. The children chased after the horses.

Reaching the edge of the city, the stallion propelled Cody through the blue bubble. It was like passing under a waterfall of slime. As soon as he emerged, Cody instantly felt the energy from the Book pumping through him. He sighed in relief—it was good to be immortal again.

The Labyrinth Mountains. They dwarfed any structure Cody had ever seen as they dominated the horizon like New York's cityscape. The mountains appeared to march toward them as The Company rode steady all morning, through the afternoon, and into the evening.

The horse's flaring nostrils snorted in a back-and-forth dialogue with Cody's growling stomach.

Then, on the break of evening, it appeared. One moment there were only mountains on the horizon—the next, a mighty fortress. The giant wall filled the break in the rocks like outspread arms holding the colossal mountains at bay. Beyond the city rose a dense pillar of smoke—Lilley.

Dace pulled his mount in front of the convoy bringing them to a halt. "We will reach the walls of Flore Gub by darkfall. Our rides are going to give out at any moment. We must rest for the final push."

"Rest within sight of the fortress? We will get *new* horses if we must, we should push on!" urged Tat.

Dace dismounted. "Wolfrick. Sheets. Fall back and watch our rear." The two soldiers nodded and took off in the opposite direction. Dace turned back to Tat. "We are all sensitive to your situation, but as the leader the call is mine. We will rest and tend to the horses."

Chazic stepped forward. "Captain, our circumstances have been valid, but we have neglected the Orb's Hymn. Perhaps now would be an opportune time to give honor."

"*This* again?" Tat huffed, the only member of the Company still in saddle. He pointed to the billowing pillar of smoke. "How can you, in clear sight of such evil, maintain your self-righteous devotion and childish rituals? I can't comprehend it."

Chazic knelt to one knee. "Just as I can't comprehend abandoning your faith at a time when hope is most needed."

"Hope is just a coward's excuse for inaction. Have it your way. I volunteered to lead you to Flore Gub and I have.

I owe nothing to any of you." Tat spat to the ground before Chazic. "Nor your orb." Spurring on his horse, Tat took off toward the mountains. The rest moved toward their horses but Randilin brought up his hand. "Let him be...."

Cody stretched his stiff legs and watched Tat ride out of sight. He felt no anger toward the guide for his departure. If their places had been switched, and Jade's fate awaited him, he had no doubt he would do the same.

Cody looked up and jerked. Xerx was standing in front of him, dragging his feet in the sand. "Um...do you need something?" Cody asked hesitantly. He folded his right hand into a fist, preparing for anything.

Xerx opened his mouth several times as though to speak, but each time he closed it without uttering a word. Finally he muttered in a rushed voice, "I've been thinking about what you said the other day, when we were with the Garga...I can train you. That is, if you still want me to...oh, never mind...."

Cody grinned. "I'm just two days away from facing the most powerful creator in Under-Earth. I can't think of anyone I'd trust more to prepare me than you...seriously," he added as Xerx seemed unsure whether to take the comment as a jest.

"Well, my first lesson would be to lose the dramatics. No offense, but sending balls of fire is entirely cliché and predictable."

Cody shrugged sheepishly. "But it sure looks impressive, doesn't it?"

"A fight is not won by style, it is won by smarts. You actually did this when you saved me from the Garga."

"I didn't have time to think. I did the first thing that came to my head and just filled their lungs with sand."

"Exactly! You did so instinctively because you didn't have time to bog it down with finesse. It was an *indefensible* move. Spouting geysers of lava may make an impression, but they can be extinguished by water. Instead, you need to use your head. For example, instead of drenching someone with water, create the water *in* them. Cause it to burst some of their veins and you defeat them quickly and easily

"I'd never thought of that, Xerx."

If Xerx's grin had grown any bigger it would have leapt off his face. Something triggered a thought in the back of Cody's mind. "You've known Master Stalkton for a long time now. You probably know him better than anyone, don't you?"

Xerx nodded. "Yeah, I suppose so. Why?"

Cody hesitated. "Did he ever mention anything about… *The-Creation-Which-Should-Be-One's-Own*?"

Xerx's smile instantly vanished. "Where did you…?"

Cody shook him off. "Stalkton mentioned it, but vowed never to speak of it again; said that the Golden King was close to discovering it. Do you know what he was talking about? Did he ever mention it to you?"

Xerx looked around making sure no one was within earshot. "Yes." He sat down beside Cody and spoke in a whisper, "You know how Stalkton can be, spends more time talking to himself than anyone else. Well, one night I heard him muttering and it caught my attention. The next couple nights I'd loop back around after my lessons and eavesdrop. Every night was the same; he would get himself worked up about *The-Creation-Which-Should-Be-One's-Own*. Kept going on about *protecting them*—whatever that means. I couldn't sleep at night. My curiosity was too great. Finally, after a lesson, I casually brought it up."

"And…?"

"Nothing. Probably told me the same thing he told you. Something about it being the doorway to destruction and such. He's never spoken of it since. I've been searching for clues, but no one ever has anything to say."

Cody bit his lip. Before he could say anything further Dace called out from atop his horse, "Mount up! We can't wait any longer. Next stop—Flore Gub."

35

Changing the Board

Captain Talgu's bloodshot eyes glazed as they stared unblinkingly at the battalion map on the table. He was by no means a fool or childish dreamer. One does not get personally appointed by General Levenworth without a reputation for rational thinking. It was that very intellect which had led him to the map's inevitable outcome: *we can't win.* The red chips within the outline of Flore Gub were outnumbered twenty-to-one by the golden stack outside it.

The Captain flinched when he heard a rattle on the door. His arm slipped on the table and knocked the red chips to the floor. *How quickly they fall,* he thought grimly. "Come in." A youthful, well-postured soldier marched in and saluted. Talgu returned the gesture. The soldier spied the fallen chips.

"Father, where is your hope?"

Talgu huffed, "Nocsic, my boy; where is your prudence? There is no cowardice in accepting reality. We both know we are no more than a picket fence—a meager gesture declaring that no trespassers are desired, without power to actually stop them when they decide to cross."

"Yes, Father, but that is precisely why I have come...he has arrived."

Talgu's eyebrows jumped to his hairline. *"The Book Keeper?"*

"Yes, Father. He and his convoy just arrived at the east entrance. How shall we proceed?" Talgu paced back to the map. *The board has changed.*

"Prince Kantan's orders were clear. You must ensure that it is done as planned."

Nocsic shifted. "And if the Book Keeper resists?"

Talgu pulled a dagger from his belt. He slammed it onto the map in the center of the golden chips, sending them flying. "That's not his decision to make."

36

Flore Gub

Cody gazed at the scene in wonder. The massive walls of the fortress would make even the great ramparts of Atlantis appear as little more than a dollhouse. Large towers jutted like skyscrapers. Situated sporadically atop the immense walls were wooden catapults.

Unlike the grubby peasants of Atlantis' Outer-City, every person in the fortress was adorned in full battle armor and well armed. The soldiers cast curious glances at the new arrivals as they marched past. Every one of their faces registered fear.

"Your arrival is *most* welcome," shouted a stranger who was the most handsome man Cody had ever seen. His fine black hair was neatly tied in a small ponytail. His chest was broad and his muscles toned to a level Cody had not seen before. The man walked with the confidence of someone well aware of these traits.

"Well, if it isn't the notorious Captain Dace Ringstar—look who finally got a vacation from the slums of Atlantis," the man called.

Dace threw his arms around the man. "Knowing *you'd* be here, Nocsic, I'd almost swear Levenworth sent me here as *punishment!*"

"Well, you would know all about receiving Levenworth's wrath, wouldn't you?" the man laughed. Dace turned to Cody. "Allow me to introduce Nocsic, son of Talgu. He and I were in the academy together."

The two acquaintances set to chatting as they strode through the castle. "What's the situation?" Dace probed.

"Not good. More enemy forces appear every night. I've never seen so many troops."

"Yet they haven't attacked?"

Nocsic shook his head. "That's the thing. We were hit hard at Lilley. They had us on the run, fleeing back to Flore Gub—and then they stopped. My father cannot gauge their strategy. They have vast superior numbers; why not attack?"

"Intimidation?" suggested Dace.

"Well, if so, it's worked. Morale is shattered. What happened at Lilley, it was...ugly. The ever-billowing smoke has stolen courage from even the most seasoned soldier. It's a battle we can't win." His eyes fell on Cody. "But my father may have found a strategy to turn the odds...."

Captain Talgu looked like a man carved from a crude stone. His skin was as gravelly as animal-hide. Although, after visiting the *Ageing City*, Cody was impressed by the waves of wrinkles definitively etched into his brow and below his deeply-set eyes.

"I forbid it," Talgu said in a low growl, sitting stiffly at his war-table staring at Cody and Dace. "You are not to leave this fortress no matter the circumstance."

Cody felt his cheeks begin to burn. "But we must! We have only two days to reach El Dorado! You can't keep us in the fortress. Jade's life *depends* on me!" Cody stepped toward the Captain, but Dace caught his shoulder and pulled him back. "Indeed Captain Talgu, our orders were to..." Dace interjected, but Talgu grunted, "The situation has changed. The enemy barricade is the only way into El Dorado's realm. As commanding officer of this fortress, I assign you to the ranks. Having the Book Keeper defending the walls is the only chance we have. We have no other choice. You will remain in Flore Gub until the siege is over. That is a non-negotiable order. Dismissed."

Cody tilted the pewter bowl and funneled *The Speaking Sands* back into its vial. It had felt good to catch up with Eva and the on-goings of Atlantis. He didn't realize how much he had missed her company, even if only through the *Sands*. Eva's soothing aura was the only antidote for his rage toward Captain Talgu's maddening orders.

The young Princess had communicated that Atlantis was becoming overcrowded and tense as refugees from throughout the kingdom sought safety from the impending El Dorado invasion. Eva also had noted that Cia had been acting odd of late, being in an unusually jolly mood and always sneaking about the palace when she thought no one was watching. Cody couldn't picture the Queen as anything but serious. *Especially at a dismal time like this.*

Cody walked to the window. He had been roomed in one of Flore Gub's three towering keeps. He looked out across the fortress walls. The sea of enemy warriors stretched off into distance like an ocean. They remained hypnotically still. *What are they waiting for?* Cody turned his vision beyond the enemy. *Where are you, Jade? What are they doing to you?*

Dace had remained behind to argue their case to Talgu, but the veteran Captain would not budge. Cody's knuckles throbbed as he clenched them into a fist. *This is time we can't afford to waste!*

A firm rap on the door startled Cody from his thoughts. He scooped up the Book and answered the door cautiously. Chazic filled the entire frame. "Follow me. Quickly. We have a problem."

37

Gone

The stench in the air was nauseating. Cody and Chazic lay on their stomachs as they peered down at Lilley. The entire village was scorched black. Any beauty it once shared had been purged by fire and smoke.

"We should have seen this coming," Cody said. Chazic had gone to Tat's chambers to apologize for their haughty parting. He had found the chamber empty and Tat's bow missing. "Are you sure he came here?" Cody questioned.

"Positive. And...*duck*!" Chazic whispered. Cody dropped as three golden sentries patrolled past. He remained motionless until the sound of the sentries' steps faded away. Chazic rolled to face Cody. "Our best shot of evading the guards is for you to sneak into Lilley alone. You're quicker and more agile—also, Tat hates me. You must convince him to return to Flore Gub. Lady Death is the only one left to greet visitors to Lilley. I'll watch from here and alert you to any approaching danger. Speed be with you."

Cody nodded. He squeezed his fists until the color in his knuckles drained to white. With a deep breath he rose to a crouch and scampered down the hill. He heard footsteps and voices but didn't dare slow down to look back.

Cody felt his stomach twist. The sight was even more sickening than it had looked from afar. If Lilley had once been a beautiful village, Cody could scarcely imagine it. The once peaceful hovels were caved in and seared and a thick haze floated on the air. Ash and rubble blanketed the ground. As he scanned the central square of the city he noticed something odd: *Where are the people?*

The ambush at Ishmael's funeral was still etched in his mind. He was all too aware of the disgusting residual of battle. The Atlantis courtyard had been cluttered with blood and mangled corpses. But as he surveyed Lilley there were no bodies amidst the debris. He knelt to the ground and examined the dirt. There were no signs of struggle. The only footsteps visible in the dirt were his own. *What happened here?*

He ventured deeper into the dreary ghost town. A loud, echoing bang made his heart jump. He spun around and looked behind him. A section of a blackened roof had dislodged and crashed to the ground. Cody slowed his breath. *I need to get Tat and get out of here—fast.*

He heard a faint gurgling sound ahead and followed the noise to the central square. In the middle of the courtyard was a half-demolished tower. Hanging against the side of the tower was a man.

The soldier was strung up against a wall by his wrists; a bloody wound had been cut into his chest. The branding in his chest was in the shape of a six-legged spider. Cody looked away in disgust until he realized the bald man was

158

familiar. It was Captain Eagleton—Captain of Atlantis' Mid-City guard. The Captain released a pained cough.

"You're alive!" Cody exclaimed louder than he meant to. His shout carried across the village like a masted ship with the breeze. He cringed as the sound slowly faded. The mangled Captain lifted his head.

"The Book Keeper? What *madness* has brought *you* here!?" he asked through struggled breaths.

Cody kept his eyes downcast; the sight of the Captain's wounds brought vomit up his throat. "What happened here? What happened to all the people?"

To his surprise the Captain began chuckling. "Gone. Every last one of them. Gone." He entered into a fit of coughing. With each gag the branded spider on his chest darkened with fresh lines of blood. "We didn't stand a chance. One second we were evacuating the civilians and bracing to fight. The next everyone was gone except for me. Just like that—*poof.*"

"What do you mean? Were they captured? Killed?"

The Captain shook his head. "Just *gone.* All I saw...was *the Impaler.* The High General...was...alone. There was a bright...light. Then they...were gone," he said between tortured gasps. "He leaves no prisoners...everyone is dead! You shouldn't have come!"

Cody shivered.

"I have to get you some help and then find my friend. Which way did he go?"

Captain Eagleton didn't answer. He was dead.

Cody turned away, nauseous by the sight of the lifeless soldier. As he did, he noticed fresh footprints leading to the outskirts of the village. *Tat's gone home.* Cody sprinted through the village, no longer caring about stealth or silence. He saw that no part of Lilley had eluded destruction. Black smoke billowed through each of the collapsed rooftops, forming a thick pillar into the sky.

He stopped; at the end of a path was a single cottage. Tat's footprints became greater spaced as they led into the home. Like the rest of the village, the cottage was destroyed. The entire left half of the roof had collapsed and the scorched door lay on the floor. Cody ran up the path, cautiously sticking his head through the door.

"Tat? Are you here?" Cody called out. He stepped over the charred debris strewn across the floor and walked up the creaking stairs. He heard a faint sound coming from the far room. "Tat? Is that you?"

Walking quietly toward the entrance, he found the door ajar. Through the crack he could see someone in the room. He inched the door open.

Tat stood unmoving with his back to Cody. He was muttering to himself.

"Tat...?"

"My precious Rali. So beautiful," he cried, without acknowledging Cody.

"Tat, we can't stay here," Cody pressed. Finally Tat turned around. His face was pale and his eyes glazed. He held out a pendant bracelet in the shape of a heart—it was shattered down the middle and the left half was missing, as though ripped in two. The faded silver was stained in blood.

"My Rali...she's gone."

38

Unleashing the Flood

Cody watched silently as Tat pressed the remnant of the bracelet against his chest. He turned; his eyes empty. "She was everything." His legs buckled and he tumbled against the wall.

"I don't know what to say," Cody pleaded, "I'm so sorry."

Tat's head bowed against the wall. "She was so tender. She never entertained an ill thought. What did she do to deserve an end like this?"

Cody understood that he was not included in the conversation. He glanced around the room and paused. "Everyone in the village is gone. Maybe she escaped? She might still be alive." Tat didn't seem to hear as he continued mumbling to himself. "Tat, we can't stay here. It's not safe. We need to…"

Long shadows stretched across the floor. Cody turned just in time to see the four golden warriors crashing through the door.

"Tat!" Cody shouted. The front golem paused, glimpsing Cody's face.

"The Book Keeper! The Bo~"

Chazic silenced the fiend with a scimitar to the jugular. Chazic twirled the blades in his hands before bringing them down like an X. He stepped over the four slain soldiers.

"We need to go *now*. There was a fifth golem who got away. He will carry news that the Book Keeper has been spotted." His voice trailed off as he looked to Tat who hadn't moved.

Chazic turned to him for an explanation; Cody motioned to the split, blood-stained bracelet. Chazic's face dropped with realization. "This evil will not go unavenged." Reaching down, he scooped the dazed guide onto his shoulder. "As long as the Orb shines, I promise you that."

"Chazic, look!" Cody pointed toward the horizon where lights were being ignited in the distance.

The Enforcer frowned. "The enemy wakes. We need to get back to the fortress—*now!*"

"Father!" shouted Nocsic. Talgu strolled across the battlements, his hands cupped behind his back. Several pinpoints of light danced in the distant dark. On the other side of the plains more lights popped up, like hundreds of fireflies. Soon the whole horizon was aglow. A low rumble began to grow, shaking the ground.

Nocsic glanced to Talgu. "Father, should I ready the men?"

Talgu brushed the perspiration from his forehead. "Immediately...and fetch the Book Keeper. I want him on the front line. This is our defining moment, son."

"Yes, sir." Nocsic raced across the wall bellowing out orders. Talgu watched him depart, smiling with pride—*A good soldier...and a good boy.*

Thump...Thump...Thump.

Talgu gazed back upon the endless mass of torch lights closing in on the fortress. *The dam has finally broken...the unstoppable flood approaches.*

39

Battle of the Borderlands

"To the wall! To arms!" The foundation of the fortress rumbled as the sea of torches came crashing toward the gate. "Ready the catapults! Fire on my mark!" Talgu stepped atop a crenellation with his arms raised. Even as the enemy charged, torch lights continued to ignite farther and farther into the unending abyss. *Orb protect us.*

"Fire!" There was a whizzing sound as the catapults launched, sending massive boulders soaring through the air toward the approaching mob. Talgu raised his arms to ready a second volley.

"Captain, look! Men approaching!" Dashing in front of the stampede were three men. Talgu frowned. *How the blazes? "Prepare the gate—the Book Keeper approaches!"*

The ground shook like an earthquake; Cody lost his balance and fell to his face. The firm hand of Chazic grabbed his collar and hoisted him back up to continue the sprint.

The lifeless body of Tat was draped over the Enforcer's broad shoulders.

The horde behind them was now close enough to hear the bellowing war cries of the warriors. Up ahead Cody saw the open drawbridge of Flore Gub. Dace stood at its mouth madly waving them forward.

From behind, the throng of golems split and a warrior on a large, black stallion galloped through. The man was a titan. In his hand was an immense sword the size of a tree trunk.

Black armor covered his enormous body, jutting out in jagged spikes like the back of a porcupine. Two pinchers curved in front of his mouth and from the back of the helmet jutted six large spikes, as though an immense spider had latched onto his head. *A six-legged spider.* Cody thought of the image cut into Captain Eagleton's chest.

"The Impaler! The High General leads the charge! Faster!" Chazic cried. There was a deafening boom as massive boulders from the catapults crashed to the ground, crushing dozens of yelling golems. The stampede continued, as the golems funneled around the boulders in an endless stream.

"Faster!" Cody could now see Dace's mouth yelling but couldn't comprehend his words as everything had mushed into a ringing clamor. Cody didn't dare look back to see how close the Spider-General was. Hundreds of arrows soared over their heads, pelting the warriors behind.

The drawbridge began to close. "Hurry!" Dace screamed as the plank lifted off the ground. Cody could hear the thundering gallop of the General behind him. Cody closed his eyes and leaped across the drawbridge into the fortress.

An endless volley of arrows crashed down on the enemy like raindrops in a fierce storm. Already bodies of the slain enemy stacked ten feet high against the wall. But each time a warrior fell he was instantly replaced by another. The enemy scaled the pile of dead comrades like a ladder up the wall.

Talgu's eyes scanned the wall until he found his son. "Nocsic! How the blazes was the Book Keeper allowed to leave the fortress?! I want him on this wall *now*! That's an order!" Nocsic nodded and departed with an escort of soldiers.

"What-in-the-name of my triple-chinned aunt Kila were you thinking, you dirt-headed oaf!" scolded Randilin, slapping Cody on the back of the head. "After Area 51, I never thought you could be any more stupid! You jeopardized the whole bloody mission by strolling across enemy lines unprotected! What possessed you to do something so reckless!?"

"It was my doing. I asked him to," Chazic confessed, but Dace shoved his way between the Enforcer and the agitated dwarf. "We will deal with your foolishness later. But we can't stay here. The fortress is overwhelmed. It won't hold."

"Book Keeper!"

Cody glanced up. Nocsic stood flanked by five soldiers. "My father requires you on the wall immediately."

Dace stepped in between. "This is madness, my old friend, and you *know* it. Cody can't change the outcome of this assault. Your father's desires are only for the glory of his legacy. There is much more at stake in this war. If Cody stays he will be killed. We *must* leave Flore Gub. Please."

The five soldiers with Nocsic pulled their weapons and aimed them toward the group. "I'm afraid that isn't an option," Nocsic said slowly, his own sword aimed at Dace's neck. There was a trample of footsteps from behind them. The remaining members of The Company, led by Tiana, came dashing around the corner.

"Cody, you're alright! What's going on here?" she stammered, eyeing up the scene. Three more armed soldiers circled around the new arrivals. Nocsic motioned to his men. "To the south wall." Sliding his sword into his scabbard he looked Dace in the eye. "I'm sorry, my friend; but orders are orders."

40

Of Loyalty and Disloyalty

A piercing screech silenced the battleground instantly. Soldiers ceased combat as the immense shape of the Hunter soared over the fortress, its giant wings casting an enormous shadow over the stronghold.

Cody pressed himself up against a wall as the Beast circled over the battlements. Nocsic motioned toward the escort. "We need to keep moving! Stay out of sight of the demon!" The soldiers closed in from behind, compelling Cody and the rest forward.

When Nocsic raised his hand to stop, The Company faced a solid, stone wall with a single, steel-barred door. One of the soldiers stepped forward. "Private Nocsic, I thought Talgu's orders were to bring the Book Keeper to the front line on the eastern wall, not to the southern wall?"

Nocsic turned to face the man. Then, without any hesitation, he pulled his sword and brought the hilt of it slamming into the soldier's nose. In the same instant, Dace dropped to his knees and brought his elbows back hard into two soldiers' kneecaps sending them to the ground.

A moment later, Cody stood shocked as the eight escorting soldiers lay limply on the floor. Dace grinned. "Oh, Nocsic, like our good looks, some things never change."

Nocsic turned to Cody. "*Orders are orders*. A code Dace and I invented in the academy whenever we had a hankering to be *less-than-obedient*. But there's no time for fanciful memories. Here's the truth. My father is blinded by fear of this invasion, but his foolishness does not stem from him only. He received the orders directly from Prince Kantan himself not three days ago. We were to contain you in the Flore Gub to prolong the defense. It seems that was the Prince's only reason for allowing your rescue mission to proceed at all. He cared nothing for your captured friend." Nocsic motioned to the door. "It leads to the dungeon. Beneath the skeleton in the far right cell is a hidden door. It's an old escape route which leads out of the castle and through the mountains to the Great Sea of Lava."

"The Lake!?" huffed Randilin, "I'd like our chances better fighting through the enemy one-by-one than that cursed route!"

Dace nodded. "It's a last resort, but it's our only chance to reach Jade in time. We have no choice." Dace embraced his long-time friend. "You're a good man, Nocsic. Your father will not be pleased."

Nocsic shrugged. "You and I both know there won't be time for discipline."

Dace clasped the soldier's arm. "Thank you. Stay alive... but if you die—die valiantly."

"I'd die no other way."

Dace looked to Wolfrick and Sheets. As he opened his mouth Wolfrick grasped his shoulder firmly, "Save your heavy conscience the grief and two ticks on your sword hilt...ol' Sheets and I *request* to remain behind with Nocsic to ensure your escape."

"And slaughter a few golden golems while we're at it," piped in Sheets.

Dace gave a slight bow. "You may be gambling drunkards, but you're two of the most valiant men I have ever had the honor to serve with. May your weapons be swift."

"And your feet swifter!" Wolfrick barked. Nocsic nodded. "Swift indeed. Now hurry!" Without looking back, The Company filed through the door and descended deep into the gloom. The last sound Cody heard was the shrilling cry of the Hunter before the thick steel door slammed shut behind them.

41

The-One-and-Only Igg

O*ne Day Remaining...*
   Whether morning had come or the night remained was a mystery as Cody trekked through the narrow crevasse. The thin, single-file passage stretched out of sight both forward and backwards, and elevated to the roof, merging seamlessly into the cave's ceiling.

Tiana paced in front. To pass the time Cody focused on the beauty of her swaying hair. Their words had been sparse since she had almost decapitated him in the *Ageing City*. Yet, Cody couldn't help feeling that their relationship had turned for the better. That it was somehow more relaxed; more—*real*.

However, at the moment, Cody's concerns were for another girl—Jade. As the convoy scurried quickly through the passage toward the Great Sea of Lava, Cody just hoped they had enough time. Dace's earlier words had been correct: they couldn't afford more delays. Time was running out.

The sight of open ground was like stumbling upon a watery oasis amidst a scorching desert. Cody stretched his arms, finally free from the constricted space of the passage. Across the vast flat clearing was a single cottage as though dropped onto the desolate wilderness by accident.

However, it was what was *behind* the cottage that caused Cody to gasp. Sprawling endlessly out of view was a smoldering, bubbling expanse of lava. The air above the fuming sea was hazy from the heat.

"Stop! *Don't* take another step!" called an unannounced, irritated voice. The door of the cottage burst open to reveal a stumpy man. The stranger marched toward them huffing and puffing with every step. His hair was frizzy and stood on end. His skin was coarse and uneven like bubble wrap paper with boils and burn marks covering half. His face was wild and in place of where his left eye should have been was an empty, gaping hole.

When the man reached them he was muttering angrily at them. "Just barging in on Igg! No appointments! Whatever happened to common courtesy...?" his words returned to incoherent gabbling.

Dace stepped forward to greet the man. "I am Captain Dace of Atlantis. We have urgent business in El Dorado. Can you assist us?" Dace scanned the barren, unoccupied wasteland. "If you are not too busy, of course."

The hermit's chest puffed like a blowfish. "*Can* Igg assist you? Do horn-backed lava beetles travel in packs?" he exhorted. "Who's traversed the Great Magma Darlin' more times than any living soul?"

Dace shrugged. "You?"

"Darn right you are, mate! Just so happens, you're in luck! As Igg doesn't have any company or business to attend to—the-one-and-only Igg K. Stalkton at your service!"

"Stalkton?" Cody questioned in surprise. "Are you related to..."

"...that crazy ol' High Priest? Do rock cakes taste best when roasted?"

Thankfully for Cody, the man once again was content to answer his own questions. "Me younger brother he is—and bonkers as a marooned seaman, too! Forever alone in that restrictive monastery...Not Igg! Nope! Can't steal Igg away from the fast life of grandeur and adventure!"

Cody suspiciously scanned the surroundings unable to find any trace of either grandeur *or* adventure.

"We must reach El Dorado by nightfall. If not, my best friend will be killed. Can it be done?" The skipper cast a disgusted look to Cody. His boil-covered finger rose and scratched the inside of his gaping eye socket as he spoke. "I can get ya' there yesterday if ya' asked tomorrow!"

"What the heavens is *that*?" Cody exclaimed staring at the jumbled piece of junk floating on the lava. The one-eyed skipper stretched out his arms like a cross. "Behold... *The Igg!*" He proclaimed. His face molded into a frown as all eyes fell on him. "Not *me*, ya' land-lovin' morons, *that!*" he motioned to the floating scrap-pile. "The mightiest vessel of them all!"

Cody looked between the human Igg and boat *Igg*. "You named the ship after yourself? Wait...*that's* a ship!?" Cody asked in astonishment.

Igg's grin widened. "That she is, sonny! And a blasting good one at that, too!" At his words, there was a loud cracking sound and a chunk of the stern of the makeshift ship broke off and sunk beneath the bubbling lava. Igg fingered the inside of his empty eye-socket again and coughed awkwardly. "Although she may be in need of some minor repairs...."

42

Across the Great Sea of Lava

Sticky perspiration spilled off Cody's body and soaked into his already drenched shirt. No matter how many times he wiped his forehead it remained coated with sweat. He looked out across the breadth of bubbling lava as the rickety ship rolled peacefully over its steaming surface. The sky had gone dark shortly after departure.

No one needed to acknowledge what every person thought: they were down to their last day. Cody hoped Igg's boasting was more than vain fluff.

"Pretty isn't it—in its own way," Tiana said, announcing her presence. She stood beside Cody looking out over the fiery sea. "You thinking about her?" Her question caught Cody off guard.

"Jade? Yeah...I mean...to have come this far. How do I know she's still okay? It'll be the first time I'll see her since...well, never mind."

Tiana placed her hand on his. "The first time you'll see her since you ran after the Book and left her standing in the middle of the battlefield? And, you don't know how she will respond to you?"

Cody involuntarily laughed. "Well, sort of...actually, *exactly* that. How did you know?"

Tiana propped herself onto the ship's railing, flinging her feet around and dangling them over the edge. Cody's heart jumped. "If I *didn't* know that, then I wouldn't be a woman," she said with a smile. "And, I was standing right there, too, remember?"

Cody played the scene for the millionth time. "When I left her, she yelled something to me. I heard her, but the noise drowned out some of her words...."

Tiana's eyes narrowed. "I remember...but it's not my place to repeat it. Some things are best heard from Jade's own mouth."

Cody nodded in disappointment. "I'm glad you decided to come, Ti—even if you almost cut my head off. You *meant* to miss...right?"

Tiana's lips formed into a slight grin and she kept silent. A foul smell proclaimed the coming of Randilin. "And a bloody shame she *did* miss," he barked. "Follow me, there's something you should see." The dwarf spun, and shuffled across the deck in the other direction.

"You go, Cody, I think I'll stay here for awhile," Tiana urged. Cody squeezed her hand before darting after Randilin, who was already standing against the adjacent railing between Igg and Chazic. The Enforcer had removed his shirt, once again revealing the large, upside-down arrow tattoo. He, however, appeared strikingly modest in contrast to the other. The Sea-skipper stood stark naked.

"Oh!" Cody cried.

The naked captain turned to face him; Cody's eyes shot toward the cave's ceiling. "Feast your eyes, son."

"*Excuse me?*" Cody exclaimed, keeping his eyes firmly focused upward. Igg turned around and pointed out over the lava. Cody looked the direction of the skipper's finger.

There was a small island jutting out of the sea. In the middle of the island was a scorching, red pool. The lava churned slowly in a sunken whirlpool.

"The prison of the banished demon," revealed Randilin solemnly.

Cody's heart rate accelerated to double-time. "The Hunter?"

Randilin nodded. "Indeed, the very embodiment of evil itself. Banished to eternal torment beneath the boiling prison of lava. For two thousand years it waited in agony; it's hunger increasing with its rage. Patiently waiting…."

"To be released by a foolish child," finished Cody gloomily.

Randilin agreed. "Aye. When Ishmael defeated the Golden King he attempted to kill the Beast. For a week Atlantis tried everything—but the Hunter didn't die…*couldn't* die. As a last resort, it was banished. Only when someone *other* than the Book Keeper attempted to read from *The Code* would the creature be released to forever hunt that person. It was meant to prevent the Golden King and his minions from stealing the Book. No one foresaw that the Book would be stolen by, well, *someone else*," he finished.

Cody felt nauseated, and not from sailing. "Can *he* control it? The Golden King?" he asked.

This time Chazic answered, "No one knows. But I've often wondered: how much, and how long, can anyone truly control pure evil?"

Cody hoped he never had to find out.

Cody silently gazed out at the rocky cliffs passing by both sides of the ship as Igg, still disturbingly nude, navigated through them. After passing the Hunter's prison, Cody had sought privacy. Unfortunately, Xerx had cornered him, eager for another training session. After an hour of lecturing, Cody had finally managed to sneak off to a quiet corner.

He had much on his mind that demanded attention. The reminder that he was the Hunter's only target, and processing his new relationship with Tiana, had his brain spinning. More importantly, he thought of Jade. He thought of the last words she had said to him.

Suddenly movement on the cliffs caught his eye. He perked up, peering through the darkness at the towering peaks. Standing motionlessly on a jutted-out ledge was a man—his wide, eyelid-less eyes looked lifelessly down on Cody, who felt an odd sensation as though the gaze had penetrated his soul.

"Randilin! Tiana! Come quickly! There's a man!" Cody yelled. There was a stampede of footsteps from all parts of the ship. "A man! Look!" Cody repeated, pointing to the cliffs as The Company reached him. But when he looked back to the ledge, it was empty.

"I swear I saw someone! He's the one who's been following me. He's..."

Dace silenced him. "I trust you, Cody. If you say you saw a man—then there was a man. What did he look like?"

As Cody described him he saw Randilin's face tighten. Before Cody could question the dwarf, Igg scurried to the ship's ledge. "*Shhh*! Something's coming...." Cody noticed it, too. Ripples in the lava washed against the ship, growing larger and more frequent. "Extinguish the lights...*quick*!" They dashed about the ship putting out the lights. Chazic heaved the ship's stone anchor over the edge, bringing the barge to a jerking halt.

Igg came running back to the ledge. "Everyone get down! Nobody make a sound." For the next few moments there was silence. Cody held his breath as he pressed himself against the deck of the ship, bobbing as the barge rose and fell gently with the ripples. Minutes passed like hours. No one dared break the quiet.

Then Cody felt it. The looming presence quietly passed the ship on both sides. Cody looked up, but from his position on the floor he could only see the tips of dark objects passing slowly one after another. *What's going on?* For several more minutes the silent parade continued like a funeral procession.

Cody couldn't bear it any longer. He quietly pushed himself off the deck and crawled to the ship's ledge, pulling himself up by the railing.

They were enormous.

43

A Golden View

They glided over the lava with eerie grace; an endless procession of gold-masted ships. Cody ducked lower behind the railing and watched as one after another of the ships passed. There were hundreds of them.

He could see the shape of golden golems marching on the ship decks. In the crow's-nest of each ship stood a Dark-Wielder chanting in the High Language to summon a steady wind against the large masts, propelling the boats forward.

Cody dropped back to the deck. He exchanged glances with Randilin who looked troubled. The dwarf pointed to the cave's ceiling and motioned with his hands like fireworks. The simple gesture was enough; Cody understood too well. At any moment daybreak would hit, and the Orb's light would expose their vessel.

Cody squeezed his eyes closed. They could do nothing but wait—and hope.

Final Day...

Bright light exploded across the sky. Cody shielded his face with his hand. He cautiously pulled himself to his feet. In the distance, steering around the bend of the cliffs, he could see the rear cabin of the final ship. They had made it.

But by the look on Dace's face, you'd think they had not. "There must have been a thousand ships at least. Even if each were only half-loaded with fighting men, which is a child's prayer of an *if*, then El Dorado has a force the magnitude of which I've never imagined even in my nightmares."

"Not to mention the mass assaulting Flore Gub," observed Tat, speaking for the first time since Lilley. His face was hard and his eyes were empty. "The attack on Flore Gub is a decoy."

"A decoy with more men than Atlantis could muster if we gave broadswords to infants. How is it possible to have assembled such a force?" Dace wondered in bewilderment.

"We don't stand a chance," declared Tat sullenly.

Chazic stepped forward. "We have hope as long as we have breath. I was appointed to protect the Book Keeper to El Dorado. I don't intend to fail my mission." The Enforcer's rich voice seemed to pump courage back into the deflated Company.

"Neither do I," declared Dace determinedly. "Igg, how much farther until El Dorado?"

The skipper was already at the helm. "Half a day's smooth sailing until shore. From there it's any man's guess how far to the Golden City. It's uncharted territory from the sea."

Cody's face dropped. "That's not fast enough!"

"I think I can help with that," said Xerx. He raised his hands, *"Byrae!"* A billowing gust of wind came careening against the barge, knocking everyone to the deck. The boat soared across the lava sea, bits of the patched-together ship breaking off as it picked up speed. *We just need to hold on a little longer.*

The instant the vessel's bow scraped against the shore Cody leapt over the edge. The moment his feet touched down against the mud shore, he started running.

"Cody, wait! It's too dangerous! Wait!" Dace called after him, but he didn't slow. He didn't look behind to see if anyone else was following. With every last ounce of stamina he could muster, he sprinted. He held up the ruby pocketwatch. The long gold hand was pointing directly north, directing his path.

He disregarded his ragged breath and burning joints, as his stumbling legs fought to keep pace with his desire. He had come too far to give up so close to the end.

As he ran, the rough dirt terrain disappeared, gradually replaced by pure, smooth sand. *I'm getting close.* He urged his body on even harder. Sporadically he passed a sprouted tree. Lush green vegetation became more frequent the farther he ran. He came to the base of a giant sand dune.

He collapsed.

Every muscle in his body seared. *Must keep moving. Jade needs me!* Pulling himself onto all fours, he crawled up the massive dune. With a final heave, he hurled himself up to the top and rolled onto his back, utterly spent. His blurry eyes gazed down.

At the bottom of the valley—was a Golden City.

The city was the most beautiful thing he had ever seen. Like Atlantis, it was surrounded by a large wall. However, from his elevated view he could see straight into the city that swirled up like a cyclone. Atop the pyramid was a dome-roofed palace. Every inch of the city was awash in light like the purest of diamonds. It was spectacular.

Cody rose to his feet. Against all odds he had succeeded. *Jade, I'm here!* Childish glee spread through his body and a smile pushed to the corners of his face. Digging into his pocket he retrieved the arrowhead Tat had given him. *I've made my choice.* He tossed his hands into the air and released a bellowing, wild cry of triumph, just as the sky went dark.

It was nightfall. He was too late.

44

Out of Time

Time was up. The darkness engulfed Cody as he collapsed to his knees. He had failed. Darkfall had come on the seventh day—he had been too slow. *I've killed Jade.*

Cody felt his cheeks begin to burn. *I could have been faster…I SHOULD have been faster!* He yelled a pained cry, his voice crackling as tears filled his eyes. "I'm sorry! Jade, I'm sorry!" His strength gave out and he collapsed.

Just before he hit the ground, he was caught by two soft hands. Tiana pulled Cody against her chest. "I'm sorry, Cody."

Her face was pale and the vessels in her eyes were red from fatigue. A tear from her eye dropped onto Cody's burning forehead. "I'm so sorry, Cody," she whispered again, her voice quivering.

Cody clenched his fist. "I'm going to kill him," he declared flatly. Tiana dried her eyes, "Cody…what are you talking about? Cody…?"

He ignored her, forcefully breaking from her embrace. His eyes peered at the palace. Tiana stood, realizing what was going on. "Cody, no. It's too far and you're too exhausted. This isn't the only way…Cody?"

Anger filled Cody like pulsing adrenaline. He lifted his hands and took a deep breath. Tiana stepped toward him. "Cody, don't. We must wait for the others. It's too dangerous...Cody!" Tiana lunged for him but she was too late.

"*Spakious!*" At Cody's command the air before them blurred as though the fabric of the atmosphere was rippling. Without hesitation Cody lunged through the portal.

The world slowly blurred into focus. Cody was lying on his stomach completely drained of strength. He was in a courtyard. Something tickled his cheek, *grass?*

Suddenly a woman dashed into the clearing. Her elegant purple robe flowed behind her, fastened by a glittering, diamond-encrusted sash. Cody could hear her panting breath from within the deep hood. She glanced over her shoulder.

A man came bursting around the corner in pursuit of her. He was broad shouldered and handsome. His eyes were fixed on the woman and burned like fire. Cody watched helplessly, unable to move, as the man overtook the woman. Grabbing her shoulders, he spun her around and pinned her against the wall. "Did you think you were going to get away that easily?" the man probed, his muscular arms imprisoning the woman.

Cody's eyelids dropped from fatigue. He fought to keep them open. The woman reached out and wrapped her arms around the man's head. Pulling him close, she kissed him. As she did, the man gently pushed her hood off.

Jade.

PART THREE
A PERFECT CITY

45

Changed

Where am I?

    Bright lights showered him from all directions. He squinted, urging his eyes to adjust to the fierce gleam. He was lying on a small, sleek white cot like a hospital bed. He sat up and examined the unfamiliar surroundings.

How did I get here?

Cody's eyebrows leaped in surprise. His filthy brown robe was gone, replaced with the most striking garment he had ever seen. The elegant white coat sparkled like a fresh morning snowfall and its silky texture soothed his skin. He traced his finger over the surplus of tiny diamonds that weaved around the tunic like an extravagant spider web.

As his dilated pupils returned to normal he realized he wasn't surrounded by bright lights—but instead by *mirrors*. Massive slates of pure crystal claimed each of the four walls from floor to ceiling. The tranquil mood immediately evaporated.

I'm in El Dorado.

Paralyzed with fear, his pale expression was mimicked hundreds of times; his stretched and distorted face reflecting off the crystal walls. Then, apart from the others, one of the faces moved.

I'm not alone!

Before Cody could react, the assailant lunged, wrapping firm arms around him, stealing his wind. Cody squirmed, fighting for enough breath to use the High Language, but the attacker's grip was unbreakable.

Cody gasped for air as the suffocating hold loosened. His head spun dizzily as he sucked in oxygen and stumbled backwards. Throwing up his fists, he braced for another attack—and gazed straight into two beautiful green eyes. "*Jade?*"

Her face was beaming. Cody's strength escaped as he tried to release all of his ten, pre-rehearsed speeches simultaneously. The result was incoherent bumbling.

Jade drew him into another tight hug, resting her head against his shoulder. "Oh, Cody, how I've missed you," she whispered into his ear.

"I've missed you too, Jade...You have *no idea* how much I've missed you." The next few moments were a dream. The warmth of the embrace communicated more than any well-rehearsed words. All of Cody's fears and worries dissipated. After three miserable weeks, his chaotic world had been instantly put back in order.

He didn't want to let go. He wanted to let the world pass around them like a gentle river around an immovable boulder. After several more still moments he reluctantly released her.

Cody scanned the room and located a door that had been camouflaged by the crystal wall. "We need to get out of here before we're discovered." He rushed to the bed and scooped up the pile of his belongings. "I can use the High Language to transport us beyond the walls and then ..." He turned back but found Jade standing still with a troubled expression. "Jade? We need to *move*. I came to rescue you...."

Jade took a step backwards. "I'm very touched. You have been *unbelievably* brave...but what if I don't *want* to be rescued?"

Cody's heart plunged in his chest. "What do you mean? I need to get you out of here! Don't you want to go home?"

Jade inched back farther. "Home? Where *is* home Cody? Is Atlantis home? Have you forgotten your mother? Have you forgotten Havenwood?"

Cody shook his head defensively, "Of course not! But..."

Suddenly the door burst open and four golden golems funneled in. Cody looked to Jade in confusion. "I don't understand...."

The soldiers encircled him, the points of their spears pricking his back.

Jade grasped his hands. "I've *found* my home, Cody. For the first time in my whole life," she paused. "Don't struggle, Cody. They won't harm you. He's not like they say he is. You really must meet him."

As the warriors forced Cody from the room, he grabbed the doorway and looked back to Jade. "Must meet who?" The last thing Cody saw before he was forced out of the room was Jade's thin, moving lips.

"The Golden King."

46

The King's Court

The immense double doors slammed behind him with a rattling boom. Cody hurled himself against them but they didn't budge—*locked*.

Turning back around, he examined the chamber he had been forced into. It was massive. Even the Great Hall of Atlantis would seem nothing more than a miniature snow-globe compared to the magnificent scale and grandeur of the Hall.

Cody carefully made his way across the vibrant, mosaic path that split the Great Hall straight down the center. Each of the lavish pillars that flanked the track were coated with polished gold and adorned with wealth as gemstones of every color spiraled toward the arched ceiling.

The Hall was mute as an art gallery, amplifying Cody's rapid breath. As he reached the end of the amethyst trail, he paused. Before him was a large throne made entirely of gold. The two armrests morphed into the shape of flaming suns.

To the left of the throne was a familiar periscope device—the tunnel-phone. Cody felt a chill. It had been through that very device that Cody had communicated with *him*. Stalkton's solemn warnings about the Golden King came racing back. *I need to get out of here!*

Cody turned to flee but something else caught his eye. On the other side of the throne was a shadowy nook. From the gloom shone the glimmer of jewels and riches. However, it was the centerpiece that had captured his gaze. The sight was eerily familiar. In the center of the nook was a podium; and upon the podium—was a Book.

The Book was made of solid gold. An elegant border was embroidered around the perimeter. In the center, formed by tiny crystals, was a large 'E.'

The Key—the second of the two Books made by King Ishmael. Cody approached the Book as though drawn to it magnetically.

The only way to defeat the Golden King is the combined power of the two Books.

The gilded Book was glowing like a firefly at midnight. Cody reached toward it in wonder. The moment his fingers brushed the golden surface, two red slits appeared from behind the podium.

"Ahh!" Cody stumbled backwards, falling to the floor. The Hunter skulked around the podium like a panther; its nostrils flaring.

Terrified, Cody shuffled back, pushing himself onto his feet as the Beast strode toward him. The Hunter purred, its five-inch tongue stroking the black lips of its snout.

Cody took another step—and collided into something solid behind him. An icy hand curled onto his shoulder, the large fingers coiling around him. The hand was made of gold.

"Welcome to my court."

47

The Two Are One

He was beautiful. Accompanying his long, fine, white hair was skin that glittered gold. His eyes shone like pure rubies only to be outdone by the gemstones that fused into his forehead forming a royal crown. His body was half human and half gold, as though caught midway through metamorphosis between caterpillar and butterfly. In every way he was perfect—the very embodiment of beauty.

"What an honor." The Golden King's voice was melodic and smooth; the words swirling around Cody and luring him into a calm trance like a siren's irresistible call toward treacherous cliffs.

From behind, the Hunter's talons scraped against the ground. The King's ruby eyes stared steadily into the Beast's flaming scarlet slits. The Hunter released a piercing shriek, snapped its fangs at the King, and then vanished.

"Lovely, isn't it?" the King purred. Cody didn't answer. Instead he stood transfixed, unable to move. The King glided toward the podium. With his fleshy hand he stroked the spine of the Book. "It senses its sister is near.

A thousand years have passed since the two halves were united as one."

As the King wove his pleasant symphony of words, Cody grabbed his backpack and unzipped it. He cautiously pulled out his leather-bound Book. The scarlet 'A' burned more fiercely than ever.

"You didn't take it...why?" The energy from *The Code* flowed through him with an intensity he'd never before experienced.

The King smiled. "For precisely the same reason I allowed you to come to El Dorado on your own accord: because deep down you and I both desire the same thing—truth."

Cody shook his head. "You're wrong. I came only to rescue Jade." Cody fought to maintain a defiant stare, but quickly dropped his eyes. "You lied to me. Darkfall came on the seventh day but you still let Jade live. Why?"

The King floated back to Cody. "Death has so many faces. I assure you, the Jade you knew before is very much dead." The King slid his silver tongue across his lips as though lapping up the savory words.

Cody felt deep dread wash over him. "What have you done to her?"

"Only what you could not — I've allowed the swan inside to break free. You will soon realize that in El Dorado you can be exactly the person you've always dreamt of becoming."

Cody's mind flashed back to the stern image of his father. Cody could hear his mother's sobs in the background. His father kissed his forehead. *"One day you'll understand, boy. You'll understand why I have to go away."* It had been the last time he had ever seen him.

Cody forced the memory from his mind. "Only I can read from *The Code*. You can't force me to use it for you."

"I don't believe that will be necessary. But what about using it for *you*? The unrestricted knowledge of the universe at your grasp; the answers to questions you didn't even know to ask. Aren't you curious?"

Suddenly a thousand questions raced through Cody's mind. He shut his eyes to block them out. The Golden King placed his hand gently on Cody's cheek, the cool gold causing him to shiver. "When the Two become One, there is no limit to the wonders they can do. The unlimited power to change the world; to make it better, to make it *perfect*. Is it not our *responsibility* to do so?"

Unwanted thoughts once again forced their way into the corners of his mind. He thought of his hard-working, single mother. He thought of the beggar, Gelph, and the rest of the impoverished citizens in Atlantis' Outer-City. *I could change things for the better.*

"Are you going to lock me up now? Torture me until I relent?" Cody challenged weakly. The King lifted his hand. As he did, the doors across the Hall swung open. The King pointed to the opened doors.

"You are free to leave anytime you wish. If you so choose, I will commission an escort of my finest soldiers to guide you safely to the Borderlands. You have but to ask. You are no more a prisoner than Jade. On the contrary, you are my most honored guest. Which is why tomorrow evening I shall host a grand banquet in your honor. The honor of a Book Keeper."

Cody stared at the King curiously.

"The moment the banquet is over I'm leaving for Atlantis."

The Golden King smiled. "I recall those very words coming from the mouth of a young woman but a month ago. You may discover that your friend may not be as keen on leaving as you think...given a week, you may realize you're not interested in leaving either."

48

Stirrings

S hhh!" The room fell silent except for the rhythmic pattern of heavy footsteps as two men marched passed the entry way of the shadowy hut. Once the sound had faded the hush was soiled by loud exhales.

"I *told you* it's too dangerous. If we're seen…"

"I know, I know! We're all aware of the risk. So let's not waste our precious time," a deep voice whispered. "It's happened. The Book Keeper has arrived. And…" The voice dropped as the noise of footsteps returned.

"This is *folly!*" a second man snapped as the strides quieted again. "We're risking *everything* tonight."

"*Shhh!* Keep your voice *down*, brother!" urged a third. "G. T. is correct. If the Book Keeper *is* here in El Dorado then it may be the only opportunity we'll get. This is the moment we've been awaiting for a very long time."

"We will need to corner him when he's alone. That may not be an easy task," observed a woman, the final member of the quartet.

The deep-voiced man cleared his throat. "I agree. But it's the only way. We must seize the moment while he's sleeping or secluded. We won't get a second chance," he concluded. "We must strike fast."

A sharp creaking noise outside the building extinguished the voices.

Two men burst into the hovel only to find it empty.

49

Confessions

---

*er green eyes locked with his. Instead of their usual fiery
state they had a soft tenderness to them.*

*When she opened her mouth, her lips quaked. "Cody...I...I...
I lo..." The sound of clashing steel echoed in Cody's ears. A limp
body fell against him. Cody shoved the body off and turned back
to Jade and Tiana. They were gone.*

The scene cycled through Cody's mind for the thousandth time. As always, it was as vivid and real as the day
it happened. He sat restlessly on the edge of his bed staring
at the closed bedroom door.

Following his audience with the Golden King he had
been guided to a specially-arranged bed chamber—a room
larger than the whole of his house back in Havenwood.
Several doors and halls led off toward unexplored sections
of the massive room. But none of that mattered at the moment. Instead, he stared at the simple note that had been
left on his pillow.

I'm sorry about earlier, I should have prepared you.
We have SO much to get caught up on.
Come to my room first thing in the morning.
I'll show you around the city—just like old times!
Your best friend always,
Jade

He lay down, holding the note against his chest. The strenuous, week-long dash from Atlantis to El Dorado was beginning to take its toll; he welcomed the comfort of the warm bed. Sleep came immediately.

After his quiet knock, Cody instantly heard loud, thumping footsteps rumbling from the other side of the closed door. Cody grinned. *Apparently the Golden King hadn't changed EVERYthing about her!*

When the door finally opened Jade greeted him with a warm smile. Her thick black hair was pulled into a neat up-do and her cheeks sparkled with glitter. She threw her arms around him and squeezed him tightly before inviting him into the room.

The weeks spent imagining the horrors of Jade trapped in a dark, isolated prison cell seemed exceedingly silly as Cody viewed the sprawling room.

He continued to examine the extravagance of the space as he searched for something to say. It was an unusual feeling. Having Jade next to him made him feel uncomfortable. He had imagined that seeing her again would somehow turn back time and things would be just as they were before. But now that the moment had come, he felt as though he were meeting her for the first time.

"This is a nice room," he muttered, finally giving up on the elusive, witty remark. Jade skipped forward and threw herself onto the bed, propping herself up on her elbows. "Yeah, it's incredible. I could fit my whole house back ho... back in *Havenwood* inside." Cody looked to the floor, unable to handle her deep green eyes. The moment he had dreaded for weeks had arrived.

"I'm sorry about leaving you in the courtyard. It was dumb." Cody winced even before the last word left his tongue. After a month of preparation he had dropped an agonizing dud.

Jade didn't seem to notice. To Cody's surprised she merely laughed. "Very dumb, indeed! But after all we've been through did you honestly think I'd be surprised?" The remark was playful and lacked venom.

Cody caught her infectious smile. "Yeah, I guess not. Remember Area 51? That was bad...."

"That *was* bad...even for you!" It felt good to be laughing with Jade again. "There's something I've wanted to ask you," he began slowly.

Jade sat up attentively. "Of course, what is it?" Cody felt his forehead burn red. He took a deep breath. *It's now or never...*

"Well, the last time I saw you, in the courtyard, you called something to me. It seemed like it was something... *important*." He squirmed; there was no turning back now. "But the thing is, with all the loud noise and fighting, I didn't hear what you said; at least not *all* of what you said. You probably don't even remember, but you called my name and said something like, *"I lo..."*

Cody lifted his eyes in anticipation. He heard Tiana's words on the boat in his ear: *"Some things are best heard from Jade's own mouth."*

Jade smiled. "Of *course*, I remember!" Cody's heart skipped. He leaned forward eagerly, but stopped at the sound of Jade's laughing. "I said *'I loathe that stupid book!'"* She chuckled again. "What else would you expect I'd say after you ran off to search for that Book and left me standing there?"

"Yeah...what else..." Cody muttered. Her words pierced his chest like a sharpened spear. He grabbed his side and as he did, he felt the shape of Tat's arrowhead in his pocket.

He wrapped his hand around it. "Jade...I need to tell you something," he pulled the arrowhead out and held it toward her. "It might be surprising at first, but I need to get it off my chest. I've made my decision, and..."

"Oh, blast!" Jade jumped up from the bed. "I completely forgot!" Cody looked to the arrowhead and then back to Jade.

"Forgot what...? What I was trying to say was that I..."

Jade dashed to the other side of the room and came back carrying a smooth, ivory bow. "I'm sorry. That just reminded me. I completely forgot that I have archery lessons with Hansi this afternoon. You can come with me!"

Cody swallowed. "Who's Hansi?" he asked, anxious to rein Jade's attention back in. Jade slapped her forehead. "How silly of me! It's been so good to see you again that I forget you haven't been here with me the last few weeks. Hansi is the Prince." Jade's powdered face turned red. "And, he's also my boyfriend."

"Oh, that's nice. Anyways, I..." Cody's words came to a jarring halt. "*Boyfriend!*? Wow, I didn't realize. I mean I wasn't...You've only been here *one month*! I didn't expect, well...*that*."

"Isn't it crazy?" Jade exclaimed. "Who would have ever thought *I'd* have a boyfriend! And a *prince!* It all happened so fast. I can't wait for you to meet him. He's an amazing guy and I think you two will get along great!" Cody tried to force a smile but it came across as cheerful as passing kidney stones. He nodded, unable to speak. Jade tossed the bow over her shoulder and walked toward the door. As she reached it she turned. "Oh, how rude of me. You were in the middle of telling me something about making a decision. What were you saying?"

Cody slid the arrowhead back into his pocket. "Don't worry about it...it was stupid anyways."

50

A Perfect City

The city was stunning, seemingly dressed up for an elegant ball. The buildings were smooth and rounded and all the homes were identical to one another. The architecture was like nothing Cody had ever seen. Each of the buildings was open-walled, providing a full glimpse into the richly-adorned homes. The citizens inside were smiling.

Cody scampered a step behind Jade as they traversed the city. As they passed, the neighbors would smile and give friendly waves or bows. Like the Atlantians, their facial features had subtle mousy characteristics but that was where the commonality ended. Each of them wore identical, lavish outfits that would have made even Atlantis' Inner-City residents look like street-rats.

Jade strutted confidently, greeting many of the people by name. Cody had never seen Jade so self-assured. He recalled the Golden King's words: *"I've allowed the swan inside to break free."*

They came to a stop in front of a street marketplace. Dozens of vendors lined both sides of the path with stalls brimming over with every imaginable treat or trinket.

A woman, who stood at least six feet tall, waved them over. Cody had the sense that she was an elderly lady, but glitter and the smoothness of her skin gave her the appearance of one much younger "Welcome, my precious dearies."

A youthful purveyor from the neighboring stall jumped in front of the statuesque woman. "Unsatisfied hunger troubling the handsome gentleman? Ol' Brodon has got *just the thing* to take your neglected taste buds on a wild adventure!" The seller was a stubby man with a bowl of exceedingly fine hair hanging evenly from the top of his head. The lanky lady shook her head. "Oh, Brodon, you're shameless...."

As always, Cody was pulled like a magnet toward the sound of flattery. "I'm starving! How much does it cost? I'm afraid I don't have any money."

The stout merchant chuckled. "You're obviously not *from* here, are ya? Look around; does it look like there's a shortage of riches? *Harmony* is the only currency here. Everything in this market is absolutely free—no strings attached. Thanks to the merciful King of Radiance, we're all equals in El Dorado." He grabbed a tart-like pastry from his booth and tossed it to Cody. "I *guarantee* just one small bite of this will change your world." To Cody's surprise, his clear reflection could be seen in the smooth, metallic-looking surface of the unusual pastry. Topping it off, in place of a cherry, was a large, polished ruby.

Brodon chuckled. "It is perfectly edible; trust me. Although, if you wish to keep your teeth, you'll want to remove the ruby first!"

The first saleswoman appeared, towering over the head of the smaller merchant. "Either way, you should probably save it for later; wouldn't want to ruin your appetite for the big banquet tonight!"

Thanking the two, Cody stored the silver tart in his backpack and scampered after Jade. "About this banquet tonight…" he said between heavy breaths, "I was thinking maybe you could meet me at my chamber and we could go to it…together?" he offered.

Jade's green eyes softened. "Oh, of course I can go down with you. I'm sure Hansi won't mind if I just meet him there."

Cody flushed. "Oh, right. Hansi. I forgot."

Jade shrugged. "We can go as a trio. You *are* my best friend, after all. It's not like he has to worry about anything. He's been dying to meet you!"

Cody forced a smile but couldn't bring himself to answer, so instead he gave a weak head nod. *Would Hansi mind if I hit him over the head with Jade's bow?* he thought bitterly.

Cody tensed up as two diamond-skinned men approached. "Dark-Wielders! We need to get out of here!"

He tugged at Jade's sleeve, but she burst into laughter. "Is *that* what they call them in Atlantis?" The two Wielders reached them and passed right by. As they did, they both gave a bow to Jade before disappearing around the corner.

"What do you mean? What are they called here?" Cody asked, still uneasy.

"The Brotherhood of Light," Jade said with a grin. "Just because Atlantis claims to be Light doesn't mean El Dorado is obligated to be Dark. And here, unlike Atlantis where the brotherhood spends all its time in a secluded monastery, the Brotherhood patrols the city making sure everybody is taken care of and happy. Sounds more worthy of Light than the other, I'd say. "

The thought perplexed Cody. *Maybe I was just seeing what I wanted to see?*

"This city is not what I expected," he admitted. Jade stopped at a ledge overlooking the city. From their elevated position Cody could see the entire breadth of the metropolis for the first time—and it was beautiful.

The city was laid out in a perfectly symmetrical circle. Every building and street had been arranged in seamlessly straight lines. Enclosing the buildings were colossal walls that seemed to reach almost to the ceiling of Under-Earth, obscuring any view of outside the city.

Near the outskirts of the city, a pillar of smoke rose into the air. The steam was rising from what appeared to be a deep pit. Cody watched as four golden golems marched to the edge of the hole carrying a smooth, silver crate. Placing the crate onto a large platform, they slowly lowered it by a pulley system into the haze.

"What are they doing?" Cody asked as the soldiers lowered the platform deeper and deeper.

"Garbage," Jade answered. "The King insists on keeping his city clean. The world's most advanced city shouldn't look like a slum," she uttered distastefully. "Everything detracting from the beauty of the city is loaded up into those silver crates, lowered into the pit, and burned in the scorching furnace. Much more civilized."

In the center of the circular city layout was a large globe-like structure. The immense building was like a gigantic crystal ball. "Beautiful, isn't it?" Jade observed. "The Monument to the Orb. Symbolically built directly in the heart of the city; a testament that it belongs to the people rather than hidden in a forbidden sanctuary for the elect and privileged."

"It seems wonderful. Almost *too* wonderful." Cody mumbled. He shook his head. *"But,* it doesn't change the fact that these people *kidnapped* you and dragged you here forcefully. Have you already forgotten that?"

"When I was first brought here I was more terrified than I've ever been in my life. I thought of you every day. It was the only thing that gave me the strength to carry on. But the Golden King was right, they weren't kidnapping me from Atlantis—they were *saving* me from it. What they did was in my best interest, even if I didn't realize it at the time. They saved me from being brainwashed. Just think about it. If this orb, whatever it is, is so sacred and all-powerful, then why are those who revere it most so impoverished, unequal, and hardened? The rulers of Atlantis could allow all of their citizens to enjoy the same luxuries as those offered here in El Dorado. So why don't they?"

Cody remained silent. He didn't have an answer.

51

A Pull-and-Shoot Kind of Guy

The man was sickeningly handsome. Like the city around him, he was so entirely flawless that it brought bile to Cody's throat. Cody despised everything about him: his wavy gold hair, his ice-blue eyes, and every one of the defined muscles that pressed tightly against his constricting vest. Cody instinctively rubbed his fingers across the sparse fuzz covering his own chin after noticing the man's full, methodically-groomed facial hair.

The angelic looking man flashed a friendly smile, revealing straight, white teeth. "Most noble Book Keeper. What a tremendous honor. Legend of your bravery is already well known in El Dorado."

Cody chomped down on his lip: *Resist! Don't be fooled by the viper's cheap flattery…Did he just say 'legend of my bravery'?…NO, it doesn't matter. He's a monster!*

"And, of course, Jade has told me so much about you," he continued. "I am Prince Hansi, and it is a pleasure to finally meet you."

Cody sneered. *Hansi? What sort of sissy name is that?! What does he think he is—a European model?*

Hansi offered his hand. Cody seized it firmly, squeezing until his knuckles grew white, all the while hoping to shatter every bone in the man's manicured hand. It was like grasping an iron pipe.

Cody glared at the man coldly. "Well, Jade and I *do* have a lot of history together."

Hansi pulled an ivory bow from his shoulder and examined the string. "And, as such, I'm sure you have much catching up to do. I'd hate to get in the way of that. Let's reschedule our lessons until..."

"No, no, no," Jade insisted. "Let's have the lessons. I'm excited to show Cody my new skills!" She pulled her own bow from her shoulder.

Hansi looked to Cody. "If you desire, I can lend you my spare bow and give you a lesson as well?"

Cody puffed his shoulders. "I'm actually already an accomplished archer in Upper-Earth. You know, with awards and stuff," he blurted. Jade's face lit up in surprise. Cody felt as though a spotlight had been focused on him. "It was before we met," he added defensively. *Strike one.*

Jade's expression deepened. "But Cody...we met in fourth grade." Cody's face reddened. *Stop talking, you idiot; don't dig yourself any deeper than you already have!*

"Yeah, well, I'm just full of surprises," he declared. *Ouch.* It had definitely sounded better in his head. *Strike two.*

Hansi slapped him on the back. "Fantastic! If you have time later, I would love to discuss the techniques and tools of current Upper-Earth archery. As a student of the craft, I'm always trying to learn and improve. Is silk thread still practiced for attaching the fletching? Do they use a nock in Upper-Earth? I have found that the groove retracts from the pure flight of the arrow, would you agree?"

Cody stared at the Prince as though he had spoken ancient Gaulish rather than English; and for all Cody knew, he *had*.

Cody pinched his lips. "I'm more of a *pull-and-shoot* kind of guy...."

Strike three.

The three targets in the distance seemed the size of dimes across the lengthy grass field. As Cody strained his eyes, each of the targets morphed into Hansi's perfect, mocking face.

Along the side courtyard a small crowd had assembled to witness the event. Cody felt each of the watching eyes as he gazed haplessly at the bow in his hands. He held the foreign object the way an in-lander holds a live catfish.

There was a rattling whoosh as an arrow exploded from Hansi's bow and soared across the yard. With a reverberating thud it lodged into the center of the target. Cody bit his lip: *I'm in trouble.*

Jade stepped forward next and lifted her bow. Whipping an arrow out of her quiver, she fitted it against the string. Hansi stepped behind her, reaching his arms around and adjusting her stance. Cody dropped his eyes uncomfortably.

Zing! Cody glanced back up to see the arrow flying through the air. *Thud*. It pierced the second target just an inch from the bulls-eye. *Yes. BIG trouble.*

Cody stepped into the center next. He squinted, trying to focus on the blurry target in the distance. He pressed the arrow against the string and aimed it toward the target. *It's now or never.*

Inhaling a deep sigh and channeling everything he had ever read about Robin Hood, he closed his eyes—and let it go.

He listened to the soft hum of the arrow cutting through the air. A loud gasp rose from the crowd. *Thud*.

Silence.

The piercing scream of a woman forced his eyes open. The target in front of him was blank, his arrow completely lost from view. *Uh-oh.* A wild commotion ensued along the sidelines. People were hollering and running around. A bewildered lady emerged from the mob. "Help! Quick!... someone's been hit!"

52

Of Air Density and Fancy Clothes

Cody's face flushed like an inferno. He felt Hansi's arm wrap around his shoulder and lead him away. "Perhaps we should call it a day."

Cody glanced over his shoulder as several Wielders rushed into the crowd, kneeling to examine the victim. He risked a glance to Jade. Her face was bordering between mortification and amusement. Her eyebrow rose. "With awards and stuff, eh?"

Hansi patted him on the shoulder. He then did the worse thing Cody could imagine—he came to his rescue.

"You know, the air density in Under-Earth is no doubt much different than Upper-Earth. As all archers know, it takes practice to get the right feel back. I'm sure you would have had it with another shot or two. But we should probably return to the palace to get ready for this evening's banquet."

"Air density!?" Cody spat as he flung his chamber door open. "You'd better hope the *air density* is enough to keep

my next arrow from soaring right between your sickeningly flawless eyebrows...." Cody jerked to a stop as the edge of a knife appeared at his throat.

"Don't move a muscle."

The blade tickled the hair on his neck as it pressed uncomfortably against his Adam's apple. A strong hand reached out and grasped his collar, yanking him into the room. The door slammed shut behind him.

With a violent shove Cody was thrown to the floor. He tried to stand but the attacker's foot pressed against his back, pinning him in place. "I surrender!"

With a harsh kick he was sent rolling across the room, colliding against the wall. Coming to a stop, he looked up, straight into the intense eyes of Tiana.

"What's gotten into you?!" she hollered, keeping her dagger drawn.

"What's gotten into *me*? You just about cut my head off!" There was a loud thud as Tiana's blade struck the wall.

"Have you already forgotten why we're here?!" she barked.

"How did you...?" Cody stammered. He grabbed the hilt of her knife and heaved on it, but it didn't budge.

"I followed you through the portal. When you passed out in the courtyard, I fled. I've been keeping tabs on you all day." She held up her sleeve to reveal a large gash through it. "Even that abomination you called archery. In an archery competition between you and a blind, three-legged horse—I'd wager my money on the horse."

Cody grimaced. "Be gentle. It's already humiliating enough."

"Well, you almost blew my cover and..."

A gentle tapping at the door interrupted Tiana's intended tirade. Cody and Tiana's eyes met. Without a word Tiana disappeared from view. Cody answered the door. A pleasant looking girl with two crater-deep dimples stood in the archway with a bundle of clothes in her arms. "I apologize for the intrusion, most noble Book Keeper, but the Ruler of Light sends garments for this evening's banquet." She handed Cody the bundle. With a curtsy she turned to leave before stopping and turning back. "The Lord of Splendor also wishes to extend his invitation to your lady friend. If she is finished snooping around the city, she is most welcome to join the feast. Clothes and bedding have already been prepared for her down the hall." With another curtsy the young girl turned and left.

As Tiana emerged from her hiding, Cody unfolded the clothes. On the breast of the garment was a golden-embroidered B.K. Amused, Cody traced it with his finger. *Now THIS is more like it.*

Tiana knocked the bundle from his hands to the floor. "Wake up! If the King knows I'm here then we're in even more danger than I thought. We *need* to get out of here."

"I know, I know," Cody muttered absentmindedly. "But after the banquet."

Tiana shook her head in disbelief. "What's gotten into you? We need to grab Jade and rendezvous with Dace and the others. Have you forgotten who the enemy is?" But Cody wasn't listening. He pulled the vest over his shoulders. The golden B.K dazzled like enchanting evening stars.

53

The Banquet

The immense banquet hall was brimming with people. It seemed as though every citizen in El Dorado was in attendance. A bouquet of fragrances swirled around the room like pirouetting spirits. Long tables, laden with mountains of food, surrounded the perimeter of the room three-fold.

Cody felt a squeeze on his hand. Tiana's fingers intertwined with his. She looked gorgeous. Her dress was made of innumerable diamonds that sparkled like stars every time she moved. A glittering tiara held her hair up and a satin veil draped down over her eyes. "This is a bad idea," she whispered under her breath.

"Cody!" Jade pushed herself through the mob. "I'm glad you made it! I'm so sorry I wasn't there to meet you. I was with Hansi and lost track of time. " Jade gave him a hug. Pulling away, she eyed Tiana. "Oh...I didn't realize you were in the city, too," she observed in surprise.

"We came together," Cody blurted. He tugged her arm, pulling her close against his side. Tiana's face registered shock, but she remained silent.

"Oh, so the two of you are still...going strong?" Jade asked.

Tiana shook her head. "Actually, Cody has recently decided that it's best..."

"not to ruin a good thing when you have it!" Cody interrupted quickly.

Again Tiana glanced at Cody quizzically but didn't refute his words.

Jade smiled uneasily. "I guess not. I'm happy for you two then," she uttered. "But we should get to our table... Hansi is probably wondering where I am." Without lingering she pivoted and marched away.

Cody began to follow but was yanked back by Tiana. "What on earth are you doing!?"

Cody's face contorted as though awaking from a trance. "I...don't know."

Tiana's face hardened. "You don't know? What's that supposed to mean!? What about your love-sick declaration in the Hall of Names? Or, on the boat? Or..."

Cody grabbed her hands and squeezed them. "I wasn't thinking. I just...well, it's complicated." Suddenly he felt the presence of someone behind him.

"Life *always* is." Cody recognized the voice instantly and felt his rage begin to simmer. He spun around to see the plump, mop-headed Prince Foz. "It's good to see you again, my friend."

The traitorous Prince was clothed in exorbitant garments. His wool-like hair had been slicked to the side with lackluster success. The last time Cody had seen the youthful Prince he had been soaring away from Atlantis in the claws of the Hunter, having betrayed and murdered his own father, King Ishmael. *Fleeing like a coward.*

Cody's fist launched toward Foz. Tiana snatched his arm, stopping his knuckles just before they struck the Prince's face.

The Prince flinched, and took an uncomfortable step backwards. "I told you we would meet again and here we are."

Cody tried to pull his arm from Tiana's grasp but she held him firm. "How dare you talk to me again!?" Cody growled.

Foz held his hands up in surrender. "I like you, Cody; I always have. That part was never an act for me. But ask yourself this, 'Are you angry with me because of what I said and did? Or because you now realize that I was right?'" Cody shook his hand free of Tiana's grip.

Foz grinned. "In time you will come to see just how great a man my uncle is."

Cody's disdainful glare was finally broken as Tiana pulled him away from the Prince. "We're in enough danger as it is. Don't make more!" she muttered to him.

At the front of the room, on the stage of the royal throne, was the head table. Jade and Hansi were already sitting. Reclining in the throne was the Golden King, staring stilly ahead at some invisible object.

Cody took a seat beside Jade. She smiled at him but remained silent. She casually reached to Hansi on her other side and positioned his muscular arm around her shoulder. Cody flushed and draped his own arm around Tiana's shoulders.

The Golden King stood from his throne. The entire room went silent. The King allowed the heavy silence to hang in the air as the anticipation grew.

"Today is monumental. For the first time in the esteemed history of our great city, the Book Keeper of *The Code* graces our noble halls." The King motioned to Cody. The crowd erupted in applause. The Golden King raised his hand and the immense room instantly returned to hushed silence.

"Let us celebrate by exalting our glorious history. From the Outer-Regions, I give you Koin and Hoin, the most esteemed *Story-Weavers* in all of Under-Earth."

Two identical-looking men were suddenly standing in the middle of the court. They shared devious faces and matching, bushy uni-brows. Their abrupt appearance startled the crowd.

One of the twins began chanting. As the refrain grew louder, the second bard stepped forward.

"Ladies and gentlemen...there is no more powerful force, above earth or below, than a rousing story. A whirling lover's waltz of *illusion* and *reality*...." Suddenly there was a striking flash of fireworks and all the lights in the banquet hall were extinguished. The room was pitch-black.

Several frightened cries echoed as furious pillars of fire burst from the floor, forming a flaming ring around the chamber.

The storyteller continued his zealous muttering and a wave of steam begin rising from the floor, casting a soft haze over the room.

"Our tale begins at the glorious dawn of the First Era. The discovery of a gateway leading to endless wonders beyond the scope of the human mind—the discovery of the Orb!" The bard let the silence build, looking each member of his captive audience in the eye before continuing.

"The Radiant One desired to share the newfound power with the people, to restore their fallen tribe to glory... but there were others who wished to hoard the power for themselves."

A flash like lightning reflected off the steam with an echoing boom. The smoke twirled like a whirlwind. When it stopped it was in the form of a man's face. He looked like Kantan, only older: it was King Ishmael.

"The Lord of Lights pleaded with his older brother, but Chief Ishmael was already consumed by his greed for the Orb's power. Claiming the power for his own, he banished The Selfless Saint to the far outskirts of Under-Earth. But from the rubble—he would rise to greatness."

A mound of dust began spiraling up from the ground and began forming like a sandcastle fashioned by invisible hands until it was a five-foot replica of El Dorado.

"It was an age of prosperity and peace...but it could not last forever. Jealousy, greed, and fear gave birth to the Great War. Before the walls of Atlantis, the Glorious One led the El Doradians on a final stand for freedom."

The dust replica shifted and was instantly a mirror image of Atlantis. Bright light erupted in the haze like a wild lightning storm and the dust replica ignited on fire. "Blood and death flooded the earth. But in the end, through trickery and falsehood, the power of darkness would overwhelm the light. Sensing the battle was lost, the Master of Mercy made one final, valiant push toward the Orb, to offer his own life as a martyr for equality. His sacrifice was not in vain—the Covenant of the Books was formed and the balance of Under-Earth was, at long last, restored."

The pillars of the flame around the room began to flicker. "But peace cannot coexist with greed…and once again Under-Earth's liberty has been challenged." A light shone down like a spotlight on the storyteller. "We've reached the part where legend and reality become blurred as one; a climactic finale longing to be written. We hope we have dazzled the imagination with our tale."

The Teller's eyes locked onto Cody. "But like all worthy tales, the trick is finding the reality within the illusion." The rising mist suddenly was sucked into the center of the room forming into a sphere. It was a perfect replica of the Orb monument in the center of the city.

The fiery fencing around the room flickered, and then burst toward the orb in large fire balls. They crashed in the middle, lighting up the Orb—then the entire room went dark.

A collective gasp erupted from the crowd. Cody heard commotion. He felt a gust of wind as several soldiers rushed past him with clanking boots. The clamor lasted for only an instant.

When light filled the room again, everything had vanished. The flames. The steam. The orb. Even the two *Story-Weavers*.

The Golden King's eyes stared firmly at the now empty floor as though there stood someone only visible to him. "A...*thrilling* tale." As the crowd cheered the sentiment Cody craned his neck scanning the banquet hall. He stopped. At the back of the room an assembly of golden golems was exiting the chamber with two men. As they vanished through the doors Cody caught a quick glance at the prisoners—Koin and Hoin. Their hands were bound and their mouths were gagged. For a moment their eyes locked with Cody's before they were led out of sight.

What was going on? Cody felt a tug on his sleeve from Tiana. She pointed across the Hall. The large doors had been pushed open and a lone man strolled casually down the center toward them. Hushed whispers spread throughout the room as the man came to a stop in front of the royal table. He bowed. "Your majesty." Cody's jaw dropped.

It was Randilin.

54

Welcoming Party

The ugly dwarf's face was smug. He sauntered toward the head table and snatched a meat-covered bone from Foz's plate. With a repulsive lack of elegance, he shoved it in his mouth and inhaled a hefty bite. "Bloody starving," he muttered between sloppy chews.

The Golden King stood slowly from his chair and beheld the dwarf with amusement. "My dear old friend, it has been far too long since you visited my halls."

Randilin sucked his plump bottom lip into his mouth, narrowed his eyes and tossed the gnawed bone onto the table before the King, saliva pooling onto the table below it. "I'm no friend of yours, ya' bloody tin boor."

The King's head tilted like a curious puppy. "Then I suppose I should have you sent to the dungeon for trespassing?"

Randilin snatched another meaty bone from the table and set to mauling it as he had the first. "The ruddy toothache of the Great Garganton, you will," he hissed. The Golden King raised his eyebrows. "Indeed? And, why is that?"

"Because I possess valuable information." Randilin pointed to Cody. "The Book Keeper didn't come alone. As I'm sure you already know, we set out from Atlantis as a Company."

The King's ruby eyes stared at the dwarf inquisitively, beckoning him to continue.

"Problem is—they have a master scout with them. So you'd have better luck finding an honest man in Yanci's Pub than capturing them." Cody breathed a sigh of relief. *"But...,"* continued the dwarf, pieces of chewed food spewing from the side of his mouth, "I not only know their whereabouts, I also know their plans."

The Golden King glided down from the stage, circling around the dwarf. "And, you will freely give this information to me? Your willingness to betray your own people continues to amaze me."

Randilin shrugged. "I have no *people*. The only ruddy person I live for is my own disgraceful self. It's a simple choice: In Atlantis I'm a despised criminal destined for a lifetime in prison or a dance with the gallows. In El Dorado I can be much more."

The King stared at him steadily. "I recall a similar scene taking place in this very court a thousand years ago. I would have thought you'd have changed. After you watched them die; after what happened to Arianna."

Randilin's fists clenched. "Don't you *dare* say that name."

The King smiled and motioned to the head table. "As you wish." Two golden golems obediently brought another chair. The King continued, "You will have freedom and shelter in El Dorado."

Grabbing Foz's arm, Randilin wiped his lips on the Prince's sleeve. "Then you better ruddy listen up. I'm only going to say this once."

He scurried through the thick shadows, his eyes scanning the daunting battlements. He halted at the base of the wall and ducked down low. He held his breath and his hand rested on the hilt of his sword. *Was I seen?*

As the silence lingered, Dace relaxed his grip on his blade and beckoned to the others. One-by-one the procedure was repeated until the entire Company was crouched against the wall.

"We need to be swift. We get in, grab Cody and Jade, and get out," Dace issued. "Randilin promised he would ensure we would be undetected on the other side."

He turned and faced The Company. "I'll go first. Wait for my signal. If anything goes wrong—flee without looking back." Dace looked up the immense wall stretching up to the cave's ceiling and grinned. On his mark, Chazic started to whisper: "*Dastanda.*"

Dirt began to spew out from the base of the wall like a volcanic eruption. *One hundred feet tall, ten feet deep.*

Dace emerged from the tunnel and immediately scanned the surroundings. The city was quiet. He peered up to the walls and found there were no guards in sight. *Randilin's a man of his word. We timed the changing of the*

guards perfectly. Dace pushed himself silently from the burrow. Lowering his face to the opening, he whistled softly.

There was a soft thud as Tat appeared beside him, followed by the others. "So far, so good. They'll surely have Cody and Jade locked in the palace," Dace whispered. "Let's go!" Dace pushed himself to his feet and dashed into the silent clearing, followed by the others.

Instantly, seemingly out of nowhere, golden warriors came streaming into the clearing. Dace reached for his sword. He heard the clattering boots as more golems circled from behind. From the ramparts and rooftops dozens of golems appeared with readied bows. They were completely surrounded.

The blockade of soldiers parted and Prince Foz strutted forward with a gloating smirk. "Welcome, my old friends!" he said. "I ask you to kindly set down your weapons."

Dace tightened his grip on his sword hilt and examined the situation. The archers on the walls readied their arrows. Finally, with an angry snort, Dace tossed his sword to the ground. "Stand down men," he ordered. The others reluctantly obeyed, discarding their weapons into the pile—except for Chazic who clung defiantly to his powerful scimitars.

"Chazic, *stand down.* That's an order. We can't win this fight." The Enforcer's eyes were pinned to Foz. "Chazic, it's not worth it." As Chazic braced himself to pounce, Foz held up his hand to signal the archers. The stalemate dragged on for several tense moments, both awaiting the other to make their move.

With a grunt Chazic threw his scimitars to the ground.

"Wise move," Foz said as he motioned to the soldiers. Several rushed forward to gather the discarded weapons and bind the prisoners. Dace kept a cool gaze on the Prince as his arms were bound behind him.

"How did you know?" Dace demanded.

Foz grinned. "Because you need to be *far* more careful in how you choose your friends." The Prince stepped aside to reveal Randilin. The dwarf stood off from the group, his hands unbound.

Dace's face was blank with disbelief. "You betrayed us? How? Why?"

Randilin dropped his eyes. "You said it yourself after Redtown; I can't be trusted. I'm a bad man. You should have taken your own advice."

55

An Under-Earth Fortune Cookie

Cody's head was spinning like a wild carousel. He squeezed his temples, trying to calm himself. *What's going on here?* The banquet had been a whirlwind. *Why am I acting so childish toward Jade? Why were the Story-Weavers escorted away?* He shook his head like a wet dog. *And what in the world is Randilin doing?*

He had been informed that Dace and the others had been detained without any violence. Yet, still, he felt a sense of guilt. He, after all, had been the one who had insisted to the others that Randilin join The Company. They had trusted him. Now, as a result, they were behind bars. But he couldn't do anything to help his friends until the morning so he pushed the worries from his mind.

His stomach rumbled. During the wild proceedings of the banquet, he had only picked at his food. And what he hadn't eaten had been promptly snatched and devoured by Randilin. *I wonder if there's a High Language word for cheese-cake?* He imagined it longingly. If there *was* such a word for it, he could imagine that it would have been one of his most important lessons. *Stalkton's been holding out on me.*

He plopped himself on his bed and dumped out his backpack. He picked up the Book and nestled it against his chest. Once again the energy was intense, like water bursting through a dam; it was almost too much to handle. He slipped it under his pillow rather than his regular nightly routine of keeping it under his shirt.

Next he raised the ruby pocket-watch. His eyes traced the direction of the short red hand toward the open chamber window. Already his thoughts of Atlantis felt like distant memories from another life.

He lifted the pocket-watch curiously as the long purple hand began slowly rotating before going still. Of the four clock-hands, the purple one alone remained a mystery.

Then, to his great delight, he discovered the final object from his emptied backpack: the silver glazed tart he had been given in the marketplace. His still-hungry stomach shouted in celebration.

He didn't have the slightest clue what the *tart* actually was, but at that moment, raw pig gizzards marinated in cough syrup would have tasted like chocolate ice cream. He crammed the whole thing into his mouth and chomped down on it.

The tart had an unusually bitter flavor. He gagged and grabbed his throat. It almost tasted like parchment. Actually, it tasted *exactly* like parchment. Cody regurgitated the half-chewed sludge into his hand. Sticking out slightly from the middle was the corner of a piece of paper.

Cody retrieved it and wiped the saliva from it. It was the size of the paper one would find in a fortune cookie. On one side were two letters: *G. T.* He flipped the paper and found a simple inscription:

EVERYTHING IS A LIE.

56

Missing

He rubbed the back of his hand across his sweaty forehead. Even though the night was generally peaceful, the slightest sound made his heart jump. He had pushed his luck—and he knew it. He tried to relax his tense shoulders. *Act natural. Don't look so suspicious!*

With another look both ways he entered into his house. "Sweetheart?" he whispered carefully. He glanced to the kitchen table. Beside his untouched and now cold dinner was a cleared plate. *She's gone to bed already.* He was relieved. It appeared more natural that way.

A rustle from outside startled him. He grabbed the kitchen table for balance, causing a loud clamor as his stale dinner plate fell to the floor. *Blast! It's too late, just leave it.*

He hurried toward the bedroom. He quickly removed his coat and looked to the bed. The lump of his wife under the covers brought him relief and comfort. "*Sweetheart, your Brodon is home....*" He stepped to the bed and tenderly lifted up the covers.

Two crystal tomblike eyes peered up at him. He screamed—then all was silent.

Cody was awake the moment the bright light of the orb shone through his window. He looked out over the waking city as he grabbed his tunic from the dresser. He realized how much he missed Upper-Earth sunrises. The abrupt arrival of mornings was incredibly unpleasant.

He picked up the paper warning from the previous night and shoved it into his pocket. He had questions that needed answering. As he stepped from his room he turned to walk down the hallway but stopped. He looked over his shoulder toward the chamber on the far end of the corridor: Jade's room.

He hesitated for only a moment before continuing on his way, alone.

By the time he reached the marketplace there were already several people roaming through the vendors' booths. Cody retraced his steps from the previous day with Jade. Skirting around a shopper he reached the location of the merchant's pastry stall.

It was gone.

In the precise spot where the booth had surely been the previous day now stood a lone tree. The solitary tree seemed out of place to the point of being comical. Cody rubbed his forehead. *I could have sworn it was right here.* He glanced down the long row of tents but the stall and its merchant were nowhere to be seen.

Cody turned to the vendor beside the vacant lot. It was the same tall elderly lady as before.

"Excuse me, ma'am," Cody began, "I'm wondering where I might find the man who was set up here yesterday afternoon."

The lady stared at Cody curiously. "Son, there hasn't been a man in that lot in a hundred years."

Cody fingered the crumbled paper in his pocket. "But there *was*! I'm sure of it! What was his name?" He rubbed his eyes searching his memory. "Brodon! That's it! He made silver-colored tarts. You must remember—you were standing right there!" Cody exclaimed, his voice raising.

The lady looked around, seemingly embarrassed by the commotion. She hollered across the clearing. "Hazig, this boy's looking for a merchant named Brodon. Do you know the man?"

The adjacent vendor looked up from his booth and shook his head. "I know every man, woman, child, vendor, or customer who's ever set foot in this market in the last one-thousand-and-sixty-four years...never been any fellow by the name Brodon."

Cody was forced to step aside as four golems carrying a silver crate passed through the market street. The woman beamed a friendly smile toward them. "Blessings on you for keeping our city clean and perfect!" The four soldiers nodded before heading on their way.

When they were gone the elderly lady returned her smile to Cody. "I'm sorry, son. I'm afraid you are somehow mistaken. But, while you're here...I've got a lovely selection of treats sure to delight!"

Cody brushed her off and left the marketplace. *What's going on here?* He reached into his pocket and retrieved the small paper: **EVERYTHING IS A LIE.** He flipped it around. *And who, or what, is G.T.?*

He looked up. Across the marketplace, standing like a statue amidst the moving crowd, was a Dark-Wielder. Its beady eyes peered directly at him.

Cody shoved the paper into his pocket and hustled the other way. The whole way down the street he could feel the burning sensation of the Wielder's eyes prying into his back.

57
A Deeper Training

As Cody stared at *The Speaking Sands* guilt nagged at his conscience. He had not contacted Eva once since he arrived in El Dorado. He knew he should, but part of him didn't want to. He pushed the bowl beneath his bed. *I'll contact her later when I have more to report*, he assured himself.

There was a knock on the door. When he opened it he found the young, large-dimpled servant girl from the previous night. "I'm sorry to bother you, but the Lord of Lights expresses his desire to see you in his Hall."

Cody thanked the servant and grabbed the Book. When he turned back the servant was still in the doorway. "Was there something else?" he questioned.

The girl squirmed nervously. "Only to thank you for coming to our marvelous city; I pray that you will be guided by the Radiant One to explore to the very *heart* of the Orb. I *guarantee* just one small sight of it will change your world." Without another word, the young girl scurried away.

Cody called after her but she was gone. The girl had spoken the very same phrase as that uttered by the missing merchant Brodon. *Could it have been mere coincidence?*

He knew it couldn't be. *There's something very peculiar going on here.*

The beautiful gold-crested Book beamed on the podium. Cody shielded his eyes. Once again he felt the increased, overwhelming power of his own Book gushing through him more and more fiercely with each step forward.

"Welcome."

Startled, Cody spun around. The Golden King stood directly behind him as though materializing from thin air. The King circled around the podium, stroking his long golden fingers across the Book's cover and tracing the embroidered *E*.

"The sensation of the Book's power flowing through your veins, filling your very blood stream, is fulfilling; nourishing, like air to the lungs, wouldn't you agree?" The energy of the Book suddenly felt amplified as Cody focused on it.

"No one else really understands it," Cody said, releasing a long-held frustration he didn't realize he had been carrying.

The King nodded. "They don't understand it because they *can't* understand it. You must realize by now that we are different from the others. We alone are the Book Keepers. There can only be two, and that sacred lot has fallen to us. We have a power they will never comprehend. We have a *responsibility* they will never carry."

Cody tracked the King's steady gaze to *The Code*. He pulled the Book protectively against his chest. The King grinned at the gesture. "Make no mistake, young Cody; while we are equal in title, we are far from being peers in creation ability and power. If I had desired to pry *The Code* from you, it would have taken but a single word the moment you entered this Great Hall."

The King's words seemed sincere, but Cody kept the Book nestled against his body. "Then, why haven't you? They told me your deepest desire was to obtain the Book. Isn't that why you started this war?"

The King laughed. "Is that what they are saying? Ask yourself this: Is it not strange that the very moment Atlantis has its Book Keeper return, and thus a means—*a power*—to counter El Dorado, they are suddenly swept into war? Has it even occurred to you that *Atlantis* is attacking *us*, to seize *The Key* for *its* own gain?"

Cody stepped back, caught off guard by the unexpected response. "Prince Kantan allowed me to leave Atlantis so that I could aid the war on the frontlines of Flore Gub," he admitted reluctantly.

The King's grin deepened. "Curious...and it is also curious that your Queen would willingly, on the dawn of war, send a band of her most valuable soldiers on a dangerous mission to rescue a single Surface-Dweller. It's poor logic... unless your band had a different reason for coming."

Cody wanted to counter the claim but couldn't. As much as he hated to admit it, the King's words made perfect sense.

"Either way, you're still at war. So I don't understand why you didn't take the Book."

"Because you have been misled; my desire is not for *The Code*—it is for knowledge. And for that…I need *you*."

"Me?"

"There are two Books and two Book Keepers. I cannot read from *The Code* any more than you can read from *The Key*. If we are to unveil the mysteries of the universe and fulfill our destined obligation to make an imperfect world perfect, we must do it together."

Cody relaxed his shoulders. "And, how would we do that?"

"I can train you. So far, your education appears to be, how shall I put this…*lacking*."

"Lamgorious Stalkton was teaching me the foundational words," Cody countered defensively.

"What your master was doing was holding you back. All the power of the universe at your fingertips and you are reduced to creating mere magic tricks. I can show you so much more. There is no limit. Indeed, there are some creations which have, as yet, eluded even *me*."

"*The-Creation-Which-Should-Be-One's-Own*," Cody blurted.

"Or so it is called by those without the courage to seek it. The albino is incapable of finding what he is unwilling to search for. The pursuit of knowledge and truth leads only as far as you are prepared to follow it."

The King placed his golden hand on Cody's shoulder. "So I ask you…how far are you willing to go?"

58

Ulterior Motives

The building was as elegant as each of the El Dorado houses. However, the presence of four walls made it stand out as something else—a prison. Cody trotted after Jade toward it.

Jade slowed down impatiently to allow Cody to catch up. "Hurry up, you snail," she chided. When Cody reached her he was huffing and puffing. Following his training session with the Golden King, Cody had returned to his chamber to find Jade waiting for him. Before departing for the prison they had stopped by Tiana's room but it had been empty, with no indication of her whereabouts.

Cody and Jade came to a stop before the prison doors. Two armed golems stood in their path. With a bow, they parted, allowing entrance to the prison.

Even the wealthiest aristocrat would have enjoyed the comfort offered within the bright, spacious, and elegantly-decorated room. Only the thick, iron bars of the jail cells reoriented one to its more solemn employment.

"Dace!" Jade exclaimed. The handsome captain reclined against the cell's wall. Having been stripped of his armor and weapons, he looked unusually youthful and plain.

Rejecting the fluffy bed provided, Chazic lounged on the floor of the cell. The Enforcer had removed his shirt to use as a pillow, once again exposing his unusual tattoos. Next to him sat Tat, whose eyes were as cold as a corpse. He stared straight ahead and didn't budge to acknowledge the visitors. There was something unusual about the trio but Cody wasn't sure what.

"Dreadful circumstances aside, it's good to see you again, Jade," Dace welcomed with a friendly smirk.

Jade clenched her fist. "I'm so sorry! I'll go straight to Hansi and have him resolve this *immediately*. He will grant your release. You have my word."

Dace chuckled. "We travel from one end of Under-Earth to the other, battling monsters, golems and Dark-Wielders, brave the Great Sea of Lava, and infiltrate the fortress of our enemy—all in name of rescuing *you*. Yet, here we are, behind bars, waiting for you to rescue *us*...just as we drew it up in the war room." Dace's ironic laughter faded as he noticed the look on Cody's face. "Something on your mind? You look as though you have a spiked mace going through your digestive system."

Cody jerked his head as he remembered the Golden King's words: *It is curious that your Queen would willingly, on the dawn of war, send a band of her most valuable soldiers on a dangerous mission to rescue a single Surface-Dweller.* Everyone's eyes were on him. "It's just, what you said just now,

241

about doing all that stuff to rescue Jade…" he paused. His forehead grew sweaty. "Is it true?"

Dace frowned. "What are you talking about? Of course, it's true. I offered myself as your blood protector. You know I would never deceive or use you…."

"Unfortunately, finding men as noble as Dace is as common as Wolfrick staying sober," Chazic added.

"What do you mean?"

The large Enforcer shrugged. "The night we departed Atlantis I was summoned to the AREA headquarters by Sli Silkian. I was not sent on this mission merely to be a body guard. I had a higher purpose."

"Which was…?"

"To steal *The Key* and return it to Atlantis." Chazic's words felt like a fist reaching out to punch Cody in the stomach. *The Golden King was right.*

He felt his anger rise. "What about the rest of you? What other lies have you been spewing? Who else was just using me to…" Cody stopped. It suddenly hit him. The unusual thing about the trio was that it *was* a trio. "Wait. Where's Xerx?"

Dace's eyes dropped to the floor. "Another notch on the sword hilt," he uttered distantly. Cody shook his head in disbelief, as though he had misheard.

"What are you talking about? That's not funny; where is he? Dace?"

Tat looked up from the floor. "In case you didn't notice; nobody's laughing, son. We were ambushed right after you left us at the boat. They were waiting for us. We weren't prepared. I'm sorry, lad, he's gone."

59

A Sacred Glen

E va pulled herself up from the floor; a tingling sensation still dancing through her limbs—the aftermath of another attack. She used the wall of the corridor for balance as her legs wobbled unstably beneath her. The room to her chamber was at the end of the hall, but, in that moment, it may well have been on a distant planet. She began staggering forward.

She had not heard from the Book Keeper in over a week—at least not directly. It was much worse, like a nightmare without escape. At any unexpected moment it would come. Always bad news. Always pain. Like a cry for help written in a foreign tongue that she didn't understand.

Suddenly her legs gave out from under her and she toppled to the ground, her face colliding hard against the wall. Her head throbbed. *Why me? Why did the accident happen to me?*

With a soft creak a door down the hall opened. She heard hushed voices released from inside. One was clearly her sister, Cia. *Who's the other?* She heard the door close with a click. The floor vibrated under the weight of heavy footsteps. When they stopped, Eva could sense the presence of someone standing over her.

Mustering all her strength she managed to raise her head in the man's direction. He wore a long black coat and a matching rimmed hat that covered much of his face. Two calculating blue eyes peered down at her. On his chest was an unfamiliar emblem with the word: CROSS.

"Goodnight," he whispered in a strange accent. Then he was gone.

"I will do everything in my power to have your friends pardoned and released. You have my word." Hansi's voice was rich and sounded genuine.

"What a saint," Cody snarled under his breath. Releasing Dace and the others would do nothing to resurrect Xerx. Cody glared at the Prince as though it had been his own sword that had delivered the killing blow.

"However, it will take some time to assure their discharge. In the meantime, there's something I've wanted to show you." As he spoke his eyes were fixed firmly on Jade. Cody shifted uncomfortably. The Prince motioned toward him. "You are welcome to come as well, of course."

Cody returned his stare with defiance.

"I would *love* to."

The trio traversed the city toward the eastern quarter. Although they had not yet explored this particular area of the city, it quickly became apparent that they hadn't missed much. The landscape was identical to all other parts of the city, down to the last detail. The painstaking symmetry was mindboggling.

Hansi led the way with Jade by his side, while Cody took up the rear several paces behind. Cody's eyes cast darts into the back of the Prince's head. He smirked and put an arm over his mouth, pretending to cough. "Cough—*Dastanda*—cough." A small patch of ground in front of Hansi became soft like sinking sand. The Prince's foot sank into the dip causing him to lose his balance and tumble to the ground.

Cody snickered softly. "Must be something to do with that air-density…." Jade's fiery green eyes shot toward him. He shrugged defensively. "*What?*"

Jade shook her head. "You can be such a child sometimes." She helped Hansi to his feet. Grabbing his hand and intertwining their fingers, she led him forward without looking back.

Cody kicked himself; his short moment of satisfaction extinguished. Jade was right. He was acting like a total jerk. *What am I doing? Why can't I just be happy for her?* He took a deep breath; *it's time to man up.* Happy with his new resolve, he jogged to catch up to Jade and Hansi. As he did, his foot slipped into the hole of sinking sand sending him face-first to the ground.

In front of the trio was a towering cluster of giant, lush-green trees; their trunks were thicker than even the majestic pillars of the Great Hall. The dense forest seemed to be surrounded by a cobblestoned wall, although foliage engrossed most of the wall's surface.

Standing in front of a thick bolted gate, Hansi turned to them. "You are about to enter into the most sacred place in El Dorado. Few have had the privilege to cast their eyes on what you are about to see."

He motioned to the guards, flashing his royal seal. The gate slowly pulled open. As they entered into the jungle the gate closed behind them.

The dense shrubbery suddenly opened up into a peaceful glen. In the center of the clearing was a large stone table. Vines and shrubbery had slithered up and swallowed its surface. Surrounding the circular table were a dozen stone chairs. Cody counted them. "The Twelve?"

Hansi nodded. "The Twelve renowned founders of Under-Earth once sat around this very table. It was *here* they debated the division of the land between Atlantis and El Dorado following the separation of the two Kings. It would be the final time the Twelve would gather in one place."

Cody began circling the table. The back of each throne had intricate engravings, worn by the ravages of time. He traced his finger along the markings of the first chair. The crude carving was of a rushing river. Crested above the picture was the letter 'I.' Cody felt a chill tickle his skin: *Ishmael.*

Cody continued to circle the table to examine the chairs. To the left of the King's throne was one marked with an 'N.' *The King's wife?* It occurred to Cody that the Queen had never once been mentioned by the royal family. However, before his thoughts could stray down that un-trekked path, he was caught off guard by the chair on the other side of the King's. The throne had the image of a budding plant and was crested with an **'R.'** *Randilin sat at the right hand of the King?*

Coming to the next set of chairs, he felt his stomach clench. The engraving was of a mountain. The letter was **'W'**—*Wesley.* His wife Sadria's chair was beside it. The face of the elderly Book Keeper appeared in Cody's mind. Without a word the face slowly began to shift, as though moving backwards through time. The face continued to grow younger until it was no longer Wesley at all. It was Xerx. Cody stepped away from the chair, withdrawing his hand. *How many in that line will die because of me?*

Cody moved on. There was a chair marked with two crisscrossed swords and an **'L,'** another with the engraving of an opened book and a **'T.'** He came to the final seat. The image was a simple circle. He was not sure how he knew, but immediately he realized it once belonged to the Golden King. He rubbed his hand along the rough surface above the etching but, to Cody's disappointment, the letter had been roughly chipped away.

Jade looked at him from across the table. "Can you imagine what it must have been like to see them all gathered together?" Cody scanned the table. He would have given anything to see that moment.

It was then he first noticed an unusually large gap between two chairs, breaking the perfect symmetry of the circle. The space was overrun with foliage. Reaching the spot, Cody pushed at the overrun bushes with his feet revealing the dirt below. In it were four deep gouges—the size of four chair legs. *There was another chair here...a Thirteenth founder.*

Cody stared at the spot in wonder. He thought of the ancient man they had discovered in the Caves of Revelation. Randilin had called him *The Thirteenth.* Had he been here, too? Had he been a Founder of Under-Earth? Who was he? More importantly: *Why has someone gone to such lengths to have him removed?*

60

The Price of a Good Story

Tiana didn't know where she was heading. She didn't care; as long as it was as far away from where she was as possible. *I deserve this.* Since she was a young girl she had casually played with fire and now she had to deal with the scorching burn. This understanding did nothing to lessen the pain.

She had watched Cody leave with Jade and the Prince. He had not asked her to accompany them, nor did she expect him to. She was not fooled by his silly, impulsive actions at the banquet. The user had become the used. Cody was using her to spark jealousy in Jade. Their time spent together on route to El Dorado seemed a lifetime ago.

She turned a blind corner and continued aimlessly down the lengthy alley. She yearned to be back in Atlantis in the comforting solitude of her rooftop dwelling, back where she could do as she pleased and be left alone. Before anyone cared about her; more importantly, before she cared about anyone.

She reached the end of the dreary passage and stepped out into a part of the city she had never seen before. *Where am I?* She glanced around. There was something unusual about it. A cluster of strange buildings with triangle rooftops had replaced the open-walled houses. The structures had four walls, but no apparent windows or doors. The night air was quiet, as though it hadn't been disturbed in a long time.

But the silence didn't last long. She detected whispered voices approaching, almost inaudible despite the placid air. She stepped back into the alley and crouched low. An instant later a silent procession passed noiselessly by the backstreet several feet from her hiding place.

The men were all concealed in dark robes, although the golden platelets fused into their hands exposed them to be soldiers. Several carried flickering lanterns dangling from large poles. The lantern light revealed two familiar men straggling in the middle of the parade: Hoin and Koin, the two *Story-Weavers* from the banquet.

The procession disappeared from Tiana's view. Peeking around the corner, she watched as they marched straight toward the city's stone wall. Then, in the blink of an eye, they were gone.

Tiana jumped out from her hiding. *What on earth?* Looking both ways, she jogged toward the wall. There was no exit anywhere in sight. *Where did they go?* She reached out and pressed against the wall. It was solid stone. *It doesn't make any sense.* She traced her hand across the wall. Then, without warning, her support was gone and she collapsed.

She was outside. The damp Under-Earth air filled her nose. She glanced behind her at the seemingly solid stone wall. From her position on the ground she could just make out the outline of a door. The opening was built on a slant and reflective mirrors were positioned on either side. As she stood the outline once again seemed to fade and disappear into the wall. *Clever.*

Off in the distance the faint lights of the procession ventured farther away from the city. Tiana pulled her hood over her head and scurried after them.

Reaching the top of the mound, Tiana looked into the yawning mouth of a dark cave. Torchlight bounced off the tunnel walls. As the lights faded around the corner, Tiana scampered into the cave in pursuit. She pressed her back against the wall and peered cautiously around the corner to where the group had congregated.

The *Story-Weavers* were shoved to the cold floor. Their mouths had been melded shut with a gold platelet fused into their skin over their lips.

The hooded men with the torches encircled the two prisoners. The leader of the parade stepped forward and removed his hood—Prince Foz.

Tiana inched back into the shadows and held her breath. The Prince knelt beside the twins. "That was an impressive story at the banquet," he said coldly. "Admirably brave... but reckless." Foz grabbed Koin's cheek and pulled his face toward him. "The first one to give me names is free to go."

The storytellers didn't budge an inch, staring defiantly at the Prince. Foz's face hardened. He grabbed Hoin by the hair and shoved his face against the dirt. "I asked you a simple question."

"That's *enough*, Foz." Another of the hooded men stepped forward. "They've made their choice." Tiana leaned in; the voice was familiar. Foz stood to face the speaker.

"I will not be bullied by you, Hansi." El Dorado's Prince removed his hood, revealing his powerful eyes. For a moment the two Princes stared steadily at each other.

There was a rumble from deeper within the cave. All heads turned toward the sound. The faces of Hoin and Koin went ghostly pale. "So be it." Foz said at last.

Tiana sunk low into the shadows as the convoy retreated past her and out of the cave, leaving the two *Story-Weavers* behind. As the men turned around the cave went pitch dark.

Tiana stood to follow but froze. From deep within the cave, she saw two glowing lights. The beams approached slowly. Tiana felt a chill come over her. The glow came from scarlet slit-like eyes.

She took off running, blinded by the dark. Her foot caught a stone and she tumbled to the ground. Pressing herself up, she ran with all her strength.

From behind she heard a low purr and then a wet crunching noise.

61

Disagreements

Cody tried to sleep but tossed and turned restlessly thinking of the Golden King. *I don't know what to believe anymore.* He felt so alone. The satisfaction of Jade's jealousy had lasted only a fleeting moment before being replaced by the deep longing for her friendship; for things to be like they were in Havenwood.

Cody's thoughts turned to Xerx. Cody recalled the young monk's boyish enthusiasm in embracing his role as instructor. Cody had seen a whole new side to his former Brotherhood rival—and now he was gone. Cody pushed the fact out of his mind. The more he thought about it the more he was forced to accept the truth.

He turned his eyes to the window and was shocked to see a silhouette filling the frame. Tiana's face appeared hovering over him.

"We've got to get out of here, *now*." Her face was pale.

"What are you talking about?" he asked. Or at least that's what he attempted to ask; what actually came out of his mouth was sleepy groaning and mumbling. Tiana grabbed his shoulders and slammed him back onto the bed. "Wake up! *It's here*. The Hunter. You've got to believe me!" she pleaded.

Cody sat straight up. "You *saw* the Hunter?"

"Yes! Well, not exactly. It was dark..." she stumbled over her words.

Cody yawned. "I think you're jumping at shadows. Are you sure you're not just seeing what you *want* to see? Maybe these people really aren't as evil as we were led to believe."

Tiana's jaw dropped, "Are you really that dense?! You of all people should know best; even in the pitch dark you can *feel* the Beast. You can feel its hatred; feel its hunger."

Cody shuddered. It was true.

There was a soft knock on the door and it began to open slowly. Tiana dove onto the bed and grabbed the hilt of her dagger. The door opened.

Jade stuck her head in. "Cody? I heard you awake. I couldn't sleep and wanted to apologize for the way I've been acting. It's just been..." her voice fell flat as she saw Tiana crouched on top of the bed. "Oh, gosh...sorry to interrupt," she said venomously.

Cody suddenly realized the misunderstanding, "Oh, no-no-no. This isn't how it looks at all!" he explained.

Tiana stood from the bed. "I only came to warn Cody that he's in danger. That *all of us* are in serious danger."

Jade raised an eyebrow. "Really? Well, by all means then, *do* tell..." she said with sarcastic politeness. Tiana ignored the slight and quickly recapped what she had seen at the caves.

Cody ran his fingers through his thick hair. "It *is* strange; all these people disappearing. But what on earth would lead to the *Story-Weavers* being treated that way?"

Jade shook her head. "It *doesn't* make sense because it's not true. The story is a fat lie. Isn't it obvious? She's miserable here and wants to go home." She stepped toward Tiana.

Tiana smirked. "Oh, I almost forgot. There was another man leading the execution with Foz…your beloved Prince Hansi." The statement effectively broke Jade's barrier of composure.

"How *dare* you…you miserable, meddling, sabotaging hag!"

Tiana's face boiled red. "Wake up, cupcake! Dunk your oversized head in the pool of reality! Do you really think this fairytale life you've been sleepwalking through could be real? *You*, living like a princess? Loved by a handsome prince? Who are you trying to fool?"

Jade's entire body shook like a wet dog and she ground her teeth. "Who's trying to fool who? Tiana, loner of Atlantis, abandoned and left alone by the big, bad world. Do you really think you're a golden girl now? You will always be the same selfish, miserable, lonesome girl you were the day I met you. All you've ever had was a pretty face…and now you're not the only one."

"I've *always* thought you were pretty, Jade" Cody blurted. His words silenced the room. His cheeks flushed as he felt the probing eyes of both girls. Suddenly reminded that Cody was in the room, both looked completely caught off guard by his intrusion into their argument. That reminder was an unwelcome one.

Without a word Jade and Tiana pivoted and left the room, marching in opposite directions. Cody, once again, was left alone. He collapsed back onto the bed. *Well, that certainly could have gone better.*

Tiana stomped down the hall toward her chamber and slammed the door behind her. *I'm going to kill that girl.* She smashed her fist against the wall. *I'm going to kill that boy, too!* She wound up to deliver another devastating slug to the wall but stopped mid-swing.

She sensed a foreign odor and immediately knew she wasn't alone. Reaching for her dagger she hurled herself to the side. Twirling in the air, she sent her blade flying at the attacker who was rushing at her from behind. The knife ricocheted off his head with a shrilling *cling.*

The Dark-Wielder collided against her, pinning her to the ground. Its firm crystal hands clutched her neck. She gasped as the Wielder squeezed tighter. *"Byrae!"* She managed to force out. A gust of wind billowed through the window sending her bed careening across the room. The Wielder looked up just in time for the footboard to collide with his face. Crystal fragments exploded like confetti all over the room.

Tiana rolled out from under the bed. Two more Dark-Wielders stood in her window frame. She jumped to her feet and dashed to the door. The Wielders pressed in toward her. She flung the door open and crashed right into Prince Hansi.

Everything became still. The Prince looked at her, at the two Dark-Wielders, and then back at Tiana. Then, without a word, he brought the hilt of his sword down hard against Tiana's temple. She crumbled toward the ground unconscious. The Prince caught her as she collapsed, and quietly lowered her to the floor.

Hansi leaned his face to her ear. "Didn't your parents ever tell you not to stick your nose in other people's business?" He motioned to the Dark-Wielders. "Dispose of her of quickly."

62

Two of a Kind

Cody was up early. His eyes were bloodshot and weary, the residual of another sleepless, troubled night. His brain throbbed from being in overdrive. He needed some space to process the radical 180-degree turn of recent events. He grabbed his backpack and left his room. He needed time to think.

There was freshness in the air as the city awakened. The streets were empty other than the merchants who peacefully set about preparing their booths. He found a soft patch of grass and sat down.

He closed his eyes to soak in the tranquil atmosphere but an explosion of giggling decimated his peace. He forced his eyes open in frustration and scanned the area for the guilty culprit.

Down the middle of the marketplace two people were walking blissfully toward him, their limbs interlocked, oblivious to the world apart from each other. Cody recognized them instantly—and groaned.

Prince Hansi tossed his head back and released a deep laugh at the unheard joke offered by Jade. Cody packed up his stuff. *Excuse me while I go vomit.* He scurried away, unseen by the two irritating lovebirds.

He gazed out across the landscape. The faded walls of the Labyrinth Mountains teased the outskirts of his vision. He knew that, despite the peaceful appearance, there was a violent battle for the Borderlands somewhere at the foot of the cliffs and men were being slain by the scores below the walls of Flore Gub.

The vast landscape was a welcome sight after looking at only the stone walls of the city for the last week. It had taken him nearly two hours and an infinite number of steps, but he had finally found his way to the top of the city's mammoth walls. Even his profound terror of heights was numbed by the exhaustion caused by the climb.

He reached into his backpack and pulled out the stone tablet—The Prophecy. At least that's how Chazic had referred to it. Cody read it for the thousandth time:

THE POWER OF FULL DIVINITY,
RESTS ENCODED WITHIN EARTHLY TRINITY.
WHERE SACRIFICE OF THE PURE ANGEL WHO FELL,
IS THE WAY TO RETRIEVE THE PEARL WITHIN THE SHELL.
WITH HUMBLE HEART AND GOLDEN KEY,
THE UNIVERSE'S MOST POWERFUL FORCE IS REVEALED TO THEE.

And for the thousandth time, Cody could make no sense of it. He rubbed his forehead. Maybe there *was* no sense to make of it. Perhaps, like everything else lately, it simply existed to further confuse and muddle his life. He raised the stone tablet and wound his arm back, preparing to catapult it off the wall and out of his life. As he brought his arm forward a grunt from behind stopped him in mid-throw. *"Randilin?"*

The dwarf looked like Cody had never seen him before. Rather than the grimy hobo he had become accustomed to; he looked clean and polished like a long-neglected set of chinaware finally cleaned. His straggly hair had been combed behind his ears and even his beard had been given some much-needed care.

The dwarf frowned. "Ruddy well right it's me; who the blazes else would I be? The bloody tooth fairy?" He snorted and added an entirely unnecessary curse, as if to assure his listener that despite his appearance, he remained the same grumpy scoffer as always.

Cody smiled. "I simply *love* what you've done with your hair."

Randilin's face flushed red and his thick fingers quickly pulled the hair out from behind his ears.

"I knew it looked ridiculous," he muttered defensively. The dwarf plopped himself beside Cody. After a moment he huffed, "Welcome to my life, son."

Cody raised his eyebrows. "Excuse me?"

Randilin held out his palms motioning to the surroundings. *"This.* Always frustrated. A disappointment to yourself and to others. Always alone." Randilin pounded his chest. "Take it from me, I'm the patron saint of miserable lives!"

Cody couldn't help but chuckle.

"What a wretched pair we make." Randilin brushed his hair back behind his ears again and grinned. "Well, at least I still have my dashing looks."

Cody smiled. "You're right; I guess things could always be worse," he laughed before pausing, "Randilin...why did you do it?"

The Dwarf's ugly smile faltered. His shoulders slouched and he pulled his hair from behind his ears again. "Why did I sell out my only friends to a man I can't stand? Why did I throw away everything for the sake of my own selfish, pitiful existence?"

Cody dropped his gaze.

"I wasn't going to put it *exactly* like that..."

Randilin snorted. "I've been asking myself that same question every day for hundreds of years. But the answer is simple—I'm a bad man."

Cody opened his mouth to protest, but Randilin shook him off. "Oh, don't bother. I've long since accepted my own curse." He took a deep breath, holding the air in his chest for several seconds before releasing it slowly. "Do you want to know the reason I jumped into the wishing well that day to return to Atlantis after centuries of banishment?" Cody leaned forward, anticipating the answer.

"Because of you."

"*Me*?"

"You deaf, boy? That's what I just bloody said! Because of *you*...because in you I saw the same curiosity and passion for life that I had so many years ago. And I saw a chance for you to become the man I never was."

Despite the leathery skin and rigid wrinkles, there was a softness in Randilin's face. But it didn't last long. The dwarf's hand shot out and whacked the back of Cody's head. "So stop moping around like a ruddy child and man up!"

Cody rubbed his throbbing head. "But I don't know what to do."

Randilin scrunched his forehead. "It was a book that got ya' into this shoddy mess…maybe a book can get ya' out. The Great Library wouldn't be a bad place to start."

"There's a library here?!" Cody asked excitedly.

Randilin grinned. "Aye laddie; the biggest stinkin' one your eyes have ever seen. More books than you could read in a million lifetimes." Randilin looked over his shoulder carefully. Cody's eyes followed. A dozen yards down the wall the glimmering crystal eyes of a Dark-Wielder peered at them from the shadows. How long it had been watching was impossible to tell. Despite his distance, Cody had the eerie feeling that their words were no longer private.

Randilin turned back to Cody and lowered his voice. "Find the library," he winked. "The beauty of books is that nothing lost is ever lost forever."

63

History Erased

Cody was awestruck. The room was immense, the walls stretching thirty floors high with spiraling balconies twisting along the side. A majestic chandelier hung from the ceiling, thousands of lights dancing on candles. The walls were crusted in gold and made entirely of cabinets. Each space was teeming with a thousand bundled scrolls.

Cody's eyes explored the room in astonishment. There must have been tens of millions of scrolls. The American Library of Congress would have appeared as a small-town kindergarten bookshelf in contrast to this breathtaking hoard of literature.

He walked in slowly, his senses overwhelmed. A long shadow stretched from behind him. When he turned an exceedingly old man was standing several feet away. He had a haunting skeletal face and his cheek and chin bones jutted out as though they would cut right through his thin pale skin. His stringy, pure white hair hung to his feet and his black eyes were wide and calculating like a cat.

The librarian's steady gaze made Cody turn back around uncomfortably. He stepped to the nearest wall and retrieved a scroll. Removing the binding, he unrolled it. The title read: *Journey to the Top of the Earth*. As he pretended to read, the shadow behind him disappeared. Cody returned the scroll and quickly ventured deeper into the boundless library.

The room was like a majestic coliseum. Each of the large archways led to another hall filled with wall-to-wall books and scrolls. At the top of each passage were titles spanning every imaginable category. In the center of the immense hall was a pavilion. Above the lone entrance were the words: *THE ANCIENTS*.

Unlike every other section, a barricade blocked the smaller building and a guard stood before it. Cody bit his lip. *Now what?* Suddenly he felt an uncomfortable sensation come over him. Cody again could feel the stare of the gaunt librarian.

Cody muttered under his breath, *"Byrae."* As he did, there was a loud boom as an entire shelf of scrolls came hailing to the floor from two balconies above. The librarian's head jolted up, and he vanished.

The moment he was gone Cody approached the pavilion. He squeezed his hand into a fist and whispered to himself. The golem guarding the room raised his pick-axe. Cody held out his hand and revealed a royal seal—a seal identical to the one Hansi had used to gain access into the sacred glen. The guard nodded, stepping aside to let him in.

The room was not large. Around the room were thirteen gold pillars. On each of the pillars was a single book. In the center of the room was a statue—three rectangles in the form of an upside arrow. Cody's breath accelerated. *This is it.*

Cody circled the room. Each of the antique volumes was tattered and the titles were faded, several to the point of being indecipherable. Of those he could make out were: *Proverbs of Boc'ro the Wise* and *Transcript of the Great Assembly.*

He stopped before the middle pillar. It was slightly higher than the other twelve and the hefty book on it was three times the width of the others: *The History of Under-Earth.* At the bottom of the cover was: *Written and Compiled by Lamgorious H. Stalkton.*

Cody hauled the weighty book slowly. He carefully flipped through the pages, unsure what exactly he was looking for, but convinced that whatever it was lay within these pages. Skimming the pages he noticed that every time *The Twelve* was written it was smudged out as though by a troublesome child with crayons. But Cody knew it was no accident: *Because it didn't say Twelve...it said Thirteen.* Somebody had gone through the painstaking process of blotting out every reference to *The Thirteen.*

Cody began to read:

It was in the third day of the first week of the discovery of Under-Earth when The T——— made the most astonishing discovery—they were not the first inhabitants of the new world. The native watched the Founders day and night— but only from afar; never making contact with the Tribe, but always looking on. His eyes were dark, and continually open, for they were not covered by eyelids. The Alac-icacs came to call him The Watching One. The age and origin of the wandering hermit remain unknown.

Cody almost shouted. *I'm not crazy! Others have seen him!* It was a reassuring discovery. He resumed scanning the pages with increased urgency. He heard noises from outside the pavilion. *I don't have much time!*

His eyes stopped at the phrase: *It was during this period when we first discovered The Prophecy....*

A footnote at the bottom of the page read: *For a detailed account of The Prophecy and the search for the Earthly Trinity, see page 2812.**

Cody quickly flipped to the page—and frowned. The page was a detailed description of the history of *de-fossilized* food. Cody licked his fingers and pressed against the page sure he had missed one. He had not. *I don't understand.* It was then that he noticed a single, jagged piece of paper, no bigger than a fruit fly, sticking out from the middle crease. He held the book up to his eyes and ran his finger down the crease. *Somebody has torn pages out of this book.*

Cody heaved the book back onto the pillar in frustration. He had been so close. He reached to close the cover when he saw it, tucked against the corner of the page and so faint he almost missed it—a penciled inscription: *Find the Fallen Angel.*

64

In Search of Answers

She had been missing for too long. No one had seen Tiana since the previous night. It made Cody uneasy. They had not parted on good terms. *Maybe she just wanted some privacy?* It wouldn't be all that unlike Tiana after all. *For crying out loud, the girl lives on a rooftop a thousand feet above all other civilization!* But in his gut he knew it was something else. *Something's wrong.* It was becoming increasingly clear that peculiar things were happening and people were going to great lengths to keep them hidden.

He was determined to get to the bottom of it. He shoved the Book into his backpack and swung it over his shoulder. It was time to find the truth.

With a soft thud his feet hit the ground. He looked up at his chamber window a hundred feet above him and the leafy vine ladder he had created weaving down the wall. "*Fraymour,*" he whispered. The vine began to sizzle before crumbling to the ground scorched and wilted.

Cody set off swiftly. Reaching the end of the palace wall he peered around the corner. It was dark and the streets were empty. Even from across the clearing he could see straight into several open-walled homes, the tenants peacefully sleeping within. He frowned. The slightest untimely noise would wake them and he would be fully exposed. There was no room for error.

He began scampering down the alley. A rumbling noise caused him to stop. With nowhere to hide he froze like a statue and bit his lip. One of the house tenants rolled over in his bed. Moments later, he could again hear the sound of soft snoring. Cody exhaled and continued forward.

Peering across the slumbering city he saw the massive gold Orb monument marking the heart of El Dorado. His mind drifted back to the banquet and the *Story-Weavers'* tale. Their ending climax had been to create an orb and then light it up from the inside. Then there was the young servant girl's peculiar advice: "Explore to the very *heart* of the Orb." Everything seemed to point to the Orb; it was as good a place to start as any.

Cody skidded to another quick stop. Directly across the alley two Dark-Wielders were approaching between two houses. Cody looked around, desperate for a place to hide, but the courtyard was empty. The Wielders were almost at the clearing. If he didn't move quickly he would be seen.

He jumped through the open wall of the closest house. The noise brought another rustle from the snoring man in the bed. Cody ducked low and held his breath. Like silent wraiths the two Dark-Wielders appeared in the courtyard.

Their gemstone eyes spied into the open houses that flanked them. Scanning the inside carefully, they glided to the next two houses in the row and repeated the process... each time moving closer and closer toward Cody.

Cody glanced around frantically. He needed somewhere to hide and quick. *Under the kitchen table!* He turned and scowled. The table elevated only two feet off the ground, surrounded by several large cushions. *OF COURSE they have to eat laying down,* he thought bitterly.

Cody glanced around but couldn't see anyone. Yet he could hear the Wielder surveying the house next door. *What do I do?!* The footsteps approached his hiding place.

65

The Heart of the Orb

The Dark-Wielder scanned the house only to find a couple sleeping soundly in bed. Their steady breathing was genuine. There was nothing suspicious there.

The Dark-Wielder's eyes moved toward the kitchen. They paused and lingered on the table. The Wielder leaned forward, its crystal eyes glistening from under its hood. Then it was gone.

After several still moments one of the cushions jiggled, and was shoved aside. Cody lifted his body out of a large hole in the floor. He watched the two Wielders turn down another alley and disappear from view. He wished he could see the house owners' expressions when they awoke to find a giant crater in the middle of their kitchen. He replaced the cushion to conceal the opening and checked that his escape route was clear. Being sure, he exited the house.

Cody continued his trek toward the immense Orb monument. The moment he reached it he realized his problems were just beginning. Stationed along the perimeter of the monument were dozens of fortified golden golems. *I must be on to something.*

Movement in his periphery caught his attention. A cluster of people marched toward the monument. Four Dark-Wielders walked at the corners of a silver crate that floated on its own accord amidst them. Leading the group was Prince Foz.

Cody watched as Foz led the procession past the line of guards, straight toward the monument. He stopped before it. Then, without a sound, the wall began to move. Two pieces spread apart revealing a crack down the middle. The next moment the seemingly solid wall had been transformed into an entrance.

The heart of the orb. Those had been the servant's words. Cody grinned. *There's something INSIDE the monument!* He needed to get inside. As the final Wielder followed Foz inside, the entrance began to shrink. *It's now or never.*

Cody focused on the inside of the monument. The entrance continued to close. It became a sliver.

"*Spakious!*" Cody dove head first through the portal.

Cody face-planted to the ground. He heard the door close behind him, trapping him inside the monument. He had made it. He stared down a long corridor. The assembly escorting the silver crate turned and disappeared into a side room several yards down the hall.

Cody crept down the long hallway and stopped at the door. It had been left slightly ajar. There was a thud as the crate was released to the ground. Cody risked peeking farther into the room that was empty except for a single, elevated bed. Hanging on the walls by hooks were various contraptions and devices. Many of them had sharp blades and needle-like ends. Cody tried not to imagine their purpose.

The four Dark-Wielders and Foz stood around the crate on the floor. One of the Wielders began muttering. As he did the crate's lid slowly lifted into the air. With a loud clank it crashed to the ground. The other three Wielders stepped toward the crate and pushed it onto its side.

Cody covered his mouth. Out of the crate rolled a limp body. Cody recognized the distinctive, deep dimples of the young palace servant girl. Her face was pale and her body was lifeless.

They've been transporting people in the crates! Cody shuddered. Foz looked down at the girl indifferently. "Let us begin." Two of the Wielders lifted the unresponsive girl onto the bed. Foz turned and walked toward the door. Cody pulled his head from sight and looked down the corridor. He didn't have enough time to run in either direction without being seen. He pressed his back against the wall and braced himself.

With a soft click the door was pressed closed. Cody didn't waste any time. The next instant he dashed down the narrow corridor, finally reaching the end. The hallway opened out into a massive domed room.

Cody's gazed over the room in disbelief.

It was horrifying.

66

A Living Sacrifice

It was utterly dark. She couldn't even see her own body through the impenetrable shroud. Tiana tried to move but her limbs were locked in place. She felt the firm squeeze of the ropes binding her arms and legs and was light-headed and dizzy. She tried to take a deep breath but couldn't move her mouth. She tried sticking her tongue out but it pressed against a hard, smooth metal surface. *Oh, no.* She had been gagged by the golden platelet that was now fused into her face.

I'm going to suffocate! She thrashed at her bindings enough to teeter her body over. Her face pressed against the cold ground.

Where am I? There was something familiar about the stale air. She relaxed her muscles. Her bindings were so tight that any struggle would deplete her energy. She needed to reserve what strength she could and wait for the proper moment. She couldn't feel her dagger against her leg, nor did she expect to. She would have to resort to the strategy she'd been using her whole life: play the weak damsel, and once the victim was lured into a false confidence—strike hard and fast. Her head continued to spin. Unless that opportunity came soon she was going to run out of air.

A noise from the dark spiked her senses. Adrenaline began pumping through her veins. *Someone's coming.* She strained her ears, trying to pinpoint the direction of the sound. *It sounds like several people.* The ground rumbled against her face. *Or one very large person.*

The muffled steps grew louder, the sound pin-balling around the damp room. Tiana braced herself. A strange, potent smell carried toward her. At that moment the horrifying realization hit her and her heart pounded in her chest. It wasn't a some*one* approaching—it was a some*thing*. From the other side of the room two red eyes appeared.

They burned with ravenous hunger.

67

Death and Life

The room was an enormous factory.

Like the skyline of a haunted city, large devices jutted up toward the ceiling producing a humming noise. Weaving between the unknown structures was a matrix of conveyer belts. Soaring a hundred feet above the workshop large containers sailed along wires that stretched across the room in countless directions like an immense spider web. Bustling around the floor were scores and scores of Dark-Wielders and golden golems. The Wielders danced their arms in the air and chanted, like maestros conducting the droning machines.

Cody dashed down a long set of steep stairs and hid behind one of the conveyor belts. *What is this horrible place?* Cody began to raise his head but quickly ducked back into place as two Wielders marched past. In their hands were large, clear vials full of a dark liquid that looked like blood. Cody gagged.

The moment the Wielders were out of sight Cody crouched and dashed across the room. Despite the loud drone of the machine-like devices, every one of his footsteps seemed to erupt, broadcasting his presence. His head twisted back and forth cautiously.

Turning a corner Cody nearly crashed into the backside of two golems. Skidding to a halt, he dove to the side and rolled behind a conveyor belt. The golems turned and scanned the area before resuming their march.

Cody exhaled. *I need to get out of here.* He braced himself to make another dash. 3…2… A hand fell on his shoulder. Cody flinched, yanking on the hand to free himself. Without any resistance the hand was pulled toward him. Cody looked down to his lap—in it was a detached arm.

"Ahh!" Cody flung the arm away and shook his body in utter disgust. He pushed himself away. Moving slowly along the conveyor belt were dozens of unattached arms. *What kind of revolting place IS this?!*

Cody covered his mouth and inched forward. There was something odd about the arms. They were hollow of any bone or muscle and the pale gray skin had a strange plastic-like appearance similar to that of a manikin.

Suddenly, Cody grabbed his ears as a harsh ringing sound pierced through the room. At the sound all the giant devices stopped droning and the area went silent. *That can't be good.* Cody dropped to the floor and rolled against the conveyor belt, his face stopping directly in sight of the thrown arm. He bit his lip to keep from retching.

Peering up he watched as dozens of Wielders and golems dashed by his location heading away from him. Cody locked every muscle in his body. *They're all leaving… why?* As the soldiers continued to stream by, none both-ered to glance back and see Cody lying in open sight. All at once the parade stopped. *This is my chance!*

Cody stood and ran deeper into the factory. He passed by another conveyor belt covered with legs and a barrel full of bare feet, both with the same unnatural appearance. He stopped as he arrived in the center of the plant.

Around the perimeter of the room were five gurneys. In the middle of the circle was a chair. Cody approached one of the cots but jumped back, startled. Occupying the bed was a wraithlike man. Similar beings filled each of the other beds, covered up to their necks in white sheets. Their eyes were hauntingly empty: *The Rephaim.*

Cody knew it was true. The dreaded, hollow men Tat had first discovered in the center of the enemy war camps outside Flore Gub. The demons Levenworth claimed were impervious to pain and fear.

In that moment Dace's bewilderment aboard *The Igg* came rushing back and everything was clear: El Dorado's suddenly innumerable fighting force made perfect sense: El Dorado was not enlisting more soldiers…it was *creating* more soldiers. Thousands of them.

There was a rumbling noise and the large devices began to click before settling back into their drone. *Uh-oh.* Then a rattling commotion sounded from behind him. Cody froze. Someone was coming. He searched around desperate for a place to hide. The approaching steps were getting louder.

Lifting the sheet from the bed, he crawled chest-down onto the cot and pulled the covers over him. The next moment two Dark-Wielders appeared in the center of the circle dragging a third man with them.

Cody looked down and his heart jumped. He was lying directly on top of the hollow man. The haunting wraith's empty eyes gazed lifelessly at him. Cody clamped his jaw to keep from screaming.

He lifted the sheet a sliver and peered out at the scene. The Dark-Wielders pushed their hostage onto the chair in the center of the circle—it was Brodon, the merchant.

He did exist! Cody squinted his eyes; the merchant was bruised and swollen almost beyond recognition. His mouth was quivering but produced no sound. The two Wielders continued moving around the chair busily, oblivious to the merchant's unspoken words.

The merchant's head tilted and rolled to the side. His eye caught Cody's. His eyebrows lifted and he increased his quiet muttering. Cody's sightline was broken as the Wielders stepped between them. They placed their arms on the merchant's chest and began chanting. Their voices were low and too muffled to comprehend.

Suddenly the merchant started thrashing violently. His back arched off the chair as though a powerful electric current bolted through him. His hands reached out and pressed against the Wielders' faces trying to shove them away, but they continued chanting indifferently. Then, just as it had started—it stopped.

The room reverted to its eerie silence. Then, with a soft wheezing sound, the merchant shriveled like paper in a fireplace. Cody retched. The innards of the depleted skeletal body had been cleanly vacuumed out. His jaw fell open and from his gaping mouth a tiny, glowing light floated out.

The glowing orb elevated toward the ceiling and stopped several feet above the dead man. With a spark there were suddenly five smaller lights in place of the one. The lights began floating across the room and headed directly toward the five beds.

Cody watched helplessly as one of the lights drifted directly toward him. He pressed his body tighter against the lifeless wraith on the bed. The light hovered over the body before dropping and disappearing into the warrior's mouth beneath him.

There was an almost inaudible moan around the room. Cody watched as the other four beds around the room begin to stir. Then, one-by-one, the hollow warriors rose from their resting place. Cody's skin went cold. The body beneath him began to twitch as the warrior's two hands shot out and grabbed him around the neck. Cody squealed.

The moment he did the room was silenced and every eye was pinned directly on him.

68

One Final Cask

The door closed softly behind him. Flickering light from three thousand white candles illuminated the room.

The chamber was as ornately elegant as it was neurotically neat. From the entirely straight angles of the furniture to the perfectly-positioned paintings spaced along the wall, the chamber appeared as though it had never before been tarnished by the irritating clumsiness of human life.

Indeed, he would have believed it true if not for the man standing across the room gazing out the window. The man's hands were clasped behind his back and his snow white hair hung straight, evidently handled with as much careful precision as the room's décor.

"You wished to see me, father?" Prince Hansi asked from the entranceway. The Golden King continued to stare intently out over the city as though it held the answer to an unsolvable mystery.

"Sit," he commanded.

Hansi entered into the room and sat in the chamber's only chair. "Have the...*imperfections* been removed?"

Hansi nodded. "Yes, father. I have seen to it personally."

"And, the girl?"

Hansi's face tightened. "I have done all you've asked of me."

The King turned and glided toward the Prince.

"You have done well, son. You make your father proud," he whispered, stroking Hansi's hair. "I believe the time has come to...move forward." The words slithered from the King's mouth like a serpent.

Hansi's back straightened. "Already? Are you sure? Perhaps if you gave me more time it would..."

The Golden King lunged forward, his face pressing close to the Prince's. "Do you question my judgment? You don't have *feelings* for the girl, do you? Have you lost sight of your assignment? Have you forgotten why we brought her to El Dorado in the first place?"

Hansi shook his head firmly. "Of course not, father. Your wisdom is impeccable. Your judgment is sound. Tomorrow I will speak to her and...."

"No," the King interrupted. "Bring her to me *tonight*."

Jade stared at the mirror suspiciously. For the first time in weeks there was a stranger staring back at her. She wiped her hand across her face, smudging her powdered cheeks.

What am I doing?

She looked ridiculous in the mirror with only one half of her face covered in the thick coating of makeup. And the realization hit her—she was caught awkwardly between an old and a new life.

Jade perked up at the sound of a tap on her door. *Who on earth could that be at this late hour? Cody?* She frantically used her fingers to comb her frizzled hair.

Giving another look in the mirror, she wiped the remaining makeup from her face. She double-checked the mirror—she looked beautiful.

She dashed to the door. Reaching it she took a deep breath to regain her composure. She opened the door. The man standing in the door was not Cody.

"Hansi? What are you doing here?" she stammered. His handsome face and dashing smile made her quickly regret having so rashly removed her makeup.

"You have been summoned to the chamber of the Golden King."

"At this time of night?"

"The King has something...*special* planned for you."

69

Packaged

Cody's head burned as he fought for breath. The hollow wraith's fingers clamped tighter around his neck, pressing against his windpipe. Cody's vision began to blur. He could faintly make out the shapes of the two Wielders and four hollow men closing in on him.

He grasped the attacker's wrists, trying to pry them away from his throat but the grip was too tight. His vision was lost and his body went limp.

Boom! Cody's ears rang at the sound of a bang. The pressure on his neck instantly loosened. Cody rolled to the side, falling off the bed and crashing to the floor. The hollow man on the bed was scorched black from head to toe. Gasping for breath, Cody scanned the room. The other hollow men and the two Wielders were scattered across the floor, steam rising from their lifeless bodies. *What in the world just happened!?*

He didn't have time to find out. He scrambled to his feet and dashed away from the area. Whatever boom had slain the men had not gone unnoticed by the rest of the factory. Disorder rose up from all parts of the domed room.

Cody looked across the vast factory and calculated the sea of enemies separating him from the corridor exit. *It's too far.*

Heavy footsteps and voices behind set him running again. He darted around the corner and leapt over a conveyor belt. His feet skidded to a stop as several golems clustered in his path. He threw himself behind cover just as they approached. Crawling on all fours Cody scurried quickly along the floor. Glancing over his shoulder he saw the shadows of four more golems.

He sprinted down the side of the belt and pulled himself around the corner, pressing his back against the ledge and covering his mouth to suppress the sound of his heavy breathing.

The corridor exit was still far away. He couldn't keep up the game of cat-and-mouse much longer. *Thud.*

Something brushed past him, knocking hard against the side of his head. It was a large steel container. Cody watched the container's path as it rose into the air and soared over the room on the complex pulley system.

Cody felt the bump of another container as it glided by. The agitated voices of the four golems were getting louder. Before he realized what he was doing, he impulsively grabbed the next container and hurtled himself over the edge.

His landing was softened by something cold and squishy. Cody sunk into spongy matter up to his neck. He grasped the side of the bin to keep from sinking in over his head. He vomited when he saw that the bin was completely full of unattached ears.

He thrashed in disgust, trying to pull his body out. *They're fake! They're just artificial, created parts….* His desperate reassurance did nothing to ease his stomach. He finally managed to pull himself up and onto the bin's ledge.

The floor was tiny below as he soared a hundred feet above it. He instantly felt queasy again. He traced the path of his bin right past the exit. He braced himself to jump. *Wait for it…wait for it…wait…for it….*

At last the bin came parallel with the corridor's ledge. Cody leapt from the bin, stretching his arms outward. He stumbled as his left foot caught the edge of the container. Suspended in the air, his face peered down at the ground.

He groaned as his body swung and crashed against the wall. His fingers burned as they held his weight and kept him from plummeting to a mushy death a hundred feet below.

He risked a glance down even though his arms shook violently from the tension. A cluster of Dark-Wielders had gathered below and all eyes were on Cody. They raised their arms and he saw their mouths begin to move.

With a pained scream Cody pulled himself onto the ledge by his fingertips and out of the sunken warehouse. The lengthy corridor stretched out before him. Cody rolled to his feet and sprinted as fast as he could. The door at the far end grew larger and larger. *Almost there!* He didn't dare look back to see if he was still being followed. He needed to escape the nightmarish laboratory—and fast.

The door was now only a dozen feet away. *I made it!* He reached out to grab it. From the corner of his eye he saw motion but was too slow to react. A fist collided against the side of his head sending him staggering to the floor, winded and dazed.

A hooded man stepped over him, grasping him by the collar and dragging him into a side room. Cody flailed his arms, swatting at the man, but his sense of balance had been knocked out of sync by the unanticipated blow.

Cody felt himself being lifted into the air and dropped back onto a hard surface. He was now in one of the silver crates. "Noooo!" His cry was suffocated as the lid of the crate slammed shut, trapping him in darkness. Cody pounded his body against the sides of the encasing, but the tight compartment confined his arms, pinning them against his side. He couldn't move an inch in any direction. He coughed as the air began to grow thin. "Help!" he tried to scream, but no sound came.

He heard muffled voices from outside the box. "Where's this crate headed?" asked a steady voice. "Should I bring it to initiation?"

"No," replied a second voice. "Not this one...send this to the furnace."

70

Stranger in the Night

The heat of the Hunter's breath burned like fire against her face. Its two flaming eyes remained still, penetrating her and savoring the pitifulness of its helpless prey.

Tiana thrashed desperately at her bindings but the work only managed to press her face harder to the cold ground. She heard the sharp sound of the Beast's talons as they cut across the ground, slowly approaching.

Her screams were silenced by the golden platelet over her mouth. It was no use. She could do nothing but wait. The approaching steps grew louder as the Beast drew closer. She felt breathing against the back of her neck and braced herself for the piercing sting of the Hunter's fangs.

Suddenly, the bindings around her loosened and she immediately wiggled them off. The Hunter squealed. Tiana jumped to her feet. She grabbed at her mouth trying to pry the platelet off.

With a rumble the ceiling of the cave began to collapse. Tiana took off running the opposite direction of the wailing Beast. Completely blinded in the dark, she staggered dizzily as her head screamed for air.

She could hear footsteps beside her but couldn't see a face or body. She stumbled into a wall but felt two hands grasp her shoulder and gently shift her direction. Tiana continued to run through the gloom.

As she ran, the stranger continued to guide her path. It was as though the invisible guide was running in beautiful summer daylight.

She didn't know how long she ran or if the Hunter was behind her. She put her faith in the invisible stranger and ran until her legs began to wobble. All at once the utter darkness was replaced by the expansive landscape.

Tiana staggered out from the cave. Down below in the valley sat El Dorado in a tranquil slumber. Tiana heaved over, clutching her head and trying to maintain her vision.

She turned back to the opening of the cave. Inches from her face, a man stared directly at her like a ghost. He had no eyelids.

Tiana shuffled back in fright. The man stepped toward her and reached his hand for her face. Tiana closed her eyes and flinched. The next thing she knew a wave of soothing air flooded her lungs.

She grabbed her mouth—the gold platelet was gone. She looked back at the stranger who motioned for her to follow. Without waiting for a response, he disappeared over the dune. Tiana glanced around, and then ran after him.

Cody felt himself bobbing through the air. He kicked at the walls of his prison and his head whiplashed and smashed against the floor, all to no avail. *Did they set me down?*

He strained to hear. He could make out quiet voices but couldn't determine whom they were or what they were saying. Suddenly the cart began to rumble and he heard a cranking noise. *They're lowering me into the furnace!*

Cody thrashed with all his strength. "Help! Help! *Help!*"

He began to sweat as he was lowered deeper and deeper into the blazing heat.

PART FOUR
ILLUSIONS AND REALITY

71

Phase Three

He watched the numbers climb like the steady ticking of a bomb: **23...24...25....** He removed his hat and ran his boney fingers through his thick, sweat-dampened hair.

He anxiously shifted his weight back and forth between his right and left legs. He was not one overly acquainted with the sensation of nervousness. Such sentiments belonged to weaker men. Yet, as the numbers continued to rise, the jitters seized control of him—**35...36...37....**

It must be a significant development, he thought, dropping his gaze to his freshly polished dress shoes. In all his years, the number of times he had been summoned for a face-to-face meeting could be counted using just his fingers. He was never eager to add to that tally.

As the digits hit **66** it was announced with a *ding.* The elevator doors slid open and he took a final deep breath before he marched out into the room. He hoped to reveal more confidence than he felt.

The back of the chair faced him, a haze of smoke rising up from the other side. He removed his hat in respect. "My master, you summoned me...?"

Another puff of smoke preceded the reply, "Indeed, my faithful Dunstan, in hopes that your lips carry good tidings." The man's voice had not an ounce of warmth. Dunstan felt his hands twitch. Phone communication was frightening, but in person, the voice, naked and untainted, was downright haunting.

"I have personally assured that the boy's journey was successful. The Book Keepers have been united at last. I obediently await further orders, my master."

"And, our man on the inside?" the master asked.

"He remains under our control. We remain in possession of the leverage. I assure you he will play his part when the time comes."

The master's hand appeared from behind the chair. The skin was like rough leather and a prominent scar ran from the top of the hand to his elbow. He dropped the cigarette butt and grasped a shiny object leaning against the desk.

There was gleam as he lifted a magnificent sword. "The time for CROSS to rise from the ashes has come at last. Begin *Phase Three*."

Dunstan felt a chill run down his spine. "Sir, *Phase Three*? Now?" He bit his tongue before another reckless sound could exit.

"You question me?"

Dunstan felt his heart racing out of control. "Of course not, master! There is no other like you. I live only to do thy bidding, my master." Dunstan rubbed the wrinkles on his forehead. "It's just…after all this time; all this preparation…."

The master brought the sword down, its blade piercing the floor. "Patience is the greatest virtue of the greatest predators; but the time has come. Go, faithful Dunstan, and do what you must do. Today the spark we ignite will become a raging inferno."

72

Resistance

Am I alive?

The consuming darkness around him was suddenly dispelled by light streaming in from above. Two hands broke through the glare and grasped his collar, hoisting him into the air. Cody gasped for air as the world blurred back into focus around him. The air was damp and heavy.

Cody looked down to the empty silver crate and then to the hooded man who had pulled him out. "Where am I? I thought I was lowered into the furnace."

The hooded man nodded, "And so you were." Without any further explanation the man urged him forward. They were in a darkened tunnel; the rocky ceiling of a cave only ten feet above their heads. "Where are we?" Cody asked again, but his escort offered no reply.

As they turned around the bend the tunnel opened up into a wider compartment. Cody gasped in surprise—there were hundreds of people.

They wore tattered clothing and their skin was shaded gray with grime and filth. Their emaciated bodies appeared as mere walking bones draped with a thin blanket of skin. Scattered about the caverns, small huts and shelters had been weakly constructed with tattered tarps and stacked rocks.

The shanty hovels and deprived people became scarcer as Cody was led to the outskirts of the parish. They came to a small nook in the side of the rocks. Cody stopped to examine the solid rock mount in front of him, running his fingers across it. It was a dead-end.

He sensed the hooded man blocking his only path out. Cody gulped. "Are you going to kill me?"

"It's possible," he stepped forward, backing Cody tighter against the wall, "but as you must now realize, nothing in this city is ever how it appears." The man removed his hood.

"Xerx...?"

The young monk grinned. Before he could say anything, Cody leapt and threw his arms around him.

Xerx forced his way out of the embrace. "Easy buddy! Don't get all *touchy-feely* on me." Cody stared at him, astonished. "They told me you were dead! Dace and the others, I thought...I mean.... I don't understand...."

Xerx grabbed Cody's shoulder. "Slow down, there will be plenty of time to explain everything." He glanced left and right before leaning closer. "After your reckless rescue attempt and capture, we knew we could never infiltrate El Dorado undetected. After you gained access all of the city's defenses were immediately tripled. We needed a way into the city. The idea was all Randilin's."

"Randilin!? But he betrayed you. He sold you out to the Golden King!" Cody exclaimed.

Xerx laughed. "One of the advantages of being a legendary scoundrel, liar, and traitor is that nobody questions you when you act despicably. Randilin not only enabled Dace, Tat, and Chazic to be safely escorted into the heart of El Dorado, he also earned the Golden King's favor and wormed his way into the King's inner council. Brilliant when you think about it."

Cody felt a sense of relief, relaxing against the rocks. *Randilin, you continue to surprise me!* "What about you? Where are we?"

Xerx scanned the area again carefully. "I was originally planning on being caught along with the others, but something presented itself that changed our plans," he motioned with his hand. "There's someone I want you to meet."

Suddenly Cody lost his balance as the cliffside shook. He jumped back as the rocks began falling toward him. He paused. He couldn't believe his eyes. The rocks weren't falling—they were *walking*. A man stepped forward, his entire body camouflaged to blend perfectly into the rock.

"Allow me to introduce the legendary Gorgo Tallsin, inventor of Rock Clothing...and leader of The Resistance."

73

Illusions Dispelled

The man was as aged as the ancient rocks that camouflaged him. His face was coated gray with dust that had sunk into each of the hard wrinkles. His armor, from his rounded helmet to his chest plate, was stone-like in appearance and all but his face seemed to morph into a large boulder every time he stopped moving.

"We have been waiting for you a long, *long* time." Despite the shakiness of his voice, it was rich and authoritative; the kind that makes a body instinctively offer a soldier's salute and stiffen to better posture. "I trust you received my message?"

A light bulb lit in Cody mind. He fingered the paper in his pocket. "G.T.—Gorgo Tallsin. It was *you*!"

Voices sounded from behind. Xerx quickly threw up his hood and without warning planted a solid blow against Cody's cheek. "If I have to tell you *one* more time then you know what's waiting for you: the factory!"

Cody's wind had been knocked out; he could no longer speak. Writhing on the ground he saw that Tallsin had once again disappeared and blended into the cliffs.

Behind Xerx four golden golems marched into sight. They paused briefly to acknowledge Xerx, and then marched on. When they had gone Xerx lent Cody a hand. "Sorry about that. I got carried away." Cody noticed a lack of remorse in Xerx's voice.

"As you can see," Tallsin said, once again visible, "circumstance prevented me from contacting you more directly. The Resistance endures only in secrecy."

"The Resistance?" Cody asked in surprise.

Tallsin gave a single, ill-humored laugh. "El Dorado— the perfect utopia; where everyone has everything they could ever need or imagine—except for *freedom*. On the surface they seem joyful and peaceful...but nothing could be further from the truth. The entire city, every part of it, is a giant illusion conjured by the Golden King. The citizens live every day in fear; a nightmare they have been forced to endure so long, it's become their only reality."

"Why doesn't anyone say anything?"

The ancient tailor chuckled humorlessly. "Oh, in the early days some did. But after those unfortunate souls suffered fates that I dare not repeat, people became resigned to their fate. The Golden King leaves nothing to chance. He is obsessive and haunted by paranoia. At all times he keeps tabs on his people. The streets are monitored every minute by the Dark-Wielders."

"I was told the Wielders went around using the High Language to help people, to give them what they needed."

Tallsin shook his head. "An insidious lie! The Wielders patrol the streets without mercy, popping into homes unannounced, keeping an ever-watching eye on the city.

Even the city's architecture was altered to leave the houses open walled, all the easier to keep tabs. In El Dorado there is no privacy, there is no peace of mind—there is only fear. You never know when a Wielder is watching you. And, if ever you should fail to play your role in the elaborate hoax, there are no second chances. People disappear from the city all the time, no word or hint about their whereabouts. But no one dares ask or acknowledge the disappearances lest *they* be the one to vanish next."

"What happens to them? The ones who vanish," Cody asked, unsure if he truly wanted to hear the answer.

"The ones who openly defy the King are eliminated. Offered as living sacrifices to his unholy monster."

"Hoin and Koin...," Cody whispered, remembering Tiana's story.

Tallsin's face hardened. "Both valuable members of The Resistance. They gave their lives willingly so that we could have *this* meeting."

"What about the others? What happens to them? Are they brought here? Down to the furnace?"

"Not all who disappear are threats...many are simply *outdated*. The Golden King obsesses over perfection. He will not tolerate anything, or any*one*, that fails to meet his delusional ideals. Anything deemed *less-than-perfect* is discarded down here to the underworld, or what some call *Under*-Under-Earth. Down here in this godforsaken pit, the imperfect either die off or deteriorate until they can serve some gruesome purpose. You witnessed the horrors within the Orb Monument. The King has recently found a new use for us. Harvesting our very souls to fuel his new soldiers."

"But how did *you* end up down here. You're legendary. Were you a prisoner-of-war?"

The old man's eyes became sorrowful. In that instant he looked every bit the ancient age he was. "History is unjust. It picks favorites. Randilin and his infamous *dark deeds* overshadow the reality that there were many who switched sides during the Great War. Regrettably, like so many others, I believed the lie that El Dorado was invincible. When the dust settled I wanted to be found on the winning side. During those first days it was everything I imagined and more. The Golden King offered me a position of prominence and I began constructing armor for the warriors.

"When the good King Ishmael miraculously overthrew his brother I was too ashamed to return. I wasn't ready to embrace a life of banishment like Randilin, so I stayed here. After The Great War, the Golden King began rebuilding his forces. He needed something new; he would not lose again in the same way. The day he discovered how to infuse golden platelet armor into his warriors' skin, any use I may have once had was gone. I was among the first banished to this ghastly pit where I've had many long years to repent of my mistakes."

"You mentioned something about a resistance…."

At the question, Tallsin's somber demeanor was transformed into a militant determination.

"For thousands of years The Resistance has grown right under the Golden King's nose. We never assemble in large groups. Often times a single conversation has been stretched over several years, spoken sporadically and by people who are careful never to draw attention to themselves. Slowly, we have infiltrated the city. The Resistance exists in the palace, in the marketplace, in the servant quarters, in the barracks, even in the King's own inner-circle. We have waited, patiently waited, millennium after millennium, buying our time, living in shadow, waiting for the opportune moment to strike," he paused, his boney hand stroking his sharp chin as a grin formed on his face. "That time has come at last."

74

Danger

———

Startled by every sound, Cody kept his eyes downcast as he scurried through the city. *Slow down, don't draw attention to yourself!* The city that once had seemed so shiny and magnificent now was pallid and haunting.

Cody felt the sting of unseen eyes burrowing into him. He fought to clear his mind, as though the eyes could peer through his skin and read his thoughts. With his head down he bumped into two people walking the opposite direction. Regaining his balance, Cody looked up to apologize—and looked straight into the eyes of a Dark-Wielder.

His body stiffened. *Stay calm!* Giving a hurried nod of apology, Cody slipped around the two hooded creatures and hastened down the street. He could hear the soft patter of steps behind him. He risked a glance over his shoulder—the Wielders were following him.

Don't overreact, it doesn't mean anything. Cody turned down a narrow back alley and picked up his pace. After several moments he once again heard the rhythm of the Wielders' steps mirroring his. Panic began to rise up in him.

Reaching the end of the alley he covered his mouth and whispered, *"Vapiroi!"* A thick cloud of smoke instantly filled the area. Cody dashed out of the alleyway and pressed his back against a wall. Through the dense haze Cody saw the shape of the two Wielders, just a foot away from him.

They scanned both directions and, without exchanging a word, they split up, each hurrying down separate paths. Cody doubled back down the way he had come. *That was too close.*

Cody dashed down the palace hallway. *Almost there.* He threw open his chamber door—and collided into Tiana. *"Umph!"* Tiana grabbed his shoulders and pulled him into the room, slamming the door closed behind them.

"Where on earth have you been!? I've been looking *everywhere* for you," she stammered. Her face was pale and her hair was crazy. Cody noticed the skin around her lips was raw and there was an unusual expression on her face.

"Ti, are you okay? You look like you've just seen a ghost."

Tiana shoved him off. "Where's Jade?" she demanded.

Cody held his hands out defensively. "I don't know where Jade is. But I really need to talk to you. You will not believe what I've found. I…"

"It doesn't matter right now! What matters is that we find Jade." The urgency in her voice was frightening.

Cody took a step backwards. "Ti, what's going on? What happened?"

Tiana eyes blazed with intensity. "Jade's life is in terrible danger!"

75

A Special Girl

Jade looked at him with wonder. The Golden King's skin shimmered in the light, casting rainbows on the wall. He stood with the posture of a man with confident authority, not unlike her military father.

"Welcome. Please have a seat." Jade looked to Hansi, who urged her forward. She walked into the chamber and sat in the lone chair. The King turned to face her.

"I apologize for the late summoning. I pray it wasn't too inconvenient?" he asked, his voice gentle as a clear lake.

Jade shook her head. "Of course not," she responded quickly.

The King smiled. "I knew I could count on you; which is precisely why I've asked you to join me tonight. Because I need you."

"*Me?*" Jade asked in surprise, "Why didn't you ask Cody? *He's* the Book Keeper."

The King laughed. "Yes, but he's not *like* you. You must understand by now...you are *very* special." His golden hand stroked her ebony hair. "Like the daughter I never had...."

The King paced around the chair placing his long fingers on her shoulders. "From the day you arrived I knew you weren't like the others. That, like myself, you were a student of science, an open-minded pursuer of answers to the questions others, like your dear friend, Cody, are far too timid to ask."

Jade soaked the words in with unpreventable pride. "My father taught me to exercise my brain. To treat it as my most valued and powerful possession," she blurted.

"You father was a wise man, and you are a wise girl. Which is what makes it so tragic that you have been restricted..."

Jade's ears perked up. "Restricted? How?"

The King glided back in front of her. "When you were in Atlantis why do you think you were ignored? Treated as a thoughtless child? Never included in important councils or trusted by the royal family?"

Jade shrugged. "Because that dumb book chose Cody and not me."

"Wrong! Do you want to know the real reason?" he lowered his mouth to her ear and whispered, *"Fear."*

The King stood. "They were afraid that your enlightened mind would see right through their truthless mask. Afraid their lies and false beliefs could not blind you like everyone else. You saw them for who they really were."

The Golden King pressed his finger against Jade's forehead. "Which is why they used the forbidden High Language to tamper with your thoughts."

Jade grasped her forehead. "What are you talking about? How can they do that?"

"Fear can motivate the most unthinkable acts. The fear of those who accuse them of being monsters can lead one on a path to become the very monster they sought to deny."

"But I don't feel anything different," Jade stammered.

The King traced his long finger across her forehead as he stepped even closer. "That's the danger of it. I had hoped when we rescued you from Atlantis that it wouldn't be too late, but the damage was already done. Whatever dark creation technique they used, your brain has been caged in a dark shroud."

As the King spoke, Hansi reached out and grabbed Jade's shaking hand.

"Can you help remove it?" she pleaded.

The King looked Jade straight in the eyes. "Yes...but it won't be pleasant. Is this what you want?" She nodded firmly. The Golden King placed his fingers on the sides of her head. "You may feel a bit of a sting...."

He began whispering in a language unrecognizable to Jade. She flinched as something pinched the back of her neck. Her head felt tight pressure and she grimaced as something began to worm its way toward her brain. She squeezed Hansi's hand as the sensation burrowed deeper and deeper into her skull.

The Golden King's ruby eyes burned as he continued to whisper. She felt his words slither over her brain and her head began to quiver. There was a searing pain.

Jade screamed in anguish.

76

The Desire to Kill

The walls blurred on both sides as Cody sprinted down the palace corridor. Flying around the corner he collided with two servant girls coming the opposite way. "Sorry!" he called over his shoulder as he continued his mad-dash.

Jade, where are you! She hadn't been in her chamber, and by the look of her things, she appeared to have left on short notice. It was unlike Jade to leave things untidy. She had too much of her military father in her.

Cody cleared a lengthy staircase with one soaring leap. Throwing out his arms to regain his balance, he continued to run. On the other side of the room he spied a familiar face; the servant who often assisted Jade. "Wait! Over here!" he shouted as he rushed toward her. She looked to him and the commotion he was causing.

He grabbed her shoulder and spun her around to face him. "Have...you seen...Jade?" Cody asked between heavy breaths.

The girl's face was full of concern. "I saw her not an hour ago..." she looked both ways before leaning forward, "she's been taken to the Golden King." Cody's heart dropped. The King's chamber was on the opposite side of the palace. He took off running.

I'm coming, Jade; I won't lose you again.

Anger...Fear...Jealousy...Glee...Passion...Pride...Happiness...Disappointment...

A carnival of emotions wheeled through Jade's head. They were like faceless spirits taunting her from the corner of her mind, just out of sight. She heard laughter; it was cruel and mocking. The pressure on her brain increased. She screamed but made no sound.

All of a sudden her father appeared before her as though passing through an invisible cloud. He knelt to his knees and began waving her toward him. His mouth was moving but his words didn't make any sense. Jade ran toward him as fast as she could but she never seemed to get any closer. He stood. His eyes were sad. Jade screamed at him as he turned away but he didn't seem to hear her. Then he was gone.

Shame...Guilt...Joy...Envy...Hope...Worry...Desire...Regret...Hatred...

Jade's body was shaking. Each of her muscles was contracting. Then Cody was in front of her. He looked different somehow, but she knew it was him. He was smiling. There was someone standing beside him. It was Tiana. Cody pulled her toward him and they began to kiss. Jade tried to turn away but her head was locked in place.

Hatred...Revenge...Envy...Hatred...Jealousy...Bitterness...Hatred...

She was so angry. She wanted to punish him. She wanted to kill him.

Then it was over.

Jade collapsed forward in her chair. She grabbed at her throbbing temples. The pain was gone. Sweat trickled off her burning forehead. She raised her tired eyes toward the chamber's entrance. Standing in the open doorway was Cody. He looked normal again. Jade felt a wave of emotion in her. She was furious at him…but she couldn't remember why.

"An…*unexpected* surprise," the Golden King uttered, his eyes fixed firmly on the doorway. "To what do we owe the honor?" Cody was crouched over with his hands on his knees panting for breath. He looked at Jade in relief.

"I…uh…I just wanted to say I'm ready to continue my training in the Books," he stammered breathlessly. The King's silent rage drained. It was replaced by a satisfied grin.

"You will not be disappointed…trust me."

The Golden King's eyes remained transfixed on the door long after Cody and Jade had scampered away. Hansi waited patiently. He knew better than to interrupt his father's silent thoughts. He had learnt the hard way as a child.

At last the King pivoted and paced back to his position in front of the large window.

Hansi stepped forward. "Father…?"

Unexpectedly the King began to laugh. The sound sent a chill over Hansi.

"It worked. At long last, it's *mine*...."

Hansi took a step away. The warmth in the room evaporated. "Father...what are you talking about?" The Golden King turned. His eyes were as cold as tombs.

"*The-Creation-Which-Should-Be-One's-Own*—I've found it."

77

The Dream Ends

Cody was still panting as he and Jade reached Cody's chamber. They had not spoken a word. They entered the room and Cody quickly closed the door behind them. He exhaled a deep sigh of relief. "That was too close."

"What happened?" probed Tiana as she emerged from an unknown hiding spot. Cody glanced to Jade. Her face was damp with sweat. She looked frail and exhausted.

"I don't know. The Golden King was doing something to her—something terrible. I was able to save her just in time."

Jade's face contorted and she shoved Cody. "I don't need saving!" she shrieked. The next instant she returned to her feeble state, but her eyes were wide with fear. "I don't know why I said that just now. I'm sorry. I didn't mean…" Cody wrapped his arms around her and pulled her against his chest.

"It's time to go. I won't let him mess with you again. I journeyed from Atlantis to El Dorado to get you out of here. It's about time I did." Jade didn't respond, but Cody felt her slow breathing against his chest.

Cody quickly recapped his experience in the orb monument and in the underworld. "This whole city is one gigantic lie, a big illusion. These people aren't happy—they're imprisoned. This city is like one giant house of horrors. We're not safe here."

He grabbed Jade's hands and stared into her deep green eyes. "Jade, I know I don't always act like it, but you know I care about you more than anyone in the world. You're my best friend. We might not always agree—but I really need you to trust me on this."

Jade didn't blink. After several moments she squeezed Cody's hands. "Okay, I trust you."

"Finally!" Tiana blurted, destroying the moment. "So, what do we do now? We need to get out of here. But how?"

"It's impossible. The Golden King has every part of the city on constant watch. There is zero chance that all three of us could go missing without suspicion. Not to mention Dace and the others still in prison. We need a plan. Everything will need to be perfect—we'll only get one chance at it. Tallsin told me to await further contact from The Resistance."

"Can we trust them?" Tiana asked.

Cody took a deep breath. "It's our only chance. Until then, we must continue on as normal. We continue to play along with the illusion. The King can't get any clue that we are onto his act. If we slip up it's over."

Tiana nodded firmly. "I'll need to stay in hiding. If the King discovers I'm still alive our cover is blown."

Cody turned to her. "We still haven't talked about how you managed to escape the Hunter. Or how you correctly knew that Jade was in danger...." He let the enquiry hang, waiting for Tiana to bite.

Her face hardened. "It doesn't matter," she responded sternly. Her fingers drifted to her eyes and she thoughtlessly rubbed her eyelids.

Cody titled his head curiously. "Tiana did you...*see* someone?"

Tiana dropped her hands as though remembering she wasn't alone. "I said it doesn't matter. I'm safe. End of story. We need to focus on getting out of this cursed city."

Cody examined her for another moment before relenting. "Okay." He made a mental note to ask her again. *Had she seen the eyelid-less man, too?*

He looked out the window over the city. "Then we wait...and pray for the impossible."

78

An Intimate Connection

It had happened. The worst thing Cody could have imagined. He walked slowly down the long hall, delaying the inevitable, unwanted destination. *Me and my big mouth.* He stopped in front of two large double doors, and stood motionlessly.

The Golden King had summoned him. He had been awakened at the first sign of morning light and informed that the King desired his presence for a training session in the Great Hall—immediately.

Does he know? The timing seemed too precise. *I was too careless last night saving Jade.* If the King suspected something Cody knew he was dancing on thin glass. Then, completely on their own accord, the two doors inched open, beckoning him to enter.

"You seem...nervous," the King said, his voice a slithering viper.

Cody felt his heart gaining speed. *Keep your cool. Stay calm!* He forced his tense shoulders into a shrug. "Just anxious about my training today," he replied in a wobbly voice. *Relax, Cody, relax!*

The King swooped around him, appearing on Cody's other side. "Then let's begin. " The King glided across the room with one smooth motion and stood beside the podium. As always *The Key* sparkled, casting bright colors against the pillars of the Hall. "I think the time has come to do that which has never before been done." The King grinned. "Let us unite the Books!"

Oh, no. Cody felt the weight of the Book in his backpack. *Not now!* "I don't know if I'm ready," he stammered.

The King strode toward him like a tracking leopard. "No? But you seemed so...*eager*...to continue your training last night. So much so that you burst into my chamber unannounced. Or was I mistaken about the purpose of your visit?"

Cody's muscles cramped. He was trapped. The King was no fool. To resist was to jeopardize their escape plans.

"I was—*am*—eager," he said, quickly correcting himself, "it's just..."

The King's face was smug and victorious. "Don't you desire one small glimpse of the endless power?"

Checkmate. There was nothing else Cody could say. "I suppose just one glimpse," he conceded in defeat.

He unzipped his backpack and removed the Book. The scarlet 'A' was glowing like a volcano ready to erupt. His fingers tingled as heat exuded from the leather cover.

A bright light gleamed from across the room causing Cody to shield his face. The diamonds forming the 'E' on the cover of *The Key* began to illuminate. The Golden King's eyes widened with zealous anticipation. He stroked his crystal fingernails down the Book's spine, arching his back and soaking in the pulsing energy.

Cody's hand trembled as he opened the front cover. The Golden King slowly opened *The Key*. Like *The Code*, the lettering was unfamiliar and the words a strange language. Cody glanced between the two Books with confusion. "How do we *use* them if we can't understand the writing?"

The Golden King's eyes burned fiercely. "How, indeed?"

Cody took a deep breath and began reading. To his surprise, his mouth pronounced the words effortlessly, as though he had known them all along, but he couldn't comprehend the meaning. The King's voice rang out as he began reading as well.

Reaching the end of the first page they stopped. Nothing happened.

"Well, now what?" The moment the words left Cody's mouth the room shook.

A beam of light shot from the scarlet 'A', shining a stencil on the ceiling. Beads of sweat poured down Cody's forehead as the heat from the book increased.

"What's happening!?" he asked nervously as the Book continued to vibrate out of control. The blinding light from *The Key* reflected off the King's eyes. They were full of child's wonder.

Cody screamed as *The Code* suddenly flew from his hands. At the same moment, *The Key* soared from the

King's hands. The two Books stopped in the center of the room and hovered in midair.

There was a deafening explosion.

The room was quiet. Dunstan stared straight ahead at the empty chair across the desk. He was alone.

A rattling noise buzzed in his ear, pulling him from his thoughts. The table began to shake. Dunstan placed his hands on the surface to steady it but the rattling increased. The entire room began to tremble. Glass shattered as a picture was shaken off the wall and forced to the ground.

The object on the center of the desk began to glow, filling the room with blinding rays of light. *What the blazes…?* Dunstan shielded his eyes and took two steps away from the desk. The light continued to grow brighter.

He took another step back and bumped into a man. Dunstan turned and looked straight into the face of his master. Another picture tumbled to the floor with a shattering crash.

The master smiled. "At last. It has begun."

79

Visions

Cody shielded his eyes as white light pelted against his eyes. As the light dimmed he realized that he was no longer standing in the Great Hall and the Golden King was nowhere to be seen. The room he was in now was somehow familiar. Across the room was a lone, sturdy table. The only other furniture was a half-built rocking chair. *I've been here before.*

He sensed a sudden presence behind him. He spun around and saw a man. Cody recognized him as well. The pieces came together in his mind. He was standing in the Caves of Revelation, which meant the man before him was called *The Thirteenth.*

Only, he looked different. He looked younger. His skin was smooth and unblemished. There was no sign of the bullet that had ended his life.

"The Books of the Covenant have been united," the man muttered.

"You!?" Cody asked, "How are you here? You were killed. I saw it."

The man tilted his head curiously. "Was I really? A pity, I suppose." He turned and scuffled across the room, lowering himself into the rocking chair. Cody scanned the room. The walls were once again covered with shelving and bins, however, the stone tablets which had previously filled them were few and scattered.

"I don't understand."

The man in the chair chuckled, "No, no, I don't suppose you do." He began rocking slowly back and forth. "As to your question of *who* I am—that is entirely unimportant." He stopped his rocking and smiled. "What *is* important is what I *can* tell you."

Cody realized he was leaning forward and drifting toward the stranger. Losing his balance, he stumbled forward. "What can you tell me?"

The man smiled. "A great *many* things. The problem is that *you* just don't know the right questions to ask!" His laughter drained. "So allow me, if you will, to bypass your unarticulated petitions and give you the answers you so greatly desire."

Cody rubbed his head trying to piece together what he was hearing. Without anything to say, he merely nodded his approval.

The man leaned forward. "The Prophecy is true—and truth can only be contained for so long. As you now see, there is also much more to your cherished Book than simple ink and leather. For one who is willing, it is the very doorway to release the Truth."

"But how do I use it? I *am* willing. I want to find the truth. More than anything!"

The man raised his bushy left eyebrow. "Do you, son? Do you *really*?" The man stood from the chair and glided toward him. "Unlocking the Truth demands a payment worthy of obtaining such a power." He reached out and placed his hand upon Cody's chest, over his heart. "The one closest to you must pay that price."

The area changed into a bright burning sun. Cody could see the silhouette of a person falling helplessly into the light, long hair streaming from her head. Then, suddenly, she was gone.

Everything went black as the firm voice of *The Thirteenth* rang out, "Unlock the Truth!"

Cody rubbed his eyes; he was back in the Great Hall and somehow the Book was back in his hands. His legs quivered and he fell against one of the large pillars.

Across the room the Golden King was standing motionlessly beside the podium holding the golden Book. His eyes peered down at it as though nothing else in the room existed. *Had the King seen the same vision he had? Had he also met The Thirteenth?* At that moment, though, the answer wasn't important.

Pushing himself to his feet, Cody scampered toward the doors, unnoticed by the hypnotized King. The vision had been painfully clear. Cody felt a lump festering in his stomach as he ran.

"The one closest to you must pay that price." The apparition's haunting words echoed in his mind. There was finally a mystery that Cody could figure out on his own: for the Prophecy to be fulfilled—Jade would have to die.

80

A Tight Spot

---

how did it go?" Jade questioned the moment Cody entered the room. Her green eyes were soft. It was the first time he had seen them so tender since he had been in El Dorado, as though scales had fallen off. He had his Jade back.

"Oh...it was fine. Just regular training," Cody replied softly. He knew in that moment that he would never tell her what he had just seen. *There's got to be another way.*

Jade's thin eyebrows pulled down toward her nose. "You may be able to fool Ms. Starky with your lies, but I know you better than anyone on earth, above or below. Something's wrong."

Cody dropped his eyes. "It's just..."

"Behind you!" Jade screamed. Cody spun around. Four hooded Wielders appeared through his window. Cody jumped to his feet and pulled Jade behind him. "You can't take her from me!"

"Easy, buddy!" cried the lead Wielder. He stepped forward and removed his hood—Xerx. The young monk cast a glance at Jade before turning back to Cody. "*G.T.* summons you. We must make haste. We don't have much time."

Cody and Jade heard footsteps and exchanged nervous glances. Xerx held up his finger and mouthed, "*Wait.*"

The next instant a convoy of four Dark-Wielders appeared with a silver crate floating between them. They moved with ghostlike silence.

Xerx kept his finger raised, as Cody, Jade and the three Resistance members held their breath. When the Wielder procession had fully passed, Xerx swung his hand down. "*Now!*"

The Resistance members dismantled the Wielders with chilling precision before the crystal beings even realized they were under attack.

Shattered crystal limbs and fragmented chunks littered the ground as the silver crate fell to the ground. The sound of a thud echoed in the air. Xerx stepped forward. "We have to be quick. More Wielders will be here any second to investigate the sound."

Xerx knelt and rubbed his hand across the ground. "*Dastanda.*" The dirt began caving in on itself, forming a pit of sinking sand. The other Resistance members quickly set to dropping the remains of the Wielders into the pit, which instantly swallowed them, leaving no trace.

Xerx motioned to Cody and Jade. "Quick! Into the crate; another sentry of Wielders will pass by here soon."

Jade's face dropped. "Are you joking? There's no way we can both fit inside that tiny crate." Xerx held up his hand to silence her. The sound of approaching Wielders could be heard around the next bend.

"Hurry!" Xerx motioned them forward frantically. Cody jumped into the silver crate and fell to his back. Jade crawled inside on top of him. They both inhaled a deep breath before being thrust into total darkness as the lid was closed.

They heard muffled voices but couldn't decipher the words. Jade buried her face into Cody's shoulder as they waited in silence. *Did they fall for it?*

After what seemed an eternity the crate was lifted. *We're moving—it worked.* Cody relaxed. Although it was too dark to see her, he felt the warmth of Jade's body curled up on him.

There was a loud cranking sound and the temperature began to rise. Cody felt Jade's hand slip into his, her fingers interlocking. He grinned: *Take this, Hansi.*

Jade's eyes were wide in disbelief as she stood and stared at the crumbling hovels and tattered shelters. The underworld exiles staggered in lines marshaled by several Wielders.

"I can't believe it," she stammered. "This is horrible."

"We need to move. We can't draw attention to ourselves," urged Xerx. They headed away from the slums toward the outskirts of the pit, but Jade stood transfixed.

Gazing at the scene, Cody grabbed her hand and gently guided her away. "We will help them, but now is not the time."

Xerx led them to the outskirts of the cave. They stopped at a dead-end crevasse in the rocks.

Jade shouted in surprise as Gorgo Tallsin materialized from the rocks.

"I'm glad you could make it. A privilege to finally meet you, Jade. However, pleasantries will have to wait. We are short on time, so let's get straight to business. Things are worse than we feared. As such, there has been a change in the plans."

The grizzly Resistance leader rubbed his calloused knuckles. "We're going to steal *The Key*."

81
A Fool's Plan

"Steal the Book!?" Cody exclaimed. "It's impossible. Besides, no one but the Golden King can read from it without calling the Hunter upon them. This is crazy!"

Tallsin nodded. "You are entirely correct. However, we have gleaned some information from within the Golden King's inner-circle that has complicated the situation. Are you aware of The Prophecy?"

Jade shook her head. "We've never heard of..."

Cody cut her off, reaching into his backpack and pulling out the stone tablet:

> THE POWER OF FULL DIVINITY,
> RESTS ENCODED WITHIN EARTHLY TRINITY.
> WHERE SACRIFICE OF THE PURE ANGEL WHO FELL,
> IS THE WAY TO RETRIEVE THE PEARL WITHIN THE SHELL.
> WITH HUMBLE HEART AND GOLDEN KEY,
> THE UNIVERSE'S MOST POWERFUL FORCE IS REVEALED TO THEE.

Jade looked at Cody in surprise and Tallsin's face hardened. "I do not know how you have this sacred text in your possession. Just gleaning knowledge of its existence was paid for by the lives of several Resistance members."

Cody felt the sting of their waiting eyes. He pushed the tablet back into his pack. "I...found it."

Tallsin's heavy stare relaxed. "Regardless. The origin or truth of this prophecy is, as yet, unknown. But our sources inside the palace report that, although the Golden King also has yet to decipher the foretelling's full meaning, he firmly believes the words *EnCoded* and *Golden Key* refer to none other than the two Books of the Covenant. If there is any truth in conviction it would be devastating. It is *vital* that we prevent the Golden King from gaining this new, ultimate power."

The ancient tailor rubbed his chin forcefully. "Everything needs to happen simultaneously. The crux to everything will be timing."

Cody took a deep breath. "Okay, so what do we do?"

Tallsin cleared his throat before beginning, "Two Resistance devotees have volunteered to sacrifice themselves for the cause. They will earn themselves the solemn punishment. With any luck, their sacrifice will draw out several of El Dorado's dignitaries. More importantly, it will keep that purple-cloaked demon occupied."

Tallsin motioned to Xerx. "When the escort has left the city, Xerx will guide a silver crate down here into the underworld where The Resistance will be waiting. We will storm the city. Our uprising will cause a diversion and draw the golden golems and Wielders to the city's outskirts. Once the riot has begun, Xerx will make haste to the prison and free Dace, Chazic, and Tat. Hagar, a stable boy with allegiance to The Resistance, will have steeds waiting outside the city walls. You will rendezvous through the secret passage that your friend Tiana discovered."

He pointed at Cody. "And, that is where *you* come in. While the city is distracted, you, Jade, and Tiana will sneak out of the palace. Word of the uprising may have already reached the palace, so you will have to be on your guard. Get out quickly. Do not linger for even a moment."

The Resistance leader took a deep breath. "The last, but most imperative move, will be to steal *The Key* itself. The King is a perpetual paranoiac. We must operate under the assumption that he won't sleep farther than an arm's length from his precious Book."

Cody shook his head. "That's certain death. Are we supposed to just walk into the Golden King's personal chamber and snatch the Book? How do we know the King even *does* sleep? It's impossible. "

Tallsin grinned. "Perhaps, unless we didn't have to break into the palace…unless the man was already positioned within the inner-council…the task will fall to Randilin."The suggestion produced a symphony of startled cries. "*Randilin*?! Can we trust Randilin with such an important task? We are all well aware of his checkered history," Xerx declared.

Tallsin nodded. "Having remorsefully made similar mistakes, I know the pain of living forever in regret. I also know the deep, soulful longing for redemption. I've learned never to bet against a man on a quest for redemption. Besides, several creators within The Resistance believe there's a chance to create a temporary decoy of the Book."

Cody shook his head. "It would never work. I can't explain it, but the connection between Book Keeper and Book is special. He would never fall for it."

"I understand your concern," replied Tallsin. "It is a long shot—but it *is* a shot. Our creators are convinced they can infuse the decoy book with enough of the Orb's energy to temporarily mimic the real Book. It's an immensely draining process, and will take them five days to complete. When ready, Randilin will make the exchange in the Great Hall. The Golden King is cocky. In his arrogance he has become blind to his reliance on the Book. He desires to be great because *he is* great—not because he has an uncommon advantage. Throughout the day the Book is left in the Great Hall on display. At darkfall it is brought to his personal chamber. Our hoax needs only to fool him long enough to break out. We must pull off a lie on the great liar. It is risky—but it's the only chance we have."

They all knew he was right. But that didn't make it any more encouraging. The plan was foolish. There were invitations for failure at every point.

"We will only get one shot at this so everything must be absolutely perfect. We will wait five nights to prepare—and then we *strike!*"

82

A Secret Language

Never before in his life had time been so conflicted—both so short and so long at the same time. There were just five nights to prepare a large-scale breakout. The waiting was unbearable. There was a different feeling floating in the air as Cody and Jade hustled through the city. *Tension*—as though the city itself sensed something huge was about to happen.

Cody and Jade came to a stop in front of the prison. The four golden golems glared at them before stepping aside to let them through. Cody leaned his mouth toward Jade's ear. "Did you count the guards?"

Jade nodded. "They've doubled the security since our last visit." It couldn't be mere coincidence. Cody frowned. *The Golden King senses that something is up.* Cody swallowed, the more pressing question was: *How much did he know?*

They entered into the elegant room and the doors closed behind them. As before, Dace, Chazic and Tat sat restlessly against the walls behind the thick iron bars of the jail.

"We're still waiting for that handsome boyfriend of yours to stroll in here with the keys," Dace remarked.

Jade shook her head. "He said he would talk to his father immediately."

"The El Doridians apparently have a different definition of the word *immediately*," Dace cracked.

Cody opened his mouth to speak but held his tongue. He saw the figure in his peripheral vision. A Dark-Wielder stood like a statue in the corner of the room, watching. Dace's eyes casually floated toward the unwanted observer as well.

Cody cleared his throat. "I was just thinking back to the time you clotheslined me. Do you remember that?" Jade's face went blank with confusion.

But before she could talk Dace narrowed his eyes toward Cody. "I do, indeed. You, scoundrel, kept trying to *flee the city...*" he let his words hang. Cody grinned.

Dace was no simpleton.

"Well, you kept coming to get me. All four attempts; all *four days* you prevented me from *breaking out*." Cody risked a side-glance to the Dark-Wielder in the room's corner. As before, the crystal-skinned zealot was motionlessly watching them with its intense eyes.

Cody fought to relax his muscles and exude calm. "We've sure been through a lot together. I remember when we met. I had stumbled down a tunnel below ground and was so shocked to find *people living there*. Remember, at first I thought you underlings were my enemies, only to later discover that you would be my greatest *allies* in my time of need...."

Dace's face remained a stone wall. He nodded. "I am your blood-protector. You will *always* be able to count on me when in need." Remaining emotionless, Dace ran his hand through his long hair. For a moment his hand shielded his face—with a slight grin, he winked.

Chazic and Tat had joined Dace's side by the cell bars. The eager look on their faces confirmed that they were not oblivious to what was being said.

Tat pressed himself against the bars, slipping his face between two. "From what I hear, when you first went *underground* you were fairly shocked not to find any children. It was almost as though they had just *vanished*, plucked from the ground like a rose or a *lily*? Did you ever find them?" Tat's knuckles were white as he gripped the bars.

Cody shook his head dejectedly. "I found children at the Ageing City. But there are still several to be found." Tat pushed himself away from the bars. "I see, what a shame." His voice was coarse. The Wielder stepped forward, moving for the first time. There was no misunderstanding the simple motion: their visitation time was over.

As Cody and Jade headed toward the exit Dace called after them, "I look forward to your next visit...."

The moment they were out of view Jade tugged on Cody's sleeve. "What was all that random chatter of old tales about? I thought the whole point of our visit was to inform Dace and the others about the escape plan!?"

"And I did. They will be ready and waiting to break out in four days."

Jade stared at Cody as though they were speaking different languages. Cody chuckled.

"Oh, Jade, how I love you and your literal mind."

Her face turned red. "What are you talking about?" she asked defensively.

Cody continued to laugh. "Just trust me."

So far, so good.

A thousand flickering candle lights illuminated the room as Foz entered through the large doors. Despite the candle flames, the temperature plummeted the instant he stepped through, as though passing from summer to winter.

Foz glanced around as he entered deeper into the chamber. Each of the tiny candles had been arranged meticulously with identical spacing and placement.

"Welcome, my nephew," the Golden King's voice sounded from the gloom, his words rushing out and swirling around Foz like a forceful breeze. Foz's eyes scanned the room but found no sign of the speaker.

Foz gave a cautious bow. "Your Majesty, we have received word from the Borderlands. The fortress is ready to fall."

The Prince continued to search uneasily for the King.

"Burn it to the ground."

Foz shivered. "And, what of the survivors?"

Turning around again, Foz came face to face with the King. The candle light illuminated his polished golden skin as he smiled.

"Leave none alive."

83

The Fortress Falls

Nocsic watched as the wooden doors bent under the pressure of another ram. The door would soon be breeched. His arm trembled under the weight of his blood-stained sword. The strain was not for fear, but from exhaustion.

The enemy had pounded against Flore Gub with the fury of an endless ocean. Weeks of unrelenting battle, yet the enemy had continued its onslaught.

He glanced to the floor to his father Captain Talgu. The shaft of the fatal spear was still lodged into his ribs. The killing blow had added his father to the crowded rank of men who had died to defend Flore Gub—men who had died in vain.

With a bang the doors exploded off their hinges. A wave of enemy soldiers flooded in. Nocsic smiled, recalling Dace's words, *"If you die—die valiantly."*

"This one's for you, my old friend." Mustering the last of his strength he brought his sword crashing down on the lead warrior, sending him limply to the ground. Twirling in place, he sliced his sword across two more soldiers' necks. Enemies continued to drop under the force of Nocsic's blade. Every time a soldier fell another would take his comrade's place.

All at once the commotion died. Nocsic was once again alone in the room. He felt cold. He looked to his body. He was covered in bloody wounds and scars but didn't feel pain.

A shadow fell over him. In the archway was a behemoth of a man. Six spikes jutted out from his spider-shaped helmet. Nocsic's heart fell. The man in the doorway was *The Impaler*—El Dorado's High General.

Nocsic tried to lift his sword but didn't have the strength. Instead he collapsed to his knees, using his blade as a cane to hold himself up. The spider-faced man stood over him. Without hesitation, he swung his blade down upon the kneeling Captain.

Cody slowly funneled the granules from *The Speaking Sands* back into the vial. It had been refreshing to speak with Eva again. The calm she always exuded made him regret having ignored contact with the Princess the last few weeks. He had quickly informed her of the pending breakout in four days' time.

He returned the pewter bowl to his nightstand and collapsed onto his bed. He needed to recoup his strength for the escape.

He jerked his head up as he heard a knock on the door. The residue in the corners of his eyes suggested that he had drifted off into a deep sleep, although it had seemed like only a blink. He rolled out of his bed and opened the door.

There was a middle-aged lady with short, curly hair like that of sheep-wool. She presented Cody with a bundle of clothing. "Here is the new tunic you requested."

Cody looked at the cloth bundle and scratched his head. "I don't remember asking for..." he began, but the lady cut him off. "The one you requested two nights ago. Please check carefully to confirm it is precisely as you wished." Before Cody could question further, the woman curtseyed and disappeared down the corridor.

Cody closed the door and spread the new garments out on his bed. He grinned. Like his current outfit, there was gold embroidered lettering. However, instead of a *B.K.* the letters read: *G.T.*

Grabbing them, Cody peeled the letters off. On the back of the "*G*"was a scribbled note:

Flore Gub has fallen. Golden King is on the move.
We can no longer wait. We must Act.
Tonight.

84

Waiting for the Sign

"It's impossible!" Jade declared in exasperation. "We're not ready! It wasn't supposed to happen this way!" She was pacing back and forth. Cody, Tiana, and Xerx sat in a semi-circle on the floor in Cody's chamber. Xerx had used the High Language to create a steel barricade on the door. Despite being alone, they spoke in almost inaudible whispers.

"Well, it *did* happen this way so there's no use in us wasting our time talking about how it *should* have been. We must do what we can," Tiana interjected.

Jade stopped her pacing and looked down at Tiana. "I was not saying that we shouldn't," she uttered defensively.

Cody pushed himself up to his feet. "Stop. This isn't the time to argue. We're all in this together."

"The decoy is still days away from being finished. We won't be able to able to steal the Book from the Great Hall. We may never get a chance like this again to gain control of *The Key*," Tiana observed.

Xerx nodded. "Tallsin agrees—which is why Randilin is going to steal the Book from the King's chamber."

"What?!" the three exclaimed in unison. "That's suicide!"

Xerx hung his head. "It is not ideal, but Tiana is right—it's now or never. You've seen the size of his forces. If the Golden King marches to Atlantis tomorrow there will be no stopping him. We *need* that Book. It's our only chance."

Cody gave his head a hard shake. "What about the others?"

"They all know. And, they will be prepared," Xerx sighed. "This Second Great War may well hinge on it."

Xerx lowered his voice when heard scuffling from outside the door. He scurried to the window and jumped up on the ledge. He turned back one last time. "Wait for the sign."

85

The Piercing Sting of Love

She was beautiful. It was not prideful or vain emotion. It was merely an acknowledgment of the truth. She gazed down at the sleek, snow-white dress that clung tightly against her body. The dress was her favorite. It had once belonged to her mother and was reserved for only the most special occasions—occasions such as tonight.

Queen Cia gave a final twirling examination of the outfit to assure that everything looked perfect. It did.

A familiar scent wafted from the entrance of her chamber announcing that her anxious wait was over. She smiled. "You're late again, Dunstan."

Two firm hands wrapped around her from behind and pulled her into an embrace. "You know how much it pains me to keep such a beautiful lady waiting...why don't we make up for lost time?" he replied eloquently, punctuating it with a jolly laugh.

He brought his hands to her shoulders and began to rub. "Tense as always, my Queen," Dunstan teased. Cia rolled her head forward, soaking in the joy offered by Dunstan's hands.

"Until the Book Keeper returns, I am afraid I must get used to it. At least I have you to help carry this burden. Anyone other than Kantan."

Dunstan kissed the back of her head. "I'd carry *all* the burden if I could. Although I'm afraid I'd be crushed under the weight!" he laughed.

Cia turned around to face Dunstan for the first time. Every time she looked into his eyes she was struck by his handsome features. There was an alluring warmth to him. When he smiled his entire face was involved in the action, not just his lips. It was comforting. It was just how she always remembered her father.

Her shoulders slouched, finally yielding to his firm fingers. "What have I done, Dunstan? Was I mad to send the Book Keeper? Atlantis' only hope...*my* only hope. Little Eva tells me the Book Keeper has infiltrated El Dorado. She still refuses to reveal how it is she speaks with him, but it matters not. That was a week ago. I have failed my people."

Dunstan pulled her against his chest. "That boy has overcome more in the last two months than most will in a lifetime. He's special. My gut tells me he is safe. You are the best queen Atlantis has ever had."

"I'm the *only* queen Atlantis has ever had!" Cia said with a smile. "What would I do without you? You've been my anchor."

Dunstan turned her around and leaned in close. "You need not worry about what you would do *without* me—but I know one thing you can do *with* me." Cia felt her heart skip a beat, but she maintained her composure. She allowed his face to slowly close the gap between them, his lips meeting hers tenderly. In that instant all worries, frets, and fears ceased to be. She completely released herself to the moment. She broke the kiss to catch her breath. "I love you," she whispered.

Dunstan placed his forehead against hers. "And I love you, my Queen."

Their lips reconnected again, more furiously, as though to make up for the brief moment of separation. She pulled him tighter into the embrace. A tingling sensation ran through her body. She stumbled back lightheaded. "You're making me dizzy!" She steadied herself. "It seems I'm not the only one love sick. Are you okay? Why are you looking at me like that? Dunstan?"

He stood like a statue, his face as expressionless as a rock. Cia grasped her forehead; her vision was blurry. She felt something warm on her brow. *I'd better not be sweating! My powder will run!* She brought her hand down and found that it was covered in a strange red liquid. She glanced at Dunstan for explanation, but he remained frozen, staring at her indifferently.

She looked down to see her pure white dress now drenched in the same red substance. She inspected it with her hand. She felt something firm and pulled on it. The moment she did, she again felt faint. The object in her hands was a dagger, stained scarlet up to the hilt.

The next thing she knew she was lying on the ground. Her body began to shiver and her eyes drooped. She felt tired. She turned her head to find Dunstan but he was gone. She was alone.

Cia rested her head on the floor, no longer having the strength to hold it up. "Daddy?" she called out silently. Her entire body now felt strange. She pulled her knees up and curled into a ball to try to warm herself. She was so cold. She squeezed her eyes closed. *Mom, I'm sorry about the dress...*

86

Less Than Perfect

Cody stared absently at the domed ceiling of his chamber. Time dragged on sluggishly; each second stretching into an eternity.

He went over the escape plan in his head. No matter how many times he worked it over, he was consumed by the same sentiment: the plan was foolhardy, it was sure to fail—but it was their only chance.

He stroked his hand over the cover of the Book, allowing its energy to sooth his cramped muscles. He inhaled deeply to steady his intensified breathing. *Relax, Cody. Relax.*

The self pep talk did little to assure him though. How could it? He knew that even the slightest mistake could doom the lives of hundreds. In a city prided on perfection, their escape could ill-afford to be anything less.

Cody perked up. Had he heard something? A soft whistle sounded from outside his room. Crawling out of bed, he tiptoed to the window and glanced out. Across the city, toward the far wall, he could see a vague procession of lights.

The parade of lights was heading away from the city toward the caves. *The sacrificed Resistance volunteers.*

It had begun.

Randilin licked his thick, dry lips. He also had heard the soft whistle from outside his window. *I'm getting too bloody old for this sort of thing*, he said to himself sullenly. He took a deep breath and puffed out his shoulders. *Well, here goes nothing.*

He strutted out of his chamber with a confident stride. Two golems that patrolled the corridor straightened their posture and eyed him suspiciously.

Randilin faked a wide yawn and scratched his rear. "My lousy toilet ain't working. Where are those ruddy Wielders when ya need them, eh?! I was just about to…"

The golems stepped aside to allow the dwarf to pass, not eager to hear any more explanation. Randilin staggered by, still grumbling as he went.

The moment he turned the corner he started sprinting down the hall. After turning the corner he stopped. At the far end of the corridor were two solid gold doors—the King's chamber.

Randilin prepared to dash to them but halted. *There are no guards.* He glanced behind him and then back to the unguarded double doors. In fact, there was no security anywhere in sight. Randilin resumed his approach with extra caution. He reached them with no hindrances.

Confirming that he was still unobserved, he pressed his ear against the door. There were no sounds coming from the room. *That arrogant tin-man doesn't even have guards at his bedroom.*

The door creaked as he slowly pushed it open. He cringed at the sound that seemed to explode like thunder against the staunch backdrop of silence. Squeezing his bulky frame through the narrow opening he entered the room, leaving the door ajar for a quick escape.

The chamber was dark and quiet. He paced into the large room slowly, every one of his senses amplified. His eyes fought through the dim. *Now, where's this bloody book?*

He froze. He had found it—*The Key*. Randilin mouthed a string of curses. The gold-coated Book was tucked under the arm of the Golden King.

He sleeps with the blasted thing? For ruddy once can't fortune smile upon me? He walked cautiously to the sleeping King. The King was lying straight on his back with his arms draped over the Book.

Randilin took a deep breath. He reached out his hand and the tips of his fingers brushed across the Book's smooth spine.

The Golden King's eyes opened.

87

From Under the Rug

The city was quieter than usual.

The golem peered out over the slumbering city. A jolt on the rope disappearing down into the deep pit returned his focus. He scowled. *About time!* He motioned to the second golem who heaved down the lever.

With a cranking noise the pulley system was thrust into motion. The chains strained under the immense weight as they slowly raised the platform toward the surface. The golem peered into the murky pit with annoyed impatience. He was eager to rebuke the crate carriers for their sluggish return. With a rattling thud the platform came to a stop.

Standing alone in the center of the platform was an elderly man. His face was smeared gray with dust and his torso seemed like a moving rock. In his hand he held a rough stone that had been crudely sharpened to a point. Surrounding the man on the platform were a hundred large boulders.

The timeworn man grinned. "Things swept under the rug have the curious tendency to reappear at the most inopportune moments." The two golems pulled their swords and rushed at the old man.

The boulders on the platform shifted as they morphed into a hundred armored men with raised weapons.

Before the shocked golems could react they were hacked down by the charging mob. The horde streamed into the city hollering and slaying the surprised sentries. The platform cranked as it was lowered back into the pit for the next load.

Gorgo Tallsin stepped onto a high ledge. He was filled with pride as he watched The Resistance crash into the city like a wild flood. He raised his weapon into the air.

"Reclaim the city! El Dorado is ours!"

88

Of Daggers and Arrows

Cody and Tiana emerged from their chambers at opposite ends of the corridor. Tiana immediately sprinted toward Cody motioning frantically with her hand. "Behind you!" Cody turned as three golem sentries turned around the corner. Seeing Cody they paused. Their hands flew to the hilts of their swords.

"*Byrae!*" Cody yelled. The lead golem's face contorted before puffing out like a blow fish. His body bulged and rippled as a whirlwind raged inside of him. "*Gai di gasme.*" The disfigured golem collapsed to the ground.

Tiana shoved past Cody. Her foot swung up, smashing the golem in the jaw. As he stumbled back she flipped her dagger into her hands and finished him with one quick, precise slice.

Her eyes widened. "Cody, look out!"

Cody spun around and flinched just as the final soldier brought his sword down on him. Before the killing blow landed, the golem was sent hurling against the wall, sliding to the ground, dead. The shaft of an arrow stuck out from between his armor.

Cody and Tiana both whirled around. Across the other side of the hall Jade stood with her bow in hand.

"Let's get out of here."

The final golem collapsed silently to the ground as Jade's arrow caught him in the neck, killing him instantly. She dropped to her stomach, concealing herself in the grass.

"Was that the final lookout?" Cody asked in a whisper.

Tiana's eyes narrowed as she scanned their surroundings, "I don't see any more. They were dispatched cleanly. Our cover hasn't been blown." Tiana looked to Jade and shook her head in disbelief of what she was about to say. "Nice shooting."

Jade grinned, soaking in the compliment.

The air was calm and quiet. In the distance Cody saw scores of golems and Dark-Wielders streaming away from the palace toward the outskirts of the city. *The Resistance must have begun the assault. So far, so good.*

Jade glanced around. "Where's Randilin? He should be here by now."

"Don't worry, he'll be here." Cody clenched his fists. *He'll be here,* he assured himself.

The minutes dragged on without an appearance by the dwarf. Lights began igniting throughout the city as it was awakened by the commotion. Cody felt a foreboding feeling rising in his chest.

Something's gone wrong.

89

Randilin's Dark Deeds

The Golden King's red eyes were wide and unblinking. Randilin stumbled back, his foot catching against something that sent him tumbling to the floor.

Randilin shouted in surprise as he landed on the floor. Only inches from his nose was the pale face of a dead body—the King's cupbearer. He was crumbled and left indifferently on the floor, his eyes bulging and his mouth gaping. His death had been slow and unpleasant.

Randilin pulled himself to his feet and diverted his eyes from the disgusting sight. Like a swift breeze, the Golden King appeared before him, stepping over the disfigured body that, to him, was no more than inconvenient clutter. His ruby eyes inspected Randilin as though the dwarf's skin were transparent and his every desire, fear, and secret were showcased.

"My old friend, you seem to be...on edge," he said softly. Randilin's cheeks reddened under the King's weighty gaze. He dropped his eyes and turned away.

"Well, how the blazes do you expect me to seem? I'm alone in a room with the man I've plotted to kill for a thousand years! I think *you* should be the one who's on the bloody edge," he snapped.

The King circled around him, once again looking him in the face. "It seems that old grudges die hard."

Randilin felt sweat break the surface of his forehead. "But we both know there is more to this intrusion than personal vendetta. There's something stirring in the air. I can smell it." The King tilted his head back, taking in a deep breath and releasing a sigh. "Enlighten me. Do so, and we will forget all about your bout of sleepwalking to-night—you have *my word*."

Randilin spat on the King's feet. "Your word is worth less than spit! You gave me your word that night...you said you would spare her life."

The King's silver tongue slid across his lips. "Mistakes happen...."

Randilin closed his eyes and found himself thrust back into the nightmare that had plagued him for hundreds of years. "You gave me your bloody word...."

~~~~~~~~~~~~~~~~~~~~~~~~~~~~~~~~~~~

1200 Years Ago...

The raging flames of the city rose up like a crazed bonfire. The entire Under-Earth sky was filled with ominous, black smoke. A flurry of ash flakes coated the ground like a December frost.

Atlantis had fallen.

Randilin dashed over the rolling dunes as fast as his stout legs could carry him. *There's not much time.* His legs were burning as he finally reached his destination—the Caves of Revelation. Without hesitating, he scaled the cliff side. Pulling himself up onto a ledge, he scrambled to his feet and resumed his haste. He navigated through the complex labyrinth of crevasses until he arrived at the mouth of a cave. He had made it.

In the blink of an eye, a dozen armed soldiers appeared, blocking his path. "Sir Randilin? What are you doing here? The Good King decreed that no one is to go in or out of this cave until after the war...."

Randilin grasped the soldier by the shoulder. "Captain Skytin. I've known you a long time—*long* before you were Captain of the Outer-City Guard. Please. My business is urgent."

The Captain stared at him for a moment before relaxing. "Stand down, men. Let him through." As the guards parted, Randilin dashed deeper into the tunnel. The narrow path eventually opened up into a small, spherical hollow. The room was softly lit by candle light. Randilin scanned the room anxiously—it was occupied entirely by women.

"Sir Randilin? What the heavens are you doing here!?" demanded a firm voice. The woman had a steady face and an aura of authority. "Answer me, boy!"

"Queen Naadirah, Your Majesty. I don't have time to explain...I need to speak with Arianna." He continued to scan the room until he spotted her. Without waiting for the Queen's response, he hurried to the corner of the room and knelt beside a woman lying on the floor.

"Sally? Is that you?" the woman questioned weakly. Randilin cupped his hand behind her head.

"No, Aria; it's me. I'm here for you."

The woman's tired eyes looked up at him. "Randilin? Where's Sally? What are you doing here?"

"El Dorado's won. The Golden King cannot be stopped. It's all but over—but it doesn't have to be for us. I've made a deal with him that will allow us to have a life together!" He reached down and lifted the flower necklace she was wearing around her neck. "We can leave this place, just like we always talked about."

Arianna rested her head against the cold ground. "Randy, that was a lifetime ago. Don't you realize, I…"

A loud noise echoed from outside the cave, cutting her off. The sound of clashing steel blasted out of the tunnel like a trumpet. "They're coming! They've found us!" cried a woman. Then the cave went silent. Nobody dared move.

A piercing scream hurled the room into chaos.

The Queen turned to Randilin, "Look what you've done! You fool! You've led El Dorado right to our hiding place! You…."

Her face contorted as she collapsed to the floor with three arrows punctured into her back. A mob of soldiers rushed into the room. Spears and arrows flew in all directions as the women ran in fear.

Randilin stood, paralyzed by shock. "He *promised* me… he gave me his word! Aria, I didn't mean for this…." A spear came hurling toward him. Randilin reflexively dodged out of the way as it flew past—a soft cry sounded from behind.

Randilin turned. Arianna's soft blue eyes were wide and her face was white with shock. The shaft of the spear still vibrated as it stuck out from her chest.

"*Nooo!*" Randilin collapsed to the floor and pulled her into his arms. "No…Aria, I'm sorry! Please forgive me! Aria…."

She didn't respond—she was already dead.

90

Ꭰistory Repeated

Tears streamed down Randilin's face as he opened his eyes. The Golden King was smiling in amusement. "She *was* a pretty girl, wasn't she?"

Randilin felt his hatred for the King consume him like never before.

The King glided to the other side of the room to where a large crate lay. A silver curtain was draped over it, like a covered birdcage. The King ran his fingers down the side of the satin curtain. "The interesting thing about history is that it is circular. It is one of the few invariable laws of this universe. Give history time, and it will always come back around and repeat. "

The King sliced the ropes of the drapes with his crystal fingernail. They fell to the floor.

"No...it can't be!" Randilin staggered a step forward. "*Sally?*"

The stout, frizzy-haired diner owner was stretched out like a star, bound by her hands and feet to the steel birdcage. Her eyes bulged and she thrashed at her bindings, but her screams were muffled by the gag in her mouth.

"Let her go or I swear I'll..." Randilin threatened, rushing toward the King. A whirling hum rang in his ear. *Thud*. Randilin skidded to a stop. A circular blade stuck out from the wall beside his head. From the corner of the room emerged a hooded man; a second circle blade in his hand and CROSS crested on his robe.

Randilin eyed the agent in astonishment. "*You*? CROSS is in league with El Dorado!?"

The agent remained silent.

The Golden King chuckled, "Did you think I would simply let you waltz into my inner court without a failsafe? I am not without my allies. So, I propose to you a game."

The Golden King reached into the cage and rubbed his hand across Sally's cheek "In my unfathomable mercy, I offer you the choice of how history will be repeated tonight: *Scenario One:* You once again sell out your people and tell me exactly what you and your friends have been so inconspicuously plotting, I'll then release her and the two of you can make a happy life for yourself here in El Dorado."

The King grabbed Sally's chin and forced her face toward his own. "Or—*Scenario Two*: you stay silent and once again watch the woman you care about murdered before your eyes. You will spend eternity knowing full well that her death was *your* fault."

Randilin stumbled, grabbing the wall to keep his balance. His body was quivering. He stared into Sally's beautiful eyes. His shoulders drooped.

The King sneered victoriously. "Now—tell me *everything.*"

91

Unforeseen Events

The five golems turned as the cloaked man stepped into the room. "All access to the prison is strictly forbidden. I command you to leave immediately or else we'll be forced to...*ah!*" The golem burst into flames. After a fury of motion, the other four guards were left sprawled lifelessly across the room.

Xerx stepped over the scorched bodies toward the cell. "*Layura.*" The iron bars of the prison liquefied and melted to the floor.

Dace quickly advanced through the opening and retrieved his sword from the table. He twirled the blade, happy once again to have a sword in hand. He begin fastening on his equipment and looked to Xerx.

"The points you lose in tardiness you make up for with style. How does Tallsin fare?"

"Things have been set into motion. But we must move swiftly."

Chazic and Tat had retrieved their weapons as well.

Dace grinned. "Then let's get going."

The streets were empty, turning the inner city into a ghost town. *The diversion worked,* Dace hoped, but still tightened his grip on his sword. The last time he observed the quiet streets he had been ambushed by a hundred men and thrown in prison. *Don't let your guard down.*

They passed under the shadow of the giant orb monument. The menacing structure towered over them. "Look out!" whispered Xerx. Dace dropped down as four golems escorting a silver box appeared. Dace motioned to the others who knelt down beside him.

The golems moved past their location. Dace eyed Tat's fidgeting hand. "There are more important things than vengeance right now. Tat...?" The guide wasn't listening. He jumped out from cover. The first golem was slain before any had time to react. Xerx uttered several words and the remaining golems instantly fell to the ground.

The same was not true for the silver crate. Tipping over onto its side, the lid fell off with a jarring crash. Dace grabbed Tat's arm. "Don't be a fool! What happened to Lilley was tragic, but you can't kill them all. Don't compromise the mission with..." He stopped as he and the others stared down at the opened crate. It was full of silver and gold trinkets and other exquisite jewelry.

"They loot the valuables of those they bring into the monument and transfer them to the palace. But we need to move!" urged Xerx. Tat knelt down and reached into the treasures and pulled out a pendant. It was half of a shattered heart. The corner was faintly stained red. Tat reached into his pocket and pulled out the bracelet he had found at his home. The two pieces fit together perfectly.

"They have my wife," he whispered. He stood slowly. "They have my wife." He turned toward the monument. "Rali! They have my wife! They have my Rali!" Tat screamed.

Dace grabbed his arm. "Stop yelling! You're going to give away our..."

It was too late. The entrance opened and hundreds of golems and Wielders poured out from the monument. Dace cursed. "Run!"

Tat shoved off Dace and charged toward the orb. "Rali!" He launched an arrow toward the mob, piercing a golem in the neck.

Another arrow bounced harmlessly off the crystal body of a Wielder. As Tat continued his charge he readied another arrow. The bow bent as he pulled the string back as far as he could, his rage fueling his strength. The arrow whizzed through the air at a Dark-Wielder who was still sneering as the arrow collided with its head. What followed was an explosion of crystal shards hailing down to the ground.

Tat reached for another arrow but was stopped by the strong hand of Chazic, who grabbed Tat's shoulders. "Let go of me!"

Chazic held firm. "Don't deprive your wife a husband. Storming that monument is suicide. I promise we'll save your wife. We must keep our heads about us."

Tat's eyes were desperate.

The legion of golems and Wielders closed in on them. Tat shoved himself from the Enforcer's grip. "Back off! I won't leave her in there!" As he turned to continue his charge, the hilt of Chazic's blade came crashing against his head, knocking him unconscious. Chazic turned to Dace, "Be swift. Finish the mission. I can buy you enough time to get out of the walls. If I don't meet you in time, don't even think of coming back for me."

Dace nodded his affirmation. He and Xerx draped Tat's arms over their shoulders and took off in the opposite direction of Chazic.

Chazic turned to face the mass of enemies. They were almost upon him. He twisted his two mighty scimitars in his hands—and waited for the collision.

92

One Simple Word

"The city is ours!" Gorgon Tallsin bellowed. His cry was echoed by a rowdy cheer from the rioters. The old tailor watched with swelling pride as The Resistance overwhelmed the enemy. Regular citizens had abandoned their houses and had joined the fight, using whatever they could find as weapons.

Hundreds of dead golems lay scattered on the ground. Tallsin watched as five Resistance fighters swarmed a Dark-Wielder. Diving on its back, they brought the zealot to the ground, their stones and household implements hacking away until all that remained was shattered crystal.

The scene was sweetened by the thousand years of patient waiting it had taken to achieve it. As the remaining enemies fled, Tallsin raised his sword. "We've got them on the run! Press toward the palace! The city is ours!" The mob cheered, holding up their weapons in pride. Tallsin smiled in disbelief. *We're actually going to pull this off. We've won.*

Suddenly the noise of the mob trickled into a hushed silence. A single man stood directly in the middle of the path blocking the road. Tallsin felt a lump in his throat.

The Golden King.

"Stand firm!" Tallsin cried. He could feel terror clogging the air. "Stay together...*charge!*" Tallsin stretched out his sword and charged. The Resistance joined in his cry and ran behind him.

The Golden King smiled.

The courtyard was littered with dead bodies.

The Golden King strolled through the courtyard, stepping over the corpses. One man twitched, releasing a pained groan. The King approached the gurgling man and looked down into the inflamed eyes of Gorgo Tallsin. A stream of blood trickled from the leader's mouth. The King knelt beside him. "Ironic...it took two thousand years for you to organize a rebellion against me—and it took me but one simple word to squash it."

Tallsin coughed, producing a spurt of blood from his mouth. "You're wrong...The Resistance was never about people...it was about an *idea*." He entered into a fit of deep, bloody coughs. "We have shown...these people...that freedom...is something worth fighting for."

"And something worth dying for?" the King asked amused.

Tallsin grimaced. "These men have been dead for a long, long time. Since the day you stole their freedom." Tallsin began to laugh, each burst causing more blood to pump over his lips. "The problem with ruling with an iron fist is...the tighter you squeeze...the more people slip from your grip. Your perfect city is over. This is not the death of The Resistance…it's only the beginning."

The Golden King's face became hard; the humor draining from it. *"Presandi!"* Tallsin's neck twisted with a crack and his eyes went blank.

The King stood and turned his eyes toward the Palace. "We shall see."

93

Trapped

S omething's wrong," Cody declared, standing up, "Randilin should have been here by now. It's been far too long. Something's happened to him." Ten minutes earlier they had witnessed an explosion from the outskirts of the city. The distant clanging and shouting had disappeared. No one needed to voice what they all knew—the escape plan was failing.

Tiana joined Cody's side. "I agree. We can no longer afford to wait. We must go on without him."

Jade shook her head. "What about *The Key?* If we leave now we may never get this close to it again. You must go back for the Book."

Cody shook his head. "Not this time." He looked at Jade. "I'm not making the same stupid mistake twice. Some things are too precious."

Jade leaned forward and planted a kiss on Cody's flushed cheek. "That was *very* sweet," she stood, "*but...* Tiana's right. We won't get another chance like this."

"But..."

Jade shook him off. "No *buts* about it...although this time I won't just let you abandon me in the middle of the battlefield," she took her bow from her shoulder, "because I'm going with you."

Dace and Xerx, arrived at the wall with Tat still draped over their shoulders. Dace scanned left and right—there were no golems in sight. Xerx looked over his shoulder into the dark clearing and heard the clanging of Chazic's scimitars cutting down foes. "Dace, we can't just leave Chazic behind."

Dace grimaced. He recalled the words of General Levenworth at the council: *"You are young and rash. A mission like this is no place for ethic codes; it is one for wisdom."* As much as he hated it, he finally understood.

"We cannot go back. What is done is done. We press on with the mission."

Running his hand along the wall Dace located the hidden passageway. They moved through the mirror-walled, jagged tunnel. The rolling dunes of the Under-Earth wasteland appeared as the trio emerged on the other side of the wall.

Across the way, against the side of the towering wall, was Hagar, the stable boy. Beside him were a dozen horses, saddled and ready to ride. "Perfect. Let's go!"

Hagar noticed them as they approached. He began waving his arms above his head and calling out to them. Dace frowned. "You fool! Stop making noise! Someone's going to hear you!" he muttered. The stable boy continued to run toward them yelling. Dace sliced at his neck with his hand, signaling to stop. "Quiet, you fool!"

As they got closer the boy's words became clearer: "Stop! Run! It's a trap! It's a..." A spear soared from the shadows and pierced him in the back. He collapsed to his face in the dirt.

Dace and Tat drew their swords. A legion of golems appeared from the darkness. Above them on the rocky dunes, a row of archers appeared with drawn bows.

Dace reluctantly lowered his weapon. "How could they be waiting for us unless...they knew our plan."

Xerx had just come to the same realization. "Cody's walking into a trap."

94

An Icy Prison

The Great Hall was eerily quiet as Cody entered. He scanned the dark room. It was empty. He looked down the lane of massive pillars. There it was. The diamond-embossed Book: *The Key*.

The King left the Book in the Great Hall! Cody immediately felt the power from *The Code* surge through him as it was brought closer to its sister. Cody approached cautiously. His eyes scanned the room for any sign of the Hunter.

He reached the podium. His fingers stretched out. His finger traced the gold *E* on the cover.

"You disappoint me." The haunting voice echoed in the Hall. Cody jumped back. His head spun but there was no one in sight. "Is this how you repay my hospitality?" The voice seemed to echo from all directions of the Hall at once.

Cody felt panic rising in his chest. "Show yourself!" he screamed out in distress.

Two hands wrapped around his shoulders. "As you wish," the Golden King whispered. The doors to the Great Hall burst open and Tiana and Jade were pushed into the room. Foz and Hansi held knives to their necks.

The Golden King circled around Cody. *"Seamour Fra-*
zan." A layer of crisp blue frost began forming on the wall
and ceiling. It continued to spread, climbing up the walls
and joining together as one. Cody could see his breath. The
thick ice had completely insulated the room.

There was no way out.

95

Forged in Ĥatred

Cody stared into the cold ruby eyes of the Golden King. "I thought we had an understanding? I thought you were ready to do great things. But how do you repay my generous hospitality? By trying to steal what is rightfully mine." The King's voice was like a calm downpour that hinted that the hurricane was not far behind.

"Everything you told me was a lie. This whole city is nothing more than an illusion," Cody countered shakily.

The Golden King's eyes flashed with primal rage. "It's *NOT* a lie!" he spat, but the eruption pacified as soon as it had begun. "It is the perfect utopia—the second Eden. It's the natural course of advancement that my brother was too weak to realize."

"Where's the line? I've seen the horrors of your *advancement*. You're *making* human beings," Cody stammered.

The Golden King beamed with pride. "The highest pinnacle of all creation—*life*."

Cody felt a chill, "You create life only to bring death. What about the innocent people? What are you doing to them?"

"Souls," the King responded, "the missing piece. I had learned to form the framework of a human body; to mold each limb and muscle. Yet the ability to fill it with a soul, with *life*, eluded me. It was perplexing, *infuriating*...until at long last I discovered the perfect solution."

Cody thought of the pretty, large-dimpled servant girl and was filled with disgust. "You implant the life of an innocent person into a cursed hollow soldier."

The King's jeweled eyes blazed with pride. "Brilliant, wouldn't you say?" He glided up to his throne. "It was many long years ago. I was young and foolish. I was obsessed with creating life. If I were to succeed, I knew it would be irrefutable proof to my arrogant brother that the Divine Creator's pinnacle act, the creation of life, was not only achievable—but able to be *perfected*. That *I* was divine master over creation!

"So, I began. For years I experimented, discovering the High Language for physical life, for animals. I was on the doorstep of succeeding. I had created a body—but it was *empty*. I was devastated. I could hear my mocking brother laughing at my bitter failure. In my bleak desperation I did the inconceivable. I infused part of *my own* soul into my creation: all my hate, all my malice, all my anger toward my brother. "

Cody felt his palms grow damp and a chill came over him. "The Hunter."

The Golden King nodded. "My beautiful first-created life. It was like a child to me. You could even say it has my eyes," the King said.

Cody shook his head in revulsion. "You've created a monster; an unstoppable demon. Can't you see? You're creating a world you can't control; a chaos you can't tame."

The Golden King laughed. "I was wrong about you, Cody. The same weakness that flowed in my brother's blood is in you, too."

Cody looked at Jade and Tiana who were still held captive at knifepoint. Jade's eyes locked with his. There was a tear in her eye as she nodded.

Cody turned back to the Golden King. "Then, I guess we have nothing more to talk about...*Fraymour!*" A ball of fire shot at the Golden King.

With a word the flames fizzled into a puff of smoke.

The Golden King sneered. "Like my foolish brother... you have chosen death."

96

Duel of the Book Keepers

Cody rolled to his left and sent two more fire balls flying toward the King.

"Seamour." A wall of water rained down from the ceiling, swallowing and extinguishing the flames.

Cody looked to the roof. *"Gadour!"* A large boulder suddenly appeared in the air, crashing down toward the King's head. The King remained still—**CRACK**.

Two inches above the King's head the boulder suddenly split down the middle; the two halves fell on either side of him. The Golden King smiled.

Does he have some sort of force field?

The King strolled leisurely to his throne and reclined in it. He uttered a few words. There was a crunching sound. Cody looked to the ceiling as several giant icicles crystalized into sharp points.

A gust of wind came billowing from behind the throne. Before Cody could guard himself the wind collided against him, lifting him off his feet and sending him racing toward the icicles.

"Gadour!" A heavy rock formed in his hands. The weight of it anchored him back to the floor. He crashed

to the ground with a loud thud. The rattle of the collision shook the Hall. The giant icicles jiggled—then came crashing down on him.

Cody shouted. A steel canopy grew over him. The icicles pelted down upon the shield, with loud clangs, denting the metal.

As the last icicle shattered on the ground, Cody rolled out and ran across the Hall. He pressed his back against one of the giant pillars, hiding himself from the King.

Cody panted, gasping for breath. Sweat soaked his brow. He glanced around the pillar. The Golden King was sitting casually in his throne with his guard down. *He's just playing with me.*

Cody pushed himself up.

The Golden King smiled with amusement. "Is this all you've got? I must confess, I expected more of a challenge from a fellow Book Keeper," he taunted.

Cody mustered all his remaining strength and readied himself. "Chew on this one...*Duomi!*" A massive explosion burst toward the King.

"*Spakious.*" A hazy portal appeared in front of the King, swallowing the explosion. An identical portal opened behind Cody. The explosion detonated out of it, sending Cody flailing across the room and slamming into another pillar.

His head was throbbing and there was a deafening ringing in his ears. His arms shook beneath him as he pushed himself to his feet. He lifted his hands into the attack position.

The Golden King grinned. "Your resilience is commendable. But I grow weary of this game." He uttered a string of words.

Instantly, Cody's entire body was paralyzed and a sense of panic overcame him. "What have you done to me?"

The King stood from his throne and walked toward him. "A wonderful substance known as Dytalisia is now circling through your blood stream. As you have now noticed, one of its many side-effects is that of paralysis." The Golden King stroked his cheek, his crystal fingernails drawing a bead of blood. "Did you really think you could defeat me?"

Cody tried to pull his face away from the King's touch but couldn't move his head. "Go ahead. If you kill me now you'll risk losing everything."

The Golden King brought his razor nails against Cody's neck. "Perhaps," the King smiled, "but I suppose there's only one way to know for sure."

Cody's confidence crumbled and his face went white. The King's nail slowly pushed beneath Cody's skin….

"Nooo! Let him go!" The King removed his hand and turned toward Jade. Her eyes were moist with fear.

The King glanced between her and Cody. "Or, perhaps there's another way…." His ruby eyes locked with Jade's and he began whispering. Jade squealed and grasped the back of her neck.

The words in the vision came racing to Cody. *"The one closest to you must pay that price."*

"No!" Cody tried in vain to twist his head but still couldn't see her. "What are you doing to her?! Stop! I'll do anything. I'll give you *The Code*. Please!"

The Golden King paused, his silver tongue sliding along his lips. "I know you will...all in good time." He turned back to Jade. She shrieked again, grabbing her head and dropping to her knees. "Get it out of me! Get it out of me!" She scratched violently at her head and screamed in anguish. A scarlet tear fell onto her cheek.

Unexpectedly, Tiana swung her head back, slamming it against Foz's nose with a crunch. Breaking free from his grip she dove across the room. Somersaulting, she jumped to her feet and grabbed *The Key* from the podium. She held it out and flipped it open. Everyone in the room froze. Jade ceased her screaming and crumpled to the floor weakly.

The King chuckled. "Brave...but pointless. Only I can read from the Book. You know full well what will happen if you even try...."

Tiana smirked. "I know—I'm counting on it." She began to read. Foz's eyes bulged. "Stop her!" He lunged at her. The room began to shake violently, knocking everyone off their feet. A cloud of mist filled the Great Hall.

An object flew through the mist toward Foz. He caught it: the golden Book. Two glowing red eyes illuminated through the haze in front of him. The Hunter lunged forward and a piercing scream rang out.

Tiana threw Jade's arm over her shoulder and pulled her toward Cody. They locked hands.

"*Spakious!*" Cody bellowed. A whirling warp-hole grew above their heads. Without hesitation they hurled themselves through the portal.

97

A Strange World

The Golden King gazed at the empty space where the three children had been moments before. Hansi approached him cautiously, as though trekking across a thinly frozen lake. "Father, nothing is beyond your power. If you desired to prevent the Book Keeper from leaving you could have done so with a single word. But you didn't...why?"

The King smiled. "My dear son, this is not a failure—it is a grand victory. Everything has gone precisely as I have intended it to go. A single *doubt* that festers and grows can be more powerful than a thousand sharpened swords. The mind has always been a more dangerous weapon than a blade."

Hansi fidgeted. "Indeed. But you had *The Code* within your grasp! And the Book Keeper!"

"The Book Keeper was never the goal."

Hansi looked to his father curiously. "If not the Book Keeper, then who? *The girl*?" Hansi paused, color draining from his face. "*The-Creation-Which-Should-Be-One's-Own*..." The King mouth rolled into the slightest grin.

"Precisely, my son. The most sacred creation which all have the power to create—is now mine...." Hansi stood a

376

step backwards. An aura of lustful power and satisfaction was beaming from the King. Even the Hunter momentarily stopped feasting, casting its scarlet eyes toward its master. The Golden King ran his silver tongue across his upper lip. "Their own *thoughts*."

"You implanted a thought into the girl's mind?" Hansi's face registered alarm. "What will happen to her now? What thought did you create in her mind? Father?"

The King turned and walked across the Hall without responding. As he did, he smiled. Yes, everything was going *perfectly*.

There was something peculiar and foreign about the smell in the air. Cody's eyes drifted open. *Where am I?* He looked to his left, straight into two bright lights racing directly toward him.

He hurled himself out of the way as the lights raced past with a piercing squeal. Cody watched the lights disappear into the distance. It was something he hadn't seen in a long time—a car.

"Cody, move!" On the other side of the road were Jade and Tiana. Tiana's face was white. Cody scampered toward them as another car whizzed by.

"What's going on? Where are we?" he asked.

Jade pointed over his shoulder. "Turn around."

He turned and his jaw dropped. Jutting into the air was Big Ben Clock Tower.

They were in London.

98

Safe

Tiana's eyes were wide with wonder. "That metal carriage was pulled by invisible horses," she stammered in disbelief.

Cody stared over the London skyline in amazement: *What just happened!* "We're back in Upper-Earth...how? Creating a portal of that size should have killed me."

Tiana held out her hands and examined them curiously. "When you took my hand, before we went through the portal, I don't know how to explain it, but it was almost as though my energy was being sucked out of my fingers." She paused and smiled. "Perhaps you're stronger than you think."

Cody rubbed his forehead. "But that doesn't explain why we're in Upper-Earth. I wasn't imagining any specific destination when I used the word, I just wanted to get anywhere but where we were. It doesn't make sense. I've never been to London in my life." He bit his lip and turned to Jade who had wandered off and was looking around.

Jade's face scrunched. "I know this neighborhood...I've been here before." She looked back and forth, scanning the street. She stopped and pointed to a large mansion at the end of the row, isolated by a black iron gate. "*That* house. I've been to *that* house."

Cody joined her side. "How can that be? Why *that* house?"

Jade took a deep breath. "Because the man who lives in that mansion is named Arthur Shimmers—and he's my father."

The steps leading to the house's large double doors were old cobblestone. Flanking the entrance were two life-sized black, stone statues of knights on horseback.

They ascended the stairs slowly. Cody glanced up. Framed in the fourth floor bay window was the silhouette of a man watching their approach. The next instant he was gone.

Cody turned to Jade. "You're *positive* your father lives here? When's the last time you even saw him?"

"It's been years, but..." She took a deep breath and grabbed the dragonhead door knocker. *Thud. Thud. Thud.*

They heard the shuffling of footsteps from the other side. Tiana braced herself for combat. Cody felt Jade's fingers lock with his. The door opened and an exceedingly old man with a stern face and a tuxedo stood in the entrance. His eyes stopped on Jade. "Little Mari? Mari Shimmers? Is that you?" his voice creaked.

Jade exchanged glances with Cody. "Do you know me?"

The old man's frail face rose into a smile. He stared at her, seemingly carried away by recollection. A minute passed as they waited for the elderly butler to return to the present. Cody coughed.

The butler jerked, startled. His eyes went wide as he remembered where he was. "Come in, come in! Your father will want to see you straight away!"

They sat anxiously in the foyer. Jade's knee shook and she was fidgeting with her hands. Cody placed his hand on her leg, stilling it. "You okay?"

Jade sighed. "It's just...I haven't seen him in a long time. What if he doesn't..."

Cody held his finger to her lips. "*Shhh.* He will be *very* proud of you. How could he not?" Cody grasped her hand. Jade smiled.

"Mari?" All eyes turned to the man now standing in the open doorway. He was tall and handsome. His wavy, shoulder-length hair was dark, as were his bushy eyebrows. Like Jade, his eyes were dark green.

Jade stood to her feet. "Father." She blushed, stumbling over her words as she tried to say something else. The man stepped forward and wrapped his arms around her, pulling her against his chest.

Cody exhaled. At long last—they were safe.

99

Unmasked

Cody felt a rush of energy pump through him the instant his foot stepped into the office. The intense static shock jolted up his spine. *What is that?* He had experienced the feeling before, but couldn't remember when.

"Oh, my gosh! Is that *me*!" Jade exclaimed. She ran over to a side shelf and picked up a framed picture. "I was such a fat child!"

Her father walked to her side. They began chatting. Cody stepped awkwardly away, feeling guilty to intrude on their reunion. His retreat went unnoticed. He eyed Tiana still standing at the room's entrance. Her pale face expressed that she was in shock and angry at being so. Cody decided to let her be. He strolled through the large room.

Cody stopped at the desk. Lying in the middle of the desk was a large, rustic book. The book's cover was made of simple wood. Cody felt his heartbeat quicken. The only marking on the cover was an image of three rectangles in the form of an upside down arrow surrounded by a runic sun. The boxes forming the point of the arrow were colored, one in scarlet and one in gold.

He suddenly pinpointed the sensation. It was the same intensity he had felt whenever he approached *The Key*. He reached into his backpack and pulled out the ruby pocket-watch. The purple hand was spinning out of control. *We're not safe.*

There was a click as the office door opened behind them. Jade's father stared intensely at Cody. "I believe you're already acquainted with my employee."

A man stepped through the door with pistol raised—it was Dunstan.

Dunstan bowed. "What are my orders, my master?"

Cody turned to Jade's father in shock. Jade's father reached to the desk and lifted a large, polished sword. "Welcome to the headquarters of CROSS."

**To Be Continued in Book Three
of the Lost City Chronicles**

Lost City Chronicles Glossary

Alac-icacs: An ancient desert tribe who once ruled over the people of the sand before coming to ruin.

Arianna: A citizen of Atlantis

Boc'ro the Wise: High Priest and councilor of the Alac-icacs

Borderlands: The land dividing the kingdoms of Atlantis and El Dorado

Brotherhood of Light: Those trained to use and protect the High Language *See High Language*

Caves of Revelation: According to Under-Earth legend, the location where the tablets containing the High Language were first discovered

Chazic: An enforcer for the AREA; understudy of Sli Silkian

Cia: Heir to the thrown of Atlantis

Cody Clemenson: A 15-year-old boy from Havenwood, Utah; Book Keeper of *The Code*

Covenant of the Books: A treaty made between King Ishmael and the Golden King dividing full access to the Orb's power between two books: *The Code* and *The Key*.

CROSS: A mysterious organization run by a powerful master

Dace Ringstar: Captain of Atlantis' Outer-City Guard

Dark-Wielders: Beings belonging to the Brotherhood of Light in El Dorado.

Dunstan: A high ranking member of CROSS *See CROSS*

Eagleton, Eli: Atlantis' captain of the Mid-City Guard

Enforcers: Grunt men for the AREA who oversee Orb worship and rules

Eva: Princess of Atlantis

Evona: One of *The Twelve*

Eyelid-less Man: A mysterious wandering inhabitant of Under-Earth; his origin is unknown

Fiery Plains: A vast desert too hot to traverse; the aftermath of a major battle during the Great War

Fincher Tople: Reporter for *The Under-Earth Rumbling*

Flore Gub: An Atlantis fortress on the borderlands

Foz: Prince of Atlantis

Gelph: A beggar in Atlantis' Outer-City

Golden golems: Foot soldiers of El Dorado with gold platelet armor infused into their skin

Golden King: The monarch of El Dorado; Book Keeper of *The Key*

Great Sea of Lava: A vast body of lava on the borderlands

Hansi: Prince of El Dorado; son of the Golden King

Havenwood: A small town in Utah

High Language: The creation words that are used to access the Orb's power

Hymn of the Orb: A chant repeated seven times every 2.5 hours in Atlantis: "Hail, the Orb of holy light, humbled we by its eternal might. Hail the Orb, let it shine forever bright. Amen."

Igg K. Stalkton: A hermit and Skipper of *The Igg*; brother of Lamgorious Stalkton

Inner-City: The innermost district of Atlantis containing the Sanctuary of the Orb and the Royal family

Ishmael: The first King of Atlantis

Jade (Mari Shimmers): A 16-year-old girl from Havenwood, Utah

Kael: One of *The Twelve*

Kantan: Prince of Atlantis; equal heir to throne with twin sister, Cia

Kingsty: A soldier in Atlantis' Outer-City Guard

Labyrinth Mountains: A large mountainous range stretching across the Borderlands

Lacen: A soldier in Atlantis' Outer-City Guard

Levenworth, Gongore: High General of Atlantis; one of *The Twelve*

Lilley: A peaceful outpost on the borderlands; the farthest point of Atlantis' kingdom

Mid-City: The middle of Atlantis' three districts; industrial center

Monastery of the Brotherhood: Home of Atlantis' Brotherhood of Light; located in the Sanctuary of the Orb

Naadirah: First Queen of Atlantis; one of *The Twelve*

Nocsic: A Private deployed at Flore Gub; son of Talgu

Outer-City: The outermost district of Atlantis

Poe Dapperhio: An Atlantis servant

Randilin Stormberger: An Atlantis citizen exiled from Under-Earth due to *Dark Deeds* committed during the Great War; one of *The Twelve*

Redtown: An abandoned town on the edge of the Fiery Plains

Rock-Clothing: Garments made entirely from polished stones; invented by Gorgo Tallsin

Sadria: One of *The Twelve*; wife to Wesley Simon

Sally Peatwee: Owner of Sally's Diner; gatekeeper of the Second Passageway *See second passageway*

Sanctuary of the Orb: The spherical structure encasing the Orb in the heart of Atlantis

Second Passageway: A wishing-well gateway in Area 51 that leads to Under-Earth

Shaheena: One of *The Twelve*

Sheets: A soldier in Atlantis' Outer-City Guard

Silkian, Sli: Head of the AREA *See the AREA*

Stalkton, Lamgorious: High Priest of the Brotherhood of Light *See Brotherhood of Light*

Surface-Dwellers: A term used by underlings to refer to those who live above ground *See underlings*

Talgu: Atlantis Captain in charge of Flore Gub's defense

Tallsin, Gorgo: Inventor of rock-clothing

Tamarah the Prophetess: One of *The Twelve*

Tat Shunbickle: A scout from Lilley

The AREA: Name used to refer to the Atlantis Rules Enforcement Association; a powerful organization enforcing Orb worship; led by Sli Silkian *See Sli Silkian*

The Code: The *Book of the Covenant* belonging to Atlantis *See covenant of the books*

The Forbidden High Language: The most powerful creation words. The words are restricted and contained within the *Books of the Covenant*

The Garga: A pagan tribe inhabiting the northern regions of Under-Earth

The Great Garganton: The deity worshiped by the Garga

The Great War: A devastating war between Atlantis and El Dorado that was won by Atlantis. In the aftermath of the war, the Covenant of the Books was sealed *See covenant of the books*

The Hunter: A horrifying beast that hunts anyone who reads from a Book of the Covenant other than its own Book Keeper

The Impaler: A title given to Kael the Invincible; El Dorado's High General; one of *The Twelve*

The Key: The *Book of the Covenant* belonging to El Dorado *See covenant of the books*

The Orb: A powerful essence at the Earth's core

The Rephaim: A rumored new class of El Dorado soldiers that feel no pain or fear

The Speaking Sands: A communication device created by Lamgorious Stalkton

The Thirteenth: A supposed additional member to *The Twelve* whom little is known

The Twelve: The twelve members of the Alac-icacs tribe who discovered Under-Earth

The Undecided One: The member of *The Twelve* who refused to join either Atlantis or El Dorado and walked away, never heard from again

The-Creation-Which-Should-Be-One's Own: A dangerous creation that is not spoken of

Tiana Hubrisa: A citizen of Atlantis

Tryin: A soldier in Atlantis' Outer-City Guard

Tunnel-phone: A matrix of tunnels that allows communication across Under-Earth

Under-Earth: The world at the center of the Earth

Underlings: A title to refer to people living in Under-Earth

Uscana: First Chief of the Alac-icacs

Wesley Simon: An elderly bookstore owner in Havenwood; first Book Keeper of *The Code*; one of *The Twelve*

Wolfrick: A soldier in Atlantis' Outer-City Guard

Xerx: A monk of the Brotherhood of Light

The High Language

Bauciv: Wood

Byrae: Wind

Colania: Cold

Dastanda: Dust/Earth

Duomi: Explosion

Fraymour: Fire

Gadour: Rock

Gai di gasme: Phrase to end creation

Illumchanta: Light

Seamour: Water

Sellunga: Metal

Spakious: Wormhole

Vapiroi: Smoke/Fog

Acknowledgments

Once again, the incalculable number of people deserving an appearance on this page is expansive enough to fill its own book. So to mention only a few:

First and foremost, to my beautiful wife, Sarah. No one has made more sacrifices for the completion of this book than you. I am so grateful for your constant support. Love you forever.

To my family: Dad, Mom, Mike, and Carrie for helping me along this journey in your own special and unique ways. You guys are the best!

To my editor, Anna McHargue, for dedicating so many hours exploring Under-Earth with me and for cleaning up the hunk of trash I continually tried to slough off as a legible manuscript.

To strong black coffee—the undisputed MVP of this writing process.

Finally, to all of you who read *Legend of the Book Keeper* and gave me such kind encouragement. During the (many) long days when I wanted to do anything BUT keep writing, your support provided the needed boost to *get 'er done*! It makes everything worth it. Thank you!

About the Author

Daniel is a fourth generation author. He grew up in the icy plains of western Canada. Daniel has published multiple books in both fiction and non-fiction genres. When not writing he enjoys reading, hockey, and playing guitar. He currently lives in Atlanta, GA with his beautiful wife, Sarah.

Follow his writing at these locations:

Danielblackaby.com

Facebook.com/danielblackabyauthor

Twitter@DanielBlackaby

Imaginationsundergroundrailroad.com